"A witty, engaging blend of history and mystery with a smart sleuth who already feels like a good friend . . . [Connolly's] stories always keep me turning pages—often well past my bedtime."
—Julie Hyzy, *New York Times* bestselling author of the White House Chef Mysteries

"*National Treasure* meets *The Philadelphia Story* . . . Secrets, lies, and a delightful revenge conspiracy make this a real page-turner!"
—Hank Phillippi Ryan, Agatha, Anthony, and Macavity award–winning author of *Truth Be Told*

"The practical and confident Nell Pratt is exactly the kind of sleuth you want in your corner when the going gets tough . . . [A] snappy and sophisticated mystery."
—Mary Jane Maffini, author of the Charlotte Adams Mysteries

"The archival milieu and the foibles of the characters are intriguing, and it's refreshing to encounter an FBI man who is human, competent, and essential to the plot." —*Publishers Weekly*

"[A] mature and intelligent sleuth, who works with historic treasures and takes her responsibilities seriously. Great pacing and placement of clues build tension as Nell uncovers the truth in this enjoyable and sophisticated mystery."
—*RT Book Reviews*

"[An] engaging amateur sleuth filled with fascinating characters, interesting museum information, plenty of action including a nice twist, and a bit of romance."
—*Genre Go Round Reviews*

Berkley Prime Crime titles by Sheila Connolly

Orchard Mysteries

ONE BAD APPLE
ROTTEN TO THE CORE
RED DELICIOUS DEATH
A KILLER CROP
BITTER HARVEST
SOUR APPLES
GOLDEN MALICIOUS
PICKED TO DIE

Museum Mysteries

FUNDRAISING THE DEAD
LET'S PLAY DEAD
FIRE ENGINE DEAD
MONUMENT TO THE DEAD
RAZING THE DEAD
PRIVY TO THE DEAD
DEAD END STREET

County Cork Mysteries

BURIED IN A BOG
SCANDAL IN SKIBBEREEN
AN EARLY WAKE
A TURN FOR THE BAD

Specials

DEAD LETTERS
AN OPEN BOOK

DEAD END STREET

Sheila Connolly

BERKLEY PRIME CRIME, NEW YORK

BERKLEY
PRIME
CRIME

An imprint of Penguin Random House LLC
375 Hudson Street, New York, New York 10014

DEAD END STREET

A Berkley Prime Crime Book / published by arrangement with the author

ISBN: 978-0-425-27347-0

PUBLISHING HISTORY
Berkley Prime Crime mass-market edition / June 2016

PRINTED IN THE UNITED STATES OF AMERICA

10 9 8 7 6 5 4 3 2 1

Cover illustration by Ross Jones.
Cover design by Rita Frangie.
Interior text design by Laura K. Corless.

Penguin
Random
House

ACKNOWLEDGMENTS

When William Penn first laid out the city of Philadelphia, he hoped that it would be a "greene Country Town," with houses surrounded by ample lawns combined with thriving commercial district and municipal buildings. He ensured that each quarter of the planned city would have a public park, as well as Centre Square in the heart of it (where City Hall now stands). But while the ghosts of Penn's grid plan and its wide avenues survive today, there are parts of the city that would horrify him now.

My father once worked at a company called Philadelphia Gear Corporation, located in North Philadelphia, now one of the worst of the blighted areas. It moved to the suburbs in the 1950s, as did so many other industries, taking with them the jobs that people in the city depended on. Years later I worked as a financial advisor to the city, so I know from experience the challenges that the city faces in fighting urban blight, and in finding a constructive way to deal with the acres of decaying buildings and trash-strewn vacant lots. A series of mayors have done their best to improve the situation, and sought state and federal funding, but the problem still remains.

But you can't give up on Philadelphia. It is rich in history, and occupies a central place in the creation of our country. In this book, my protagonist, Nell Pratt, believes that the wastelands of the city are worth fighting for, and she tries to find a way to let the citizens of the city and the state know that there should be hope that these parts of the city can be saved; she has the historic records to show what those neighborhoods once were—and could be again. As an author, I know this kind of fiction doesn't usually involve trying to solve a real-world problem, but I wanted to try.

As always, I owe a debt of gratitude to the Historical Society of Pennsylvania, which houses many of the materials that document the city's past. Kudos to its outstanding staff (including the president, Page Talbot), and to Sandra Cadwalader, whose commitment to the city and its history has never flagged. Thanks also to Jessica Faust of BookEnds, who has long championed this series, and to editor Tom Colgan, who let me run with this story. And I salute all those mayors and local activists who have tried to make a difference in a city they care about.

CHAPTER 1

The wind scoured my face as I walked briskly from Suburban Station, across City Hall Plaza, toward the Pennsylvania Antiquarian Society, where I worked. Where I was president and responsible for seeing that my forty-plus employees worked. Where it was hard for anybody to work since construction was still going on—construction that had begun a couple of months earlier, when the Society had received a generous grant from a grateful patron, whom I'd kind of helped out when a dead body was holding up his mega construction project in the suburbs. It was a wonderful gift, but the resulting construction process had produced a lot of noise, dust, and disgruntled Society members. I was hoping—praying—that it would be finished by the end of the year, only a month or so away. Or at least, all but the painting, and that would be quiet, wouldn't it? And then, of course, the monumental task of sorting and reshelving all of our treasures, collected over the course of more than a century, would begin. I refused to think about the chaos that would involve.

November was always a tricky month for getting back and forth to work. James, my—drat, we still hadn't settled on labels for each other. Lover? No, not fit for proper company. Partner? That sounded like a business arrangement (although one could argue that marriage was one as well, with a legal document attached). Boyfriend? No, too high school. Sweetie? Plum dumpling? Cuddle bunny? No, too silly for two mature adults, one of whom was an FBI agent. Special Agent Cuddle Bunny? I snickered; that was *so* not going to work. And I was a seasoned professional, a member of the Philadelphia cultural community, an historian, a manager, and an independent woman, who happened to be living with a smart, handsome, capable man. We'd bought a house together a couple of months earlier and were still settling in and getting to know each other. Neither of us had lived with anyone else for a long time, so we were moving cautiously. It had taken us a while just to pick furniture to fill most of the rooms of our gorgeous Victorian in Chestnut Hill, and then we'd mutually decided to take a breather before we tackled the task of choosing wall and window treatments. Thank heaven the kitchen had been modernized before we'd bought the place, or we might have found ourselves living on takeout and microwave meals.

We often commuted together into the city by car, but on this particular morning Special Agent James Morrison had an early meeting elsewhere, so I took the train rather than drive. I liked riding the train to the city, because it gave me time to read the newspaper and the stack of magazines that kept accumulating. The only problem was when I had to walk from the train station to the Society building during the colder months. Luckily there were underground passages that would take me right to the building, but using the passages signaled the end of summer and the beginning of the cold season, which I was reluctant to accept. At least I'd had the foresight to haul out my warm coat. It would have been handy if I had found my gloves. I made a mental note to look for them when I got home.

I arrived at the Society building nice and early. One of the pluses of walking was that I could approach from Broad Street and admire the building's solid brick walls and imposing bluestone pillars. It had been built to last— and to protect the collections it sheltered—more than a century before. I had been relieved when the architects involved in the renovation had declared it structurally sound and fit to weather another century. It was the interior storage for collections that had fallen behind the times. And the roof. And the heating and ventilation. But we had money in the bank and a good crew, and all would be remedied shortly.

I greeted Bob, who stood watch over our front desk (he was a retired police officer and provided a reassuring presence), then took the elevator up to my office on the third floor, which housed the administrative offices. My assistant, Eric, was already at his desk. We vied in a friendly way to see who could arrive first, because when he started working for me, nearly two years earlier, whoever arrived first had to make the coffee. Now we had a sparkly new single-serve coffee system in the break room we all shared, and it did make decent coffee. But I had to admit I kind of missed the old system—the uncertainty about whether the pot waiting would be fresh or ancient, and whether you would exhaust the contents and feel compelled to brew the new pot, which took time. Modern technology did make life simpler, but it changed other things, too.

"Good morning, Eric. What's on the agenda for today?" I was not a scatterbrain, but it could be a challenge to keep appointments straight in my head.

Eric flipped through his notebook. "I would have said it looked like a free day, but you just got a call from someone who works with the City, who wants to meet with you ASAP. I penciled them in, but I can cancel if you'd prefer." Eric looked at me anxiously. He was relatively young, from the South, and very polite. And very grateful to have the job, since his work history was patchy at best. I'd hired him on gut instinct, and he hadn't let me down.

"If I don't have anything else scheduled, I might as well go ahead and see them. Did the person say what this was about?"

"No, ma'am. Just that it was a matter that had to do with the Society, and they needed to resolve it sooner rather than later."

City government: everything always had to be done immediately, except then you waited six months for the paperwork to clear. "When should I expect them?"

"Any minute now. You want I should get you some coffee first?"

"Why don't I wait and see if our guests want anything? You can go down and escort them up here when they arrive."

"Yes, ma'am."

I went into my office and hung up my coat, neatly, on a hanger. I really liked my office, although I felt I didn't belong in it. It was on the corner of the building, so it had decent views and plenty of light. It was furnished with some very nice antiques from the Society's collections, which scared me to death: I was always worried that I'd spill food or something worse on a priceless piece. But I had to admit they looked extremely handsome, and they certainly impressed visitors. The more mundane items, like a computer printer and files, were discreetly concealed in modern mahogany cabinets. Best of all, it was always clean and neat, a haven of peace in the midst of what could be a chaotic job, which for reasons that continued to mystify me had included solving more than one murder. I had to admit I'd closed my door and hidden out in my office now and then, just to find some peace.

I busied myself clearing off some items of business Eric had left on my desk, and it was only a few minutes later that he announced he was going downstairs to escort the visitors to our meeting. That was one of the few stabs at security my earlier predecessors had made: researchers were not allowed to wander at will throughout the building. Some stacks were open for them to use; unique, rare, or valuable materials were housed in closed stacks, and the researchers would have to submit a request and wait for a librarian or assistant to retrieve what they wanted. The administration areas were strictly off-limits to most people, and one could not get past the second floor without a special key. It didn't exactly stop thieves in their tracks, but it made it a little harder for them to invade spaces where they shouldn't be. Of course, the general public often assumed that we had video cameras watching everyone, but that was far from the truth. Such a setup was on our wish list, but well behind a lot of other items. That kind of security equipment was expensive, plus we'd need someone to actually monitor what was going on, and adding staff was equally expensive. Somehow there was never enough funding to go around.

Eric ushered a man and a woman into the office and asked if they wanted coffee. They said yes, so presumably they weren't in my office to complain about something. I looked them over discreetly: both appeared to be in their thirties, dressed in business casual, and carrying leather portfolios. And both were black. Of course the Society had black employees, but most of our patrons were not. We did hold some significant collections relevant to the city's abolitionist movement, but it would be jumping to conclusions to assume that was what had brought them here. Researchers didn't usually make appointments with the presidents of institutions. In any case, I didn't recognize either one of them, but that didn't surprise me. I'd had dealings with Philadelphia's government under more than one administration over the years. I'd met the current mayor and respected him, but most of my interactions had been with committee members a lot farther down the management charts. The Society didn't have any issues outstanding with the city. We applied for and received an annual grant for cultural institutions in the city, but it was small—not that any money was too small to welcome in the nonprofit sector.

We made polite small talk until Eric had delivered the coffee. Then I sat back in my chair and asked, "What can I do for you?"

The two exchanged a glance, and the woman nodded to the man. He spoke first. "My name is Tyrone Blakeney, and I'm the head of the North Philadelphia Neighborhood Partnership, which you've probably never heard of." He smiled pleasantly.

"And I'm Cherisse Chapman," the woman said quickly. "I work for the City's Licenses and Inspections department."

I still had no clue why they were sitting in front of me. "What brings you to the Society?"

"Are you familiar with the Funeral for a Home project in the city?" Tyrone began.

"Only what I've read in the *Inquirer*," I said. "Something to do with mourning the last properties in neighborhoods that have changed radically over time?"

"Do you know how many derelict or abandoned properties there are in Philadelphia?" Cherisse demanded.

I guessed that they'd made this pitch before. I felt like they were ganging up on me, coming at me from two sides, although it wasn't fair to them for me to feel that way. "No, I don't, although I'm guessing there are a lot, based on what I've seen personally." At the very least, I knew that there were some neighborhoods I as a woman alone did not want to venture into, even by daylight, with all my car doors securely locked.

"More than forty thousand. Forty thousand!" Cherisse said indignantly. She spoke with the fervor of a true believer. "And that's just the abandoned ones. There are many, many more that are falling down, and yet people—families, even—are still living in them because they have nowhere else to go!"

Tyrone gave her a stern look—apparently she was getting ahead of the script—and Cherisse subsided.

"I understand that it's a problem," I told them, "but what does it have to do with the Society?"

"We should take a step backward and explain," Tyrone said. "As she told you, Cherisse works for the city, in the department that is responsible for inspecting and all too often condemning buildings that are too unsafe to occupy. Ideally they would be torn down to make room for new units of affordable housing, but I'm sure you can understand that that is often impossible, given the city's financial constraints. Which is a shame, because it means that not only homes are lost, but so are entire historic neighborhoods—the rich diversity that Philadelphia's past offers."

Tyrone clearly cared about this subject, and I was beginning to see a glimmer of light. "You said you were in charge of a partnership? What does that do?"

"The partnership is a nonprofit coalition of agencies and individuals such as real estate developers who are seeking to salvage the old neighborhoods before they are lost forever, by rehabbing whatever buildings are viable and creating new structures that emulate the styles that came before. The ones that once created a sense of community. I'm sure you know what I mean—triple-decker row houses with porches or front steps where people could sit for an evening and interact with their neighbors. Corner stores that provide the essentials. Pocket parks that offer children a safe place to play, not too far from home. Day care. Schools. Simple restaurants."

I realized I was confronted by a pair of zealots, but I had to admire them for trying. "I love your vision, but how do you make it happen?"

"By using a multipronged strategy," Cherisse took up the thread eagerly. "The city has the properties on its books and doesn't want them. But we know the legal processes necessary to gain clear title, and we have the clout to follow through. To go after absentee landlords, or those people who have walked away, unwilling to pay taxes or maintain the buildings. Tyrone here has the vision to see the possibilities and the connections to the neighborhoods—and the charm to sell it to the people who matter."

"The ones who have the money, you mean."

Tyrone grinned, which made him look boyish. "Well, yes. It takes money to make something like this work, but not as much as you'd think. We'd love to be able to use laborers who live in those very neighborhoods, so they have a stake in the outcome. The big chain stores are scared to step up and move in, but we can recruit smaller ones, or single-shop owners—again, ones who live there, who want to raise families in a place that feels like home. Not a slum with bars on all the windows. Everyone wins."

His enthusiasm was infectious. "Well, I'll tell you up front that we have no money, if that's what you're looking for."

"We know that—you're a nonprofit, just like we are. But you have the resources to provide the history of the neighborhoods we're targeting. And before you protest, we aren't going to try to do this all over the city, all at once—that would be a recipe for disaster, spreading ourselves too thin. We want to start with a single showcase neighborhood and do it right. Bring it in on budget, retain the old residents, and attract new ones. Show what *can* be done. We've got some smart businessmen on board, and they've been crunching the numbers. We've got some journalists, both print and electronic, on our side, so we'll get press attention. But what we need from you is a way to flesh out the story, to show what the place once was— which most living people never knew or have forgotten— which will show them what it could be again."

Without committing myself, I was already mentally reviewing what resources we had in the building, and who might have the time to commit to a project like this, even if it was only part-time, like a day a week. Lissa Penrose would be one possible choice. And when I thought of her, I realized that Eliot Miller could be a real asset (unless he hated the whole idea—I hadn't spent enough time with him to know his philosophy of urban development or redevelopment). Eliot was a professor at the University of Pennsylvania, and he was seeing Marty Terwilliger, uber–board member of the Society, and a tireless cheerleader for those projects she cared about. Eliot had been nominated for a vacant seat on the Society's board, and I thought his academic area of expertise—urban planning— would complement the roster of lawyers and business people we already had on the board, in addition to Marty, who brought an encyclopedic knowledge of Philadelphia history plus three generations of board commitment. If I could get all of them on the same page . . .

I was already building castles in the air when I realized that Tyrone was speaking to me. "Excuse me, I got caught up by what you were planning. Could you repeat what you said?"

"I was saying that we think North Philadelphia is the best neighborhood to start. It's close to Center City, and there's already some interest in turning it around, so we could see substantial results fairly quickly. And you—or, rather, the Society already has a stake in it."

"We do?" I said, bewildered.

"Yes," Cherisse said. "The Society owns a property right in the middle of the neighborhood."

CHAPTER 2

I tried to maintain an intelligent expression while I processed that statement. Nope, that didn't ring a bell.

"I'm afraid I don't understand," I said. "You're saying that the Pennsylvania Antiquarian Society owns a piece of property? I may be wrong, but I was under the impression that the Society had divested itself of all property holdings quite a few years ago. Long before my tenure here."

Cherisse gave me a perfunctory smile. "If you're familiar with our office, you might be aware that things have been known to fall through the cracks. Your organization may well have sold off its holdings, but it could be that the original property transfer *to* the Society was not recorded correctly, so it was not included in whatever list you had. But when we began looking into this particular neighborhood in more depth, we made a thorough search, and the original record turned up."

"Ah," I said. "I can understand how that might happen. But what is it you want us to do about it? Give it to the city, or to your organization? Sell it to you for a dollar?" Other, more troubling ideas came bubbling up, like whether we would be responsible for back taxes for who knew how many years, or fines. "I can assure you that we were unaware of this oversight."

Tyrone hurried to step in, after sending a warning glance at Cherisse. "Ms. Pratt, I'm sure we can resolve that question without any penalty. However, the process could take some time—time we don't have. The building you own is in perilous condition, and slated for demolition, if it doesn't fall down first. Let me explain, since you aren't familiar with it. It's a single row house that's lost its row. It's the last of its kind on an entire block, the only survivor of a once-vital part of the neighborhood. As such, it has some symbolic value, and we're planning a couple of public events around it, once we clear up this title business— kind of a funeral for the building. Since it appears that the Society is the owner of record, you have the opportunity to step up and do some good."

I gathered my thoughts. "Mr. Blakeney, since this is news to me, I need some time to process this information. Before any decisions can be made, I need to inform our board of the issue and provide them with details, and I have to explore what options we have, and I should probably talk to our lawyer as well. I assume you have a timetable, but we may not be able to meet it. And I probably don't need to tell you that we don't exactly have a lot of money available to us, and much of what we have is restricted to specific uses, so I'm not sure what kind of help you think we can give you."

"Call me Tyrone, please. Like I said, we don't expect money, and we don't want to see you penalized for a mistake somebody made decades ago. But I want you to understand that this is a piece of Philadelphia's history! If I understand it right, your institution is charged with preserving that history!" It was very clear that he was passionate about his cause.

He had a point, and it hit home. But I couldn't remember any project like this that the Society had taken part in, and I wasn't ready to commit to anything. "I agree in principle, Tyrone, but that doesn't mean that I'm in a position to do anything about it, certainly not on such short notice. Surely if you're part of a nonprofit organization you know that. Under normal circumstances there would be a procedure: we would assess the situation, and *if* the board approved action, we would most likely engage in a fund-raising campaign to raise money to support your efforts. I can see from your perspective that we could be a good ally."

Tyrone reined in his zeal. "Ms. Pratt, I do understand your position. But we don't have that kind of time. I know that money is tight for everyone. What I'm hoping you can do is help us to generate public awareness of this situation. Your institution has the potential to do immeasurable good, with your archival resources and your membership. We're not asking for money, and the building is beyond salvage. But if our organizations could work together, your efforts could help us to reach a wider audience than we could hope to on our own."

I was pretty sure that our memberships didn't overlap. Was he asking me to share our donor list? Or was he trying to lean on the Society as an absentee landlord, even though we hadn't been aware of it? Still, I smiled at him—he was persuasive, and he certainly seemed to be sincere. "I appreciate your faith in our clout, but you have to recognize that we're an old organization and we simply don't move quickly. I need to discuss what role we could play with other people before we make any decisions."

The poor man looked deflated. Cherisse finally spoke again. "Ms. Pratt, maybe it would help if you could come see the property, and put the problem in perspective? I understand your reservations—and as a City employee, I know that bureaucracies, large or small, can move at a glacial pace. But this particular project has a time limit that was not of our choosing." She glanced at her companion. "Would you be willing to come with us and take a look at the site? It won't take more than an hour of your time—it's not far away. Then you can review our documentation and proposals with a clear eye."

While I was still not enthusiastic about the idea, I did see her point. "When would you want to do this?"

"Today? This afternoon?" Tyrone had come back to life, seeing a glimmer of hope.

"Let me check with my assistant, who keeps my calendar. I'll be just a moment." I stood and walked to the door, pulling it nearly shut behind me as I approached Eric's desk. "What's my afternoon look like?"

Eric pulled up the calendar on his computer screen. "You don't have anything specific scheduled. Why?"

"Our guests have invited me to see a decrepit building that the Society owns, in an area if town I'd rather not be in."

"Would you like me to give you an excuse not to go?" Eric volunteered, his voice low.

I was tempted, but I said, "No, I guess not. If they're right and the Society actually does own it, there may be legal issues, and I might as well deal with it now rather than later. Thanks, Eric."

I squared my shoulders and returned to my office. "It looks as though my schedule is clear for the rest of the day. What do you suggest?"

Cherisse and Tyrone exchanged glances. "We have a meeting at eleven," Tyrone said. "Why don't we stop by and pick you up at, say, two?"

Obviously they had no plan to wine and dine me, to win me over. "That sounds fine. It will give me a chance to go through our records here and figure out what happened, if I can. Could you give me the address, so we can check our files?"

Tyrone rattled off an address, and I jotted it down. Then he and Cherisse stood up simultaneously. "Excellent," Tyrone said. "We will be here at two, and we'll take you to the site. I think our plans will be much clearer to you when you can get a sense of the area."

"I'll look forward to it." *Not*. "See you later, then." We all shook hands, and I escorted my guests out to Eric, who in turn led them to the elevator and downstairs.

The whole situation troubled me—I didn't like surprises, not if they involved money and lawyers, which it appeared this one might. I wandered down the hall to chat with my director of development, Shelby Carver. Shelby had joined the Society at about the same time as Eric—they were my first hires when I'd been bumped up to the president's office, and she had filled my former job. Shelby was from the South, too, and had proved to be an asset as a fund-raiser. She was also smart and observant, which more than made up for her somewhat thin résumé. I often used her as a sounding board for some of my ideas.

When I rapped on the door frame, Shelby looked up from the stack of documents she was sorting through and said, "Business or pleasure?"

"Development business, I think. You have a moment to talk?"

"Anything for you, Madame President," Shelby said with a grin. "Sit." She waved at a chair.

I pulled the chair closer to her desk. "I just had an odd visit from two people who work for the City. Or maybe one person with the City and another with a non-City agency, but they're working together. Anyway, I have been informed that the Society owns a building in a blighted portion of the city. I looked like an idiot because I didn't know we owned *any* real estate, except for the property where we sit. Can you provide any enlightenment?"

"Lady, if you don't know, after you put in several years in my job, how the heck am I supposed to know?"

"Well, I didn't know during those years, so now we're even. I will admit that I have some vague memory of a discussion years ago, that in the past a lot of people chose to remember the Society in their wills with real estate rather than cold cash. Could be that was their only asset, or maybe they couldn't unload it and figured their generous gesture would look good in their obituary or whatever. Anyway, my visitors said that somehow one—at least, I hope it's only one—transaction didn't get filed properly, so apparently we still own it."

"And the problem is what?" Shelby asked. "Can't you just sell it now and be rid of it?"

"Nothing is ever that simple, Shelby," I told her. "It's located in an area where I think I'm pretty safe in saying that there is no active market for property sales. That is, a slum. Maybe if these people hadn't tracked me down, the property would have defaulted to the city and they could do whatever they wanted. But some eagle-eyed researcher found the mix-up, so now we're on the hook for it."

"What do they want you to do?"

"That's kind of tricky, I think. If I understand it correctly—and mind you, I've spent all of half an hour with these people—they kind of dangled the hope that they would work with us to expedite the legal aspects if the Society would throw its weight behind some kind of neighborhood redevelopment effort."

"Publicly, you mean?" Shelby asked.

"I think so. Kind of add some prestige to their efforts, and maybe give them some historic ammunition in their efforts to rebuild what was once a fine old neighborhood."

"Hmm," Shelby said thoughtfully. "Is that a bad thing? I mean, the Society would get some visibility, and it would look like we're fulfilling our mandate to preserve local history. They didn't ask for money, did they?"

"I told them flat out that we don't have that kind of money. I guess our only bargaining chip is our standing in the cultural community."

"What happens if we don't play nice with them?"

"I don't know. Somebody may really want this property to complete a larger lot for some plan we don't even know about, although I don't think anyone will offer to buy it from us. We could give it away, to the city or a private developer, if there is one, or to some kind of community organization, but I don't know how the board will feel about that. I can't make an executive decision anyway, so I have to take it to them. If we do nothing, we might get cited and fined for neglecting it. If something were to happen to someone there, we could have some liability. Obviously I have a lot more questions than answers."

"Did they tell you that?" Shelby asked. "Smells a bit like blackmail."

"I didn't get that feeling from either of them. I think they really are trying to do something good."

"So why'd you come to me? I know diddly-squat about how Philadelphia government works."

Shelby hadn't lived in Philadelphia for very long, so that wasn't surprising. "I know. I don't either, really, and I've lived here a lot longer than you. What I was thinking is that you could go through the development records and see if there is anything on the original gift. And in addition to that, you can pull what we have about North Philadelphia."

"I know enough to stay out of the place," Shelby said firmly. "Apart from that, that's a job for a researcher."

"I know—if we move forward with this, which I haven't promised, I was thinking it might be a good project for Lissa. But for now, just see if you can find anything on the property in our files, will you? I'm going to go see it this afternoon, and maybe after that I'll have a better handle on things."

Shelby sighed, mostly for effect. "All right, I'll check on it. What's the address?"

"387 Bickley Street, in the city."

Shelby wrote a note on a pad. "It's not some gorgeous decaying mansion, is it?"

"I'm told it's a row house, minus the rest of the row. Kind of like the last tooth in an old neighborhood's mouth."

"My, you have a way with words. You want to grab lunch first?"

"Sure. I'll need my strength. I'll meet you back here at noon."

I went back to my office and sat at my desk, thinking. I was not a native Philadelphian. Although I had lived and worked in or around the city for more than a decade, I wasn't intimately familiar with the histories of the individual neighborhoods, though I could give a pretty fair summary of the history of the city in its earliest years. But for the twentieth century and the early twenty-first century, I had little to offer. I knew vaguely that some areas had once been home to prosperous industries, and that their workers had lived nearby. I also knew that such neighborhoods, in Philadelphia and many other major cities, had their own life cycles; that the industries had become obsolete and closed, or had migrated to the suburbs during the last century, leaving behind neighborhoods that had declined slowly and inexorably. I had a feeling I was going to see one of those today.

I grabbed a couple of books about Philadelphia history from my shelves. Leafing through them, I found a useful list of major manufacturing establishments in the earlier twentieth century. I was surprised to see that sugar refining topped the list by a wide margin, until I remembered that the Jack Frost refinery had once occupied a substantial piece of land just the other side of the Schuylkill River. Now long gone. If I recalled correctly, it had been shut down in the 1980s. Iron and steel mills ranked next—also gone. The rest of the list made interesting reading: it included paper, leather and textile makers, meatpacking, ice cream—that made me smile, because Breyers Ice Cream had been founded in Philadelphia right after the Civil War and was still making ice cream products. The city's northeast district had consistently been one of the most populous since the nineteenth century.

I felt mildly embarrassed as I read along. I knew about the early settlement of the city, along the waterfront, and its gradual migration inland as the city grew, but much of my knowledge ended with the construction of City Hall, finished in 1901, which was kind of hard to miss. I had never had much cause to pay attention to the rise of industries and their shifting distribution, and had given little thought to the impact of those changes on the inhabitants of various parts of the city. Did that make me a snob? Concerned only with the rich and important citizens and what buildings and artifacts they'd left behind? It seemed that I was not doing my job, or not all of it.

Shelby and I went out and grabbed a quick sandwich, and then returned to our respective desks. I did a little more reading, so at least I could ask the right questions during our excursion. At five before two I was waiting in the lobby for my zealous escorts.

CHAPTER 3

Tyrone and Cherisse arrived in a nondescript four-door sedan that had seen better days. I wondered if that was a reflection of their modesty, or recognition that we were headed for a neighborhood that would welcome a high-end car—for all the wrong reasons, like seeing it as a source of spare parts.

North Philadelphia begins only a few blocks north of Market Street, which runs east to west and extends for miles. This I knew from looking at maps and reading the papers. I couldn't recall that I'd ever set foot in any part of it, unless I was with someone who was most likely lost. It could be Mars for all its kinship to Center City. It is a slum, a ghetto, a blot on the city.

Once upon a time, long, long ago, it had been a prosperous family neighborhood, full of tidy row houses that housed working-class people, and neighborhoods revolved around the factories, the churches, the union halls, the front stoops, and for some, the bars. Now, after the early families had fled to the suburbs, the factories had moved to China, and poorer minorities had moved in, it was known as the Badlands, or Killadelphia. Those guys we passed, standing on street corners, were drug dealers, and they weren't hiding it. Much of the time the cops were part of the problem rather than the solution. Not only was there widespread corruption, but I'd read very recently that the US Justice Department had reviewed shootings by cops in the city and found that while New York's population and police force were each five times larger than Philadelphia's, Philadelphia had far more police shootings.

And the Society owned a property smack in the middle of it. I was ashamed. And I had to do something about it.

"Is it far?" I asked Tyrone, who was driving.

"Closer than you might think. You didn't find anything in your records?"

"Not yet. I have my director of development looking into it, but I didn't have much to work with. What is it you want me to look at here?" Apart from the poverty and crime and depressing ugliness.

"What do you know about row house history?" Cherisse asked, turning in her seat to face me.

"Less than I should, I'm sure. What can you tell me?"

"Short version?" Cherisse asked. I nodded. "Row houses were built to accommodate a growing artisan and commercial population—you could call them early middle class," she began. "They were built quickly—which is not the same as badly—and often left unfinished so that the purchasers could add their own details. There were also a lot of row houses built as rentals, and they tended to be plainer. Usually three rooms deep, but narrow, with a small yard behind and an alley at the back between the rows. Front room was fancier, and that's where the heat was. Dining room and kitchen behind—the kitchen was usually pretty small, more an ell than a room. Or even in the basement, sometimes. Upstairs, two bedrooms in the front, either side of the staircase, and a bathroom at the back, over the kitchen. That pretty much sums it up. That's what you've got."

"I see." I did—but I saw much more. I saw streets where vacant lots alternated with abandoned buildings interspersed with a few houses that looked like someone was living—or squatting—in them. People hanging around, watching any car that passed with suspicion. Trashed cars parked at clumsy angles to the sidewalks. A few scraggly trees, usually at the back of the properties, where they'd sprung up untended. It was possible to see that these houses had once been nice, or at least respectable, but not anymore. "Can you answer something honestly for me? Are you taking me along the worst possible route, or is this actually typical?"

The two in the front seat exchanged glances. "Half and half," Cherisse answered. "I know it's going to sound racist, or maybe I mean elitist, but you people in your nice, pretty antique buildings or your shiny glass skyscrapers in Center City really need to get out and see the real world now and then. This is it, and it's not pretty."

Was she trying to annoy me? "Point taken. I get it. So where's our house?"

"Next block over," Tyrone said, and we all fell silent for the remaining short distance.

He pulled up at the curb in front of the house, its number painted roughly on the stucco front. An orange sign tacked to the door said the building was condemned. The houses on either side were long gone, their lots now grassed over. At least there were some mature trees behind the building, providing a small amount of softness. The only window on the ground floor was covered with plywood, but in the upstairs windows tattered lace curtains fluttered, which made me sad. Someone had once lived here, cared for the place. Now it was an eyesore, unsafe, and about to be destroyed. And it belonged to the Society. I wasn't sure yet when the Society had come into possession of it, but I thought it was a safe bet that nobody had been collecting rent or paying taxes on it for a long time. It had truly fallen off the map for both the Society and the City.

"This is kind of far gone to save, you said?" I noticed that neither of my companions had made a move to get out of the car.

Tyrone turned in his seat. "To be honest, yes. We weren't exactly pitching it to you that we could 'save' the building. That's why we're calling it a 'funeral.'" He made air quotes. "But we wanted to make a point. Obviously this building has been neglected for years. The houses that stood next to it have long since fallen down or been razed. I could tell you who owned them, years ago, but those people are either dead or untraceable. You and your Society were easy to find, once we located the record. I wanted you to see firsthand what neglect and abandonment can do, not just to one building but to the whole neighborhood. You can multiply what you see here over many, many city blocks in any direction from here."

Gee, thanks for the guilt trip, Tyrone. "What do you want me to do, apologize? I didn't know. Back when the Society divested itself of what it thought was all its real estate, conditions were very different, and the properties were at least livable. I agree that this is tragic, on many levels, but I'm not sure what you expect from me. You want me to step up and do public penance in the papers and the media?" I was really getting upset, although I wasn't quite sure why. Maybe I was mad at myself: I'd made a point of avoiding looking at scenes like this not only because they were dangerous, but because they were damned depressing. They certainly clashed with the calm and dignity of the Society and what went on within its walls, where I was privileged to spend my time. This was as much a part of the city as the Society's environs.

Cherisse had been quiet for a few minutes, letting Tyrone carry the ball, but now she nudged him. "Tyrone, that car's driven past us before." She nodded toward a nondescript dark sedan coming toward us, moving slowly. Tyrone and Cherisse exchanged looks again.

"What?" I demanded. They were making me nervous. I glanced around the street. The nearest corner was maybe a hundred feet away, ahead of us. There were few people on the street, none on this block, and I could count only a few parked cars in the distance. Okay, so a car circling the block at this particular location was suspicious—I got that.

"I think we've seen enough," Tyrone said, and turned the key to start the engine.

Not quickly enough. I could see the same car rounding the corner ahead of us again. Then, like a bull in a ring, it accelerated rapidly toward us. Its windows rolled down, and a hand with a weapon emerged from the backseat. For a second I froze—could this really be happening?—but then I realized we were all like goldfish in a bowl, targets for whoever it was. The only thing I could hope to do was to get myself out of the line of fire—let Tyrone and Cherisse fend for themselves. I ducked, quickly opened the door on the curb side, and rolled out and lay flat on what was left of the pavement, just as the first bullets hit the car. And continued to hit it, sending window glass spraying, thunking against metal, until I estimated any and all magazines had been emptied—I hoped. If someone got out of that car to check, I had nowhere to go.

Luckily the shooters seemed satisfied, because they revved their engine and sped off down the block, tires squealing, leaving heavy silence behind. I lay there for a moment, taking stock. I couldn't see anyone up or down the street, much less a concerned citizen who would already be calling the police. I wasn't hurt. Lying flat on my face had been a smart move, although I didn't recall thinking, only acting. I rose to my knees and peered into the front seat. Windshield reduced to shards, blood everywhere. Tyrone seemed to be moving, but Cherisse was ominously still. I crawled over to the open rear door I'd thrown myself out, retrieved my purse, found my cell phone, and punched in 911. When someone answered, I said in a voice that was surprisingly calm. "There's been a shooting at three eighty-seven Bickley Street. Two wounded, one possibly dead. The shooters are gone." Although they could come back.

The dispatcher on the other end made soothing noises and told me to repeat the information, which I did. Cool under pressure, that was me. No problem, although I noticed as if from a distance that my hands were shaking, and I wasn't sure I could hit a phone button. She promised she was sending someone. She asked me to stay on the line. I hung up on her—and hit James's speed dial.

"Nell?" he answered in a cheerful voice. "What's up?"

It took me a moment to string words together. "There's been a shooting. I'm, uh, kind of on the scene."

James's next words could have come from a different person, as he snapped into official mode. "Are you hurt?"

"No, but the other people in the car are."

"Have you called the police?"

"Yes.

"Where are you?"

I gave him the address.

"I'll be there in ten. Rough neighborhood. If you have to move, let me know." He hung up.

I slumped back against the car after looking both ways. Still nobody in sight who seemed to care. Apparently random shootings were the norm here. Was I supposed to attempt first aid on Tyrone and Cherisse? Not one of my strengths. Besides which, I was pretty sure that Cherisse was beyond help. *Nell, what about Tyrone?* my inner conscience demanded. I wanted to tell her to shut up, but then I considered how I would feel if Tyrone bled to death within a couple of feet of me while I cowered on the pavement. I'd have to live with that. I didn't want to.

I hauled myself to my feet and glanced around again, then came around to the driver's side and opened the front door. Tyrone was held in by his seat belt, but he seemed to be bleeding from more than one place. When I touched his neck, feeling for a pulse, his eyes opened and focused on me. "What the hell . . . ?" Then he appeared to remember where he was, and he turned quickly, wincing, to Cherisse. "Damn," he whispered, then reached out and brushed a lock of hair from her face. His hand lingered on her cheek for a moment before he turned back to me. "You call the police?"

He hadn't asked whether I was all right, but the fact that I was standing in front of him with no blood on me was probably enough. "Yes. And the FBI." Tyrone raised one eyebrow, so I explained, "My boyfriend's an agent."

Tyrone leaned back and shut his eyes. "Boyfriend'll probably be here before the cops."

The blood on his clothes kept spreading slowly, but at least there was no spurting. I had no idea what I could do to help—I was more likely to do harm than good. It seemed like an eternity but was probably no more than five minutes before a black-and-white and James arrived at the same time. The cops looked wary, peering in all directions, hands on their weapons, as they approached. "Are you the one who called in the shooting?" one asked.

I nodded and gestured toward the front seat. "No ambulance?" I asked in a hoarse croak.

"Sorry. We get a lot of false alarms in this neighborhood. Sometimes they just want to draw us in and take potshots at us. We'll call for one now. You okay?"

I nodded. "I wasn't hit. Just them."

"You were in the car with them?"

"Yes, in the backseat. I saw a car approach slowly, and then I saw the gun. I ducked."

"Did you see the shooter?"

"One guy in the backseat, plus the driver. I don't think I'd recognize him. I was too busy ducking."

And then James was there, wrapping me in his arms and pulling me close, and I burst into tears.

"Uh, excuse me, sir," one of the cops began, and without letting me go, James flashed his badge. The cop retreated.

I tried to burrow into James's chest. I didn't want to open my eyes. Or maybe I did, because with my eyes closed I kept seeing the same scene of car and guns over and over.

"You're not hurt?" James's voice rumbled through his chest. I shook my head.

"But you saw what happened?"

I nodded. "Part of it," I mumbled. "I kind of got out of the way before the shooting started."

"Smart woman," James said.

I snorted. "If I was a smart woman, I wouldn't be here at all."

"Why are you here?" he asked.

"Long story. What happens now?" I pulled back maybe an inch, which kind of helped my breathing.

"The police will want to know what you saw. Are you up to it, or do you want to go home? I can stall them if you want."

I made a quick assessment. Part of me really, *really* wanted to go home and curl up with my ratty bathrobe and a fuzzy blanket and drink a large Scotch or two, neat, with James's arms around me. The grown-up part of me vetoed that. I swabbed away tears with the back of my hand. "I think I'd better get this over with now—I might forget something."

"I've got your back," James said. "I'm going with you."

"Thank you." I had no idea what to do with my hands or any of the rest of me. I grabbed James's lapels and kind of tugged on them—assuring myself he was real?—and then realized my hands were bloody from when I'd looked for Tyrone's pulse. "Oh, sorry."

James didn't say anything, just pulled me closer again.

I could hear the sound of an ambulance approaching, but I didn't think that would help Cherisse.

CHAPTER 4

James escorted me to his car and settled me in the front seat, treating me as though I would break if handled carelessly. Then he went over to talk to the two cops. They all nodded like bobblehead dolls, and then James came back to the car and settled at the wheel.

Before he started the engine he said, "They're going to oversee the process here. The ambulance will take Blakeney and Chapman to the hospital, and then the forensic people will take a look at the scene. These guys will call it in to headquarters, and we'll go over there now so you can give your story. All right?"

I nodded and swallowed. "Is she . . . ?" I couldn't bring myself to say it.

"I'm afraid so. Did you know her?"

I shook my head. "I only met them both this morning."

"I'd ask you more questions, but I think it would be better

if you only had to go through it once. You sure you're all right?"

"Physically? Sure, I guess. The rest of me is kind of numb." I laid a hand on his arm. "Thank you for being here."

"Nell, why wouldn't I be? I love you. I want to help. And if anyone comes down hard on you, I'll be all over them."

"My knight in shining armor." I managed a weak smile. "In a peculiar way I feel responsible. If only someone had gotten the paperwork right a century ago, none of us would have been here this afternoon."

"I don't begin to understand that statement, but let's save it until we get to the Roundhouse." He started the car and pulled away from the house. A few people had gathered on the nearest corner, keeping a wary eye on the flashing lights down the block, and they watched us drive by, their faces blank, their eyes cold.

Philadelphia's police headquarters, often called the Roundhouse, was only a matter of blocks away, and I'd been known to walk there from the Society. I wish I could say I didn't know the building fairly well, but somehow I kept ending up there. At least I hadn't been arrested yet, but I'd provided evidence for more than one homicide. No one had ever mentioned that working for a staid nonprofit organization could be dangerous; I was learning the hard way.

James parked and handed me out of the car. I stood up and smoothed my clothes. There wasn't much I could do about the bloodstains. He took my arm and led me to the entrance, where he explained our presence to the gatekeeper while I stared blindly into space. Three minutes later my favorite (well, the only one I knew personally, thank goodness) homicide detective emerged from an elevator.

"I can't believe it's you two again. Can't stay out of trouble, eh?" Detective Meredith Hrivnak greeted us. Then she noted the blood and our grim expressions—she actually was a pretty good detective—and escorted us through the entry procedure, alerting the desk to James's weapon. She remained silent as we took the elevator up to her floor, and she led us to an interview room. "You want coffee? Something else?"

I was about to decline when James nodded. "Coffee for her. With sugar. Thanks."

She hesitated a moment, then nodded and went off to get it.

"Standard treatment for shock?" I asked.

"It helps. It also helps to have something to hold on to, and to do something that requires some coordination, like swallowing. Trust me."

I clasped his hand under the table. "I do. Are you just going to observe?"

"Yes. I wasn't there and I don't know what happened. I'm here strictly for your sake, not in any official capacity. And I think Hrivnak plays fair, so she's not going to badger you. Just tell her what you saw."

"That I can do." We lapsed into silence again, James's hand warm in mine, until Hrivnak returned with coffee in a foam cup. I took it and sipped. It tasted of sugar more than anything else, but at least it was hot. James was right.

Having to focus on getting it to my mouth and down my throat helped, in a weird way.

Detective Hrivnak took a chair opposite the two of us and looked us over. "Okay, I got the preliminary details from the street cops. Bad neighborhood, drive-by shooting, one dead, one wounded. And you. What the hell were you doing in the middle of it, Nell Pratt?"

I sat up straighter in my chair. "This morning Cherisse Chapman and Tyrone Blakeney came to my office to tell me that the Society owned the property where the shooting took place. I didn't know, because I thought we had disposed of all real estate decades ago, but apparently the paperwork got messed up on this one."

"So you had to go running over to look at it?"

"Not exactly. Normally I would have called our attorney and let her handle it, but Mr. Blakeney and Ms. Chapman wanted something more. Apparently they are—or were—both involved in some kind of neighborhood rescue program, to reclaim dying neighborhoods, and once they discovered the Society's connection, they thought maybe we could be useful to that effort. We didn't have time to get into the details, but the fact that we owned a piece of it gave us a reason to get involved, at least in their eyes. Of course, I told them that it wasn't my decision to make, that the board would have to be involved in anything like that, and that would take time. They were impatient, since I gather that house is scheduled to be demolished shortly, and they asked me if I wanted to see it, to get a sense of what they were talking about. Since I don't know that neighborhood well, I agreed—it seemed fair. They picked me up and drove me over at two."

"Why am I not surprised that you don't know that lovely neighborhood?"

It was a snide comment, and I didn't know what to say, so I settled for saying nothing.

"Okay, then what happened?" Hrivnak resumed her formal interrogation.

"We drove over to the house and parked. Tyrone and Cherisse didn't seem eager to get out of the car. I didn't see anybody around, or at least, not very close. Then Cherisse noticed a car that had driven past before. It drove past us slowly—that was the second time—and then went around the block. The next time they went by, the guy in the backseat of the car started shooting." James's hand tightened on mine.

"How many shooters?" Hrivnak barked.

"Just the one, in the backseat."

"Weapons?"

"Hard to tell, it happened so fast. And I don't usually see them from the barrel end. It wasn't a rifle or an Uzi, but it looked pretty big to me."

"How many shots?"

"Lots. More than enough. The shooter kept on firing. I'd guess fifteen rounds."

James and the detective exchanged a glance, but I wasn't about to explain why I knew that. "Blakeney and Chapman were both hit multiple times. Why'd they miss you?"

"Because I threw myself out of the car onto the

pavement, and waited until the shooting stopped. Either they didn't notice me, or they didn't care."

"Then what?"

"I waited to see if they were going to get out of the car or come back. They sped off. I don't know which way they went. When I thought it was safe, I got up and checked on the others. I was pretty sure that Cherisse was gone, but Tyrone was conscious. Then I called nine-one-one." And James.

"Describe the car the shooters were driving."

I did, to the best of my ability. I'm not a car person, so I couldn't give more than general details. Dark, oldish, no distinguishing marks that I could remember. Of course I hadn't thought to look at the license plate—and then I remembered that Pennsylvania didn't even require front plates, so I couldn't have seen it anyway.

"The guys in the car—black, white, something else?" Hrivnak asked.

"I think black. Not kids—maybe in their thirties? Male. They were wearing something with long sleeves— maybe sweatshirts, but I couldn't tell you what color. Not pink or yellow at least. If they had tattoos, I couldn't tell. I really only glanced at them, when Cherisse first pointed them out. After that all I saw was the gun."

"So you didn't recognize them?"

"No. As I said, I've never been in that neighborhood before."

"You think they recognized Blakeney? Or the woman?"

"You think one of them was the target?" I countered.

"Too soon to tell. "

"Do you know anything more about them, beyond what they told me?" I asked.

"Chapman is—was—a City employee in L and I. Blakeney was part of a nonprofit community redevelopment organization that's been working to save neighborhoods around the city. Just like you said. The two of them worked together—the City knew that Chapman was doing it, part of some city-sponsored program. Even got some good PR about it. Made them look like they cared."

That fit. "I can't see why anybody would want to hurt them. Weren't they trying to do something good?"

"As far as we know, but it's early days. We'll be checking into their backgrounds now. Based on what you've told us, this doesn't sound like a random drive-by, not if they scouted you out first. They didn't say anything?"

"Not that I recall."

"Question is, did they see you?"

I felt a chill. "I'm not sure. Again, as I said, I got out of the car and hid, and they didn't come back after me. So either I didn't matter, if they had a plan, or they didn't see me. I'm pretty sure it's the first. They didn't know me, they had no reason to know who I was or why I was there. And it wasn't worth eliminating me."

"You want to look at mug shots? Try a sketch artist?"

I shook my head. "I don't think I saw enough. Maybe if I saw the driver again, I'd know him, but I doubt it."

"Would he know you?" Hrivnak said, surprisingly quietly.

Now my stomach was churning. "I . . . don't know. You think he'd come after me?"

"If he knew Blakeney or Chapman, maybe worked with one of them, he could find out who you are—you kind of stick out in that neighborhood. He doesn't know that you didn't see squat."

Maybe I should try to convince myself that it really had been a random drive-by. No, that wasn't working. "What am I supposed to do about that?"

"First, give us some time to do our jobs. Second, watch your back. Third, you've got him"—she nodded toward James—"to cover you at home, right?"

I wondered how she knew that. "How long is this going to go on?"

"'Til we catch the guys."

"And if you don't?" Philadelphia Homicide did a fair job of clearing cases, but this one didn't offer much to work with.

Hrivnak looked at me directly, her expression serious. "You know I can't answer that, and I won't sugarcoat it. We'll do our best." She stood up. "I think that's enough for now. You can come back and sign your statement tomorrow. You gonna be at work?"

I hadn't really thought about that, but I realized I'd feel safer behind the solid walls of the Society than rattling around our more isolated Victorian in the near suburbs. "Yes, I will. Listen, will this be on the news? Will my name come up?"

Hrivnak cocked her head. "You want it to? Or you want to be kept out of it?"

"I'm not asking for any favors. But I should give my staff a heads-up, if there will be news coverage, and maybe figure out what we should say in our own press release." I looked at my watch and realized it was already five o'clock—too late to alert anyone. I'd have to send an e-mail from home to Eric and ask him to distribute it to the rest of the staff—but there would probably be some kind of report on tonight's news broadcasts. Damn. Would whatever this program was go on without Tyrone and Cherisse? The neighborhood issues of Philadelphia were far larger than two people.

"Any word on Tyrone's condition?" I asked suddenly.

"Not that I've heard. He's in no shape to talk to us. Maybe tomorrow."

I nodded. "Will you keep me informed? After all, I'm part of this."

"I'll tell you what I can, when I know anything," Hrivnak promised.

James stood up, putting his hand under my elbow and helping me to my feet. "Nell, we should go. You've had a rough day, and there's nothing more you can do now."

Too true. My earlier vision of curling up in his arms flashed by. "Take me home."

I could feel Hrivnak's eyes on us as we left, and I realized I had no idea if she had a husband or partner or children waiting for her at home. She knew far more about me than I knew about her.

The ride home to Chestnut Hill was slow due to the usual traffic delays. James was a soothing companion; he didn't ask stupid questions, and he didn't talk just to make noise. I knew he would let me find my own way as I processed the fact that I could easily have died earlier today for no apparent reason. Okay, we all know, on some level, that life is uncertain and could be derailed without notice, but as a professional in the cultural community I did not expect to be shot at while doing my job. Not surprisingly, I didn't like it. I didn't like watching a person, and maybe another, die in front of me. I did not like trying to make myself invisible, plastered to the pavement, hoping nobody would notice me and shoot me.

It did not matter that I had done nothing to bring this about. I'd been doing my job as a responsible manager. Was I supposed to stay out of large parts of the city where I worked because they were dangerous and dirty and scary? And where did I draw the line? Where was it safe? I'd spent time in other cities—New York, Boston, Washington. Was I supposed to map those out, too—chart the places I couldn't go? Would it be different if I were a man? If I carried a gun?

I felt James's hand on my arm. "Nell, we're home."

I dragged my imagination back from what-if land. "Then let's go inside."

I hoped I'd feel safe there.

CHAPTER 5

I managed to walk into the house, and then stood wavering in the middle of the hall. I had no idea what to do. Eat? Sleep? Pitch a fit? Were there instructions? I looked up to see James watching me with a worried expression. Oh God, how had I dragged him into this? Our first major crisis since we'd officially become a couple. (Well, my saving him from a knife-wielding psycho had occurred before we were really together, so I wasn't going to count that.) And he was supposed to take care of me? Me, who had always prided myself on my independence and self-sufficiency. Funny, I hadn't made a plan for dealing with near-death experiences.

James didn't say anything, just came up to me and held me.

"I'm not going to cry again," I said into his shirt.

"You can if you want. I won't think less of you. I never did admire stoic people."

"Gee, thanks. I'll hate myself if I blubber; you'll hate me if I don't."

"Nell . . ." he said helplessly.

"I know, I'm being completely unreasonable. You're doing everything you should." I didn't want him to let go. I didn't want to need him so much. Who the heck was I?

After some endless amount of time, James cleared his throat. "Nell, here's what I suggest. We go upstairs and change clothes—we've both got blood on ours. We can burn them if you want. Then we get some food into us. Strong drink if you want it. Then we can talk, but only if you want to. I'm not going to tell you how to handle this—it's up to you, and there's no one right way. But I'm here. You can't offend me, but I hope you won't push me away, shut me out."

"You are too good to be true. All right, I approve your plan. Let me get out of this and scrub the blood off my hands. God, I never thought I'd say that again, after . . ."

"Yes, I know," he interrupted me. "Let's get comfortable, and then I'll make you dinner. One step at a time, okay?"

"Deal."

We managed to make it up the stairs, and in our bedroom I stripped off my stained clothes as fast as possible. The shirt and jacket were beyond salvage, or at least, I didn't want to try. In reality the stains extended only a bit beyond the wrists—how was it possible that those two people could have bled so much, so fast? I pitched the clothes into a heap on the floor, and pulled on warm sweats, socks, slippers. Comfort clothes. The damage to James's wardrobe was confined to his shirt, which I also tossed onto the pile. In the bathroom I turned on the hot water in the sink and scrubbed my hands with a nailbrush until they were red, but at least not with blood.

Then on to comfort food. Childhood food: scrambled eggs and English muffins. And Scotch. I didn't need to think coherently; I didn't want to think at all.

Dinner didn't take long. We retreated to the living room, where we'd finally put a well-padded couch that could hold both of us. I refused to turn on the television. Maybe there was something on the news that I should hear, but I didn't want to. I'd been there; I knew what had happened. None of it was my fault. How could anyone spin any part of it to make me or the Society look bad? Maybe there was a form someone had forgotten to fill out back in 1923, but he was long dead, so it was a little late to point the finger at him.

"Nell," James said softly, his arms around me.

I was feeling warm and mildly drunk, enough to take the edge off. "James," I replied.

"It's hard for you to lean on someone, isn't it?"

I'd already figured that out. "Yes. For a long time, there wasn't anyone to catch me when I fell. You learn to take care of yourself. You should know that."

"I do. We're alike in that way. Plus I'm supposed to be a professional defender of the law, and I carry a weapon. Double burden. No self-doubt allowed."

"I know. But I don't like feeling helpless."

"You're not helpless, you're human. You've been through

something awful. If you didn't have a strong emotional reaction to that, I'd be worried about you."

"Mmm," I said by way of answer. I was definitely feeling better now than I had a few hours earlier. How I'd feel in the morning was anybody's guess. But, as the quote went, tomorrow was another day.

The phone rang.

"Damn," I said. "It can't be the press, can it? They don't know where to find me, and I don't think anyone who knows this number would give it to anyone."

"I'm going to hazard a guess that it's one of those people who does have this number."

"Marty," I said.

"Exactly," James replied.

"I guess I have to answer it," I said, disentangling myself reluctantly and wandering toward the phone. I checked the caller ID: yup, Marty.

Martha Terwilliger occupied a unique place in our lives, individually and together. She was a board member of the Society, as her father and grandfather had been before her. Her family name was on one of the largest and most significant collections the Society had. She knew everyone worth knowing in the greater Philadelphia area, past and present, and was related to half of them. And somehow she and I had become partners in sorting out crimes—starting with one that led to her orchestrating my elevation to president of the Society—and she had introduced me to James, who happened to be her cousin. That all added up to Marty assuming she had a right to know all the details of whatever happened at the Society as well as to James, to me, and to us as a couple. She was a good-hearted person, but sometimes I wished she'd put a little distance between us.

I pushed "talk."

"That was you, right?" Martha Terwilliger said without preamble. She had a way of cutting through the underbrush and getting straight to the point.

I didn't need to ask what she was talking about. "How'd you guess?"

"Trouble seems to find you. You all right? Is Jimmy there?"

"I'm managing. And yes, James arrived in time to scrape me off the pavement—literally—and hold my hand at the police station, and guide me home."

"I'm glad," she said, uncharacteristically softly. Then she ramped up the volume again. "So, what the hell were you doing in that neighborhood at all?"

"Society business. Something you and I need to talk about, and probably have to take to the board."

"You're kidding. Aren't you?" Marty asked anxiously.

"I wish I was. Even I know enough to stay out of that part of town, unless there's a really good reason, but this kind of was. The shooting part was unexpected. I have no idea whether it has anything to do with the Society, but it seems unlikely."

"The news says somebody was killed. Who was it?"

"A woman named Cherisse Chapman. Do you know her?"

"Sounds familiar . . . Wait—she worked for the City? Short, in her thirties, smart?"

"That's right. How do you know her?"

"She was . . . oh, now I get it. She was working in neighborhood redevelopment, handling vacant properties. That's why you met her?"

I had long since given up being surprised that Marty knew everybody in Philadelphia and what they were doing, and half the time, what their parents and grandparents had done. "Exactly. We were looking at a property that she said the Society owns. Yes, before you interrupt, we all thought we'd gotten rid of all of those, but something got fouled up years ago, and we're still the owner of record. Of a place that's about to collapse, in the middle of a dangerous slum. And Cherisse is dead."

"What a waste," Marty muttered. Then she collected herself. "Well, you must be a wreck. I'll come by the Society tomorrow and we can figure out what happened. You going to produce a press release?"

"Oh, shoot—I meant to work on that tonight, so I can send it to Eric and he can get it out first thing in the morning. Although I have no idea how coherent I can be, and how much I can say."

"Hrivnak on this one?"

"Who else? I seem to be her special project, and I'm keeping her busy these days. I'd better go draft that release. Talk to you tomorrow."

I hung up, suddenly exhausted, before she could say anything more. Somehow James was behind me again.

"Want me to unplug the phones?"

"We can just ignore them. Unless it's our favorite detective, calling to let me know that they've solved the case and everything is taken care of. But I think that's beyond even her superpowers."

"Then come upstairs."

"I've got to draft a press release so Eric can get to work on it."

"Saying what?" James asked. "That you were a witness to a shooting that had nothing to do with you? That's not exactly the kind of news you want to announce."

"What if it did?"

"Involve you? Why on earth would you think that?"

"Because that's the way my luck works? I don't believe I'm the center of the universe, but I do seem to keep stumbling into dangerous things. And they don't exactly involve me, more often the Society, but in a way I *am* the Society—the public face. I'm responsible for what goes on there, both inside and outside."

James grabbed my shoulders and turned me to face him squarely. "Nell Pratt, somebody tried to kill you today. It doesn't matter whether he knew who you were, or was aiming at you, or just liked the noise his gun made when he pulled the trigger. You could have died. Don't try to brush that off. If it doesn't matter to you, it does to me."

"Oh," I said. I couldn't meet his eyes. He was right, in a way: I was being selfish by trying to pretend it didn't matter that I'd come within inches of dying. I hadn't taken his feelings into account. If he loved me (*If, Nell?*), he would have been deeply hurt himself. I'd laid my life on the line when I'd stopped his attacker a few months earlier, and I had no doubt he would do the same for me. He was probably angry with himself that he hadn't been there on that street today to protect me, even though that was ridiculous.

Damn, this relationship stuff was tricky!

So inside I let something go. He was right: the stupid press release could wait. Right now we needed each other. "I love you, James. I'm just still trying to get my head around being 'us' instead of just me. I'm sorry."

"We're learning together, love. Now come upstairs, will you?"

"Of course."

We spent some time celebrating life. After, I lay awake for a while, watching James sleep. I'd been happy on my own, hadn't I? Not long before, I would have said yes. Now . . . well, it was a whole new world. He was a good man—smart, capable, strong. And he loved me. And I loved him, thought I didn't say it enough. Something else to work on. I drifted off to sleep . . .

———

The next morning James had turned off my alarm but woke me with a cup of hot French roast coffee. He sat at the foot of the bed, watching me sip it. "You're going to work, I assume?"

"I thought so. Why? Do you think I shouldn't?"

He gave the question some thought. "Part of me would like to lock you up until we figure out why yesterday happened at all. I realize that is ridiculous, but that doesn't stop me from feeling that way."

I smiled. "That's all right. Part of me would like to crawl into a cave—preferably with you—and wait it out.

But we're grown-ups, so we can't do that. And I do have obligations that involve this incident that are going to be more pressing than they were yesterday morning. Are you going to be involved?"

"It's unlikely that Detective Hrivnak would enjoy my participation."

"Hey, she didn't bite your head off yesterday."

"No, but you will notice I kept my mouth shut. I was there to support you, not to solve a crime. I can see only one circumstance that would even suggest the FBI's involvement."

"Which would be?"

"If this was determined to be a hate crime."

Much as I would like his active participation, I didn't see much chance of that. "Black men shooting at a couple of black people in a largely black neighborhood. I don't think I was the target."

"You're saying you think the only kind of hate crime involves race?"

"Oh. Well, no, not exactly. But this is Philadelphia, so it's never far away. What else qualifies?"

"Congress has defined a hate crime as 'a criminal offense against a person or property motivated in whole or in part by an offender's bias against a race, religion, disability, ethnic origin, or sexual orientation.' Civil rights violations may also fall in that category, but the FBI can investigate only if it applies to an individual, not a group."

"I don't see how any of that fits, but who knows? I'll keep you informed if anything pops up."

"Are you okay with going in today?" he asked.

"I'll be all right, James. But thank you for worrying."

"I'm driving you to work."

"I won't argue. Now, let me get ready, will you?"

I took a shower, then chose my clothes with an eye to appearing on camera, although I hoped that wouldn't happen. I was not the news here—the bright lights should focus on Tyrone and Cherisse and the cesspit that was North Philadelphia. I was sure the police would make all the right noises and would put on a show of looking for the shooters. I had little faith that they would find them. But right now I had a smaller, simpler task to focus on: what to do with that cursed property.

CHAPTER 6

James dropped me off in front of the Society. If there had been a parking space open, I had no doubt that he would have escorted me into the lobby and handed me off to Front Desk Bob, who had once been a cop. As it was, he had to content himself with a serious kiss, and then he stayed at the curb, idling, until he saw me walk in the door. Apparently yesterday's events had really rattled him, which surprised me. And moved me: he really was worried about me.

Inside it was cool, clean, and peaceful. Bob was already at his desk. "You all right, Ms. Pratt?" he asked.

"I'm fine, Bob, just shaken up."

"Bad part of town," he said. I realized I didn't know exactly where he lived. I doubted it was in that part of town, but as a former cop he would know exactly how bad it was there.

"Yes, it is. I guess I hadn't realized how bad. Thanks for asking."

I went through the main reference room and headed for the elevator. If Bob's solicitous reaction was any indication, it was going to be a very odd day.

My arrival in front of Eric's desk confirmed my suspicion. I was afraid he was going to jump over his desk and hug me. While I considered us friends, we weren't exactly on hugging terms, but I braced myself just in case. Luckily he settled for jumping out of his chair.

"Nell, are you all right? I heard the news, and then when you didn't call or leave an e-mail or a message or anything, and you weren't on the late news, I really started to worry."

"I'm sorry, Eric. It never occurred to me that other people would be worried. Well, Martha Terwilliger called, but she's a special case. I didn't mean to scare you. I thought about sending you a draft of a press release, in case the public is interested, but I decided it could wait until this morning. We're only a footnote to the story."

"Well, I'm glad you're okay. I'll go get you some coffee right away." He hurried down the hall, leaving me feeling both guilty and amused.

Shelby arrived next, and she didn't hesitate to hug me. "What were you thinking, lady? I'm pretty new to Philadelphia, but even I know better than to wander into North Philly."

"It was business, Shelby," I said feebly. "I wasn't exactly sightseeing. And I didn't know where they were going to take me." Although I probably should have guessed, after what we'd discussed.

"Business, my butt. And you gave me the address yesterday, remember? You should have known."

"Well, yes, but that doesn't mean I recognized where it was. I don't know every street in the city. Especially in neighborhoods I've never seen."

"Well, next time you go off like that, do your homework, will you? Or better yet, send a large lawyer to handle it. We need you here. Did Mr. Agent Man swoop in and save the day?"

"Kind of, after the fact. After the shooting stopped, I called the cops and then I called him. And he got there fast. He was so sweet." His simple kindness brought new tears to my eyes.

"You've got a keeper there, Nell. So, what happens now?"

"With what?"

"That blasted property that started the whole thing."

"I haven't a clue, and I haven't had time to think about it. But I'm here, and I'm going to look into it."

"Why am I not surprised?" Shelby rolled her eyes, then winked at me. "Let me ask you this," Shelby said. "Do you have any reason to think that this shooting had anything to do with you, the Society, or that particular property?"

"Not that I'm aware of. It could have been a random event, and that's what the police are likely to think. I suppose there's a slim chance that it was directed at either one of the other people in the car with me. I don't know anything about them, although Marty seems to have met the woman. But that's for the police to look into, not me. James and I went over to police headquarters yesterday and I gave them my statement, which I still have to sign, and that may be the end of it, at least for the Society, and for me. You didn't happen to find anything interesting about the house or the street, did you?"

"Not yet, but I've just started. Not that I'm expecting much. But I'll keep looking, and I'll check with the business office to see if they have anything on file. At this place you never know what might turn up."

"Thank you, Shelby. I was wondering if I should get the staff together and tell them what happened, in case anybody asks them about it. Even simple questions like *What was Nell Pratt doing there?*"

"I think you should, just so everybody can see you're still alive and kicking. People were worried, you know."

I fought back more tears. I was beginning to wonder just how long I'd feel so emotional, but as James had told me, I had the right to be upset. "That's really nice of them. Okay, I'll ask Eric to tell people to gather in the boardroom at ten so I can get this out of the way."

"Sounds good," Shelby said. She wavered a moment, then dove in for another hug. "I'm so glad you're all right—this place wouldn't be the same without you." Then she fled to her own office.

I went back out to Eric's desk and said, "Could you send out a staff e-mail and ask everyone to gather in the boardroom at ten? I might as well get the story out, in case any patrons ask about it. I haven't dared look at the paper this morning—is there any mention of me or the Society in the news coverage?"

"Way down at the bottom. You were described as a witness."

"Well, that much is accurate, I guess. Tell the staff I'll keep it short, will you?"

"Yes, ma'am!"

Back in my office, I sat down in my damask-clad antique mahogany chair and tried to think. My mind was blank. Whatever I'd been doing yesterday seemed incredibly trivial right now, but I needed to get my head back in the game.

Much as I hated to think so, Tyrone and Cherisse had made a good point yesterday, when they came to see me. The Society had a measure of status in the Philadelphia cultural community, not to mention a wealth of varied resources—and not all high-end silver and genealogies of famous people. We also had accounts from small businesses, and architectural histories, and shipping and bank records. I realized that it would be easy for us to pull together a sort of profile of almost any neighborhood in the city, based on our own collections. Which, as Tyrone had suggested, would make the Society a very useful partner in any redevelopment project. I was somewhat surprised that no developer or neighborhood group had approached us before now, looking for ammunition to use in their own efforts. It would be a smart move, to craft an appeal not just to community activists but also to the higher-end movers and shakers who cared about the city and its past but weren't familiar with what had happened to the old neighborhoods because they didn't want to see it and were looking the other way. In other words, a lot of our members and donors. Tyrone and Cherisse had no doubt wanted to recruit me as an ally, and they were right to do so. We could help, if the project they had described was going to go on.

Which of the two had been the prime mover, Tyrone or Cherisse? They had made a good team, because they approached the problem from different directions, and each of them was in a position to know the real issues. But alliances between the City and private organizations were rare. What had brought them together? What were the specific details about the project they had most likely intended to pitch to me, if our tour hadn't ended in disaster?

By the time I was done wading through this thought process, it was time for the meeting I had asked Eric to arrange. I marched down the hall to the modern boardroom (far less formal, but also less attractive, than the former boardroom on the ground floor) and walked in to find the majority of the staff was already assembled—and they burst into applause at my entrance. I didn't know whether to laugh or cry.

"Thank you, I think. I didn't do anything but duck, but I seem to do that pretty well."

"What happened?" Felicity Soames, our venerable head librarian, asked. "The news reports were kind of vague."

I launched into a brief description of the visit by Tyrone and Cherisse the day before, which had culminated in the tour of the dying neighborhood, and the events that followed. When I was done, our relatively new registrar, Ben, asked, "What were they hoping to accomplish, dragging you down there?"

"Ben, I think they wanted to drive home the point that that part of the city was once a vital neighborhood, and now it's a disaster area. I'm sure you all know better than I do that we're talking about a large area within a short walk of some of the nicest and most visited parts of town." I turned from Ben and looked at each of the others around the table. "Before you start protesting, I know that it's not our responsibility to take on all the problems of the city of Philadelphia. We're scrabbling to keep up with what goes on within these walls. And we're not in any way a political organization. But we are the keepers of the city's history, and we can provide a wealth of information about any part of the city. I think that was all Tyrone and Cherisse wanted, although we never had a chance to get to the details. And maybe they were on the right track: we should be more proactive about it, instead of waiting for some of the activists out there to stumble over us. I'm betting that a lot of those activists are not among our regular patrons. But we as an institution need to broaden our reach and increase our visibility if we're going to survive." I stopped, surprised at myself. Where had that speech come from?

Latoya Anderson, our vice president for collections, who happened to be a black woman, had come in while I was speaking. I was trying hard not to sound racist, and many of the neighborhoods of the city had flourished under a wide range of ethnic groups, but I knew Latoya could be prickly and occasionally defensive.

I was pleased when she said, "I think you make an excellent point, Nell. I know in recent years we've focused most of our energies on keeping this institution viable, financially and physically, and that's an ongoing challenge. But we may have lost sight of our mandate along the way. We do have an obligation to all populations in this city, both past and present, and this might be an excellent way to fulfill that."

I smiled at her. "I'm happy to hear you say that, Latoya. Look, everyone, I haven't had time to think this through since yesterday, and it may come to nothing, but I'd love to hear your ideas on the subject. Feel free to spitball. I hate to say it, but I'm not even sure which neighborhoods each of you live in. How many of you live within city limits?" About half of the people around the table raised a hand. "So you know what the real day-to-day issues are—that's great. Anything that pops into your head, anything you come across while looking for something else, write it down, and we'll see where it leads, okay?"

"Give those ideas to me," Latoya said. "I'll be happy to coordinate."

That was a surprise: Latoya seldom volunteered to take on anything outside of her job description, although that job was certainly demanding. "Thank you, Latoya—that would be great." I turned back to the others. "As I said, think creatively. I don't want to sound crass, but stories about people in the neighborhoods, small shops, festivals, even plant openings—we can pull those together. We have the information, but we have to dig it up."

I swallowed. "What happened yesterday was awful. A woman died. A man was seriously wounded. I was lucky to escape without harm. The news will focus on those two, not me. If anyone comes to you and asks, *What was Nell Pratt doing there?* tell them I was acting as an histori- cal consultant, okay? You don't have to say anything more. Unless, of course, you want to give them the full descrip- tion of our amazing collections." Several people laughed at that. "Okay, that's all I have. We'd all better get back to work now."

The staff members drifted out of the room, a few stop- ping to speak to me. I was surprised that Latoya lingered until they were gone. "Thanks again for stepping up, Latoya," I told her. "You think anything will come of it?"

"Maybe. You're right about the role we *could* play, but it remains to be seen whether anything happens. Look, I wanted to tell you that I know Tyrone Blakeney . . . We've been friends for years. We even dated for a time, long before he married. He's a good man, and a smart one. I haven't seen him for quite a while, but the press might dig up our connection. I didn't want you to be surprised."

"Thank you. I've had more than enough surprises already this week. But it seems unlikely that the press would dig so deep into Tyrone's past life. Does he have anything to hide?"

"Not that I know of. He's been an activist of one sort or another for years, but not a troublemaker or a rabble-rouser.

He honestly believes in the causes he pushes—it's not just for his own glory. And if it means anything, I think he grew up in North Philadelphia, so he has his own history there."

"Is there anything I should or shouldn't tell the police about him, if they come calling? Not that I believe they will."

"Just tell them what you know. I believe Tyrone is an honest man. That's all I wanted to say."

"Thank you. Let me know if any interesting ideas pop up, will you? It's not urgent, but I'd like to be ready if an appropriate opportunity turns up."

"Of course, Nell. And I'm glad you're all right." She turned and left. While I wouldn't say it was a warm and fuzzy talk, she'd been more open with me than at any time I could remember. Interesting.

I went back down the hall to my office. "Anything I need to know?" I asked Eric when I paused in front of his desk.

"Some calls from the media—I said you were in a meeting, which was true, and I put the messages on your desk. Let me know if you want to put any of them through to you."

"Thanks, Eric." In my office I sat down at my desk and sifted through the short stack. None of the calls seemed urgent; probably staff writers were looking for a tidbit to flesh out a story. Their interest in me would probably die down quickly, so I figured I'd ignore them.

The next time I looked up, Marty Terwilliger was standing in the doorway.

CHAPTER 7

She slouched against the door frame and grinned at me. "To mangle Mark Twain, the reports of your death are greatly exaggerated."

"I'm so glad you noticed. Come on in and have a seat."

She did. "Seriously, Nell, I'm glad you weren't hurt. That must have been a scary thing."

I wasn't about to lie. "Yes, it was. Of course, I only realized that afterward—the shooting part happened so fast that I didn't have time to think. I just threw myself out of the way."

"Good instincts. Make yourself a smaller target."

"Assuming the bad guys didn't hang around. If they had stopped and come around the car to finish me off, there wasn't a lot I could have done. And I don't know how I would have coped without James."

"Knowing you, you would have put on a stiff upper

lip and tried to pretend being shot at was a normal event in your life." In a softer voice she added, "I'm glad Jimmy was there for you." Even though she had a wealth of cousins, Marty had a soft spot for James.

"Probably. I think it's called denial. I'm told that's bad for your mental health. So, what brings you here this morning?"

"Apart from making sure you were alive and functioning? My usual rounds to be sure the reshelving of the collections is on schedule and checking that the Terwilliger papers are safe."

Marty's family had been among the leaders of Philadelphia for more than two centuries, and she could recite the entire family tree and tell you which houses they had lived in and what china patterns they had used. But she was not a pretentious snob, and she was involved in a number of worthy causes, quietly. When she couldn't give money, she gave her time and energy, which was boundless. Her grandfather and father had left the extensive family papers to the Society, but they had each in turn kept an eye on them, as Marty was doing now. Terwilliger funds were paying part of the salary of an intern, Rich Girard, to help with processing the collection, but the recent renovations to the building had made that more complicated than usual. It was no surprise that Marty was keeping a sharp eye on both the collections and Rich.

"And I wanted to kick around some way to follow up on what happened yesterday. To talk about Eliot's board nomination. That enough for one morning?"

"Well, you've already made sure that I'm alive, and that

James is looking out for me, so let's focus on your next point. How much do you know about what happened yesterday?"

"Start from the beginning."

I complied, filling her in on the first contact with Tyrone and Cherisse, and my agreeing to visit the site, and everything that had gone wrong after that. She didn't interrupt.

When I was done, she said, "I have a vague memory of some comment at a board meeting that the Society had unloaded all the properties. It made sense: there was no way to try to manage them, especially when the staff was a lot smaller, and nobody wanted to pay someone else to do it. But there were quite a few of them, as I remember it. I can't say I'm surprised that the paperwork got misplaced for one of 'em. Might be more, if anyone goes looking."

"I hadn't even thought of that, but I suppose we should check now, just in case. Who should I ask to look into it?"

"Start with the law firm. If they don't have the records, they'll tell you who to ask next."

"Not someone at the City?" I asked.

She cocked an eyebrow at me. "Seriously? You know how backlogged they always are. Why do you think it took so long for them to notice this little snafu? I'm not criticizing, but the problem keeps growing, and the staff and funding don't. Start with the lawyer."

"Will do. But on that note, I talked to the staff this morning about what we should do about neighborhood projects like this one." I gave Marty the gist of what we had discussed earlier in the morning. "Is that just my guilt talking, or do you think it makes sense?"

Marty smiled. "A little of each, but it's not a bad idea. I don't think there's any way we can or should work with the City itself, but we can probably carve out a niche for the Society, and we all benefit. Make us look more relevant—and less like a bunch of old fogies looking up their family history."

"That's kind of what I was thinking," I said. "If life hands you lemons—or in this case, bullets—make lemonade. So, Eliot? Things going well there?"

"With the Society or with me?"

"Take your pick." I knew that Marty and Eliot had been seeing each other for a while, but Marty was surprisingly closemouthed about what was going on with them, although she'd had no reservations about prying into my evolving relationship with James. It was Marty who had suggested recruiting Eliot as a board member.

"Professionally he's a good fit, right? Professor, specializing in urban planning, respected in the community, well liked by his students, no skeletons in his closet or scandals on his résumé."

"Hey, you don't have to convince me. I like the guy, and I think he provides a much-needed balance to the traditional historians and lawyers on the board. Have you been hearing any resistance from other board members?"

"Nope. Of course, they might not say it to my face. You haven't heard any rumblings?"

"No. I can't imagine why anyone would object. Well, except for the issue of the two of you . . ."

"You're thinking that if we put him on the board, will I be putting myself in an awkward position?"

"Yes. And that can be taken in more than one way. If you're a couple, somebody might object—nepotism, or undue influence, or something like that. If you're no longer a couple, you're stuck with running into him regularly for as long as his term lasts."

"Let me worry about the personal side of things."

"Fine. We'll nominate him and vote at the board meeting next week." Then I had another thought. "You know, I told you I was talking with the staff this morning, about reaching out more to neighborhood redevelopment groups, offer them what we know of the history of various neighborhoods. But it occurs to me that neighborhood activists can be rather narrowly focused on more practical matters, like housing the people displaced or finding developers who will do the work at a reasonable price. Eliot might be a great person to serve as a go-between."

"Because he's a minority?" Marty asked.

Eliot was the son of an American soldier and his Korean war bride. I couldn't honestly say that I and others at the Society hadn't taken that into consideration when proposing him for a board seat: our board, and our membership, was definitely skewed toward middle-aged Caucasian men. But Eliot's credentials spoke for themselves. "No, of course not. Because it's his field of expertise. He's respected and published. And we have untapped resources that he can use."

"Let me run the idea by him. Any word on Tyrone Blakeney's condition?"

I was embarrassed that I hadn't even given that a thought this morning. "Not that I've heard, but I don't expect anyone to contact me with updates. Do you know him?"

"No. I told you I'd worked with Cherisse, though—too bad about her."

"They made a good team, based on what little I saw. Did you know that Latoya once dated Tyrone?" This didn't count as gossiping, did it? Latoya seldom doled out personal information. It was Tyrone who had inserted himself into our lives, and I thought Latoya was right in mentioning the prior connection, in case the police happened to stumble on it.

"I did not know that. Interesting—I wouldn't have thought he was her type. So, what now?"

"I have no idea. I might have had a plan yesterday morning, but that kind of flew out the window. I've got to pull together reports from departments, and from the construction guys, to send to the board this week. We're hatching a new outreach effort, maybe, but it's too soon to say anything about that. I don't want to talk to the media. Can I go home now?"

"Not hardly. Listen, I wanted to talk about . . ." And Marty was off and running. She was a tremendous asset to the Society, the third generation of her line to take a hand in managing the place, and she knew more about the Society than I ever would, even though I'd been working here for more than ten years now. But sometimes her exhaustive knowledge of details was simply . . . exhausting. I sat back and let her words flow over me.

I don't know how long that would have gone on if we

had not been interrupted by a phone call. Eric stuck his head in the door. "Nell, Detective Hrivnak is downstairs, and she wants to see you."

Marty and I exchanged startled glances. "Maybe she's just delivering my statement to sign?" I suggested.

"You believe that?" Marty shot back.

I shook my head. "Not the way my luck runs. I'd better go see what she wants. You going to wait here?"

"Of course. She knows who I am, and she knows you're going to tell me everything anyway. This saves time. Bring her on up."

I passed Eric's desk and told him I would be collecting the detective, then took the elevator down and walked to the lobby. She was deep in conversation with Bob at the desk, but she looked up quickly when she saw me approaching.

"Detective, what can I do for you today?" I said.

"We need to talk," she said bluntly. I'd heard that line before from her, and it didn't bode well.

"My office?" I suggested. I knew Marty was lying in wait there. Did I think I needed protection? Or a witness?

"Okay," the detective agreed. She followed me silently to the elevator and up, then down the hall to my office. When she walked in she was startled to see Marty there, but she didn't protest. "Ms. Terwilliger."

"Detective," Marty replied, equally curt.

"Detective, do you mind if Marty hears whatever you have to say?"

Detective Hrivnak waved a dismissive hand. "No problem. But this is off the record, kinda, for now."

That was curious. "You know you can trust us. Please, sit down. Do you want some coffee? Anything else?"

"Nah. Let's just get this sorted out. Ms. Terwilliger, you know what happened yesterday?"

"I do. Nell filled me in this morning. Please call me Marty—it'll save time."

"Right. Marty. Okay, a drive-by shooting in North Philly. Not exactly a rare event. One dead—a City employee named Cherisse Chapman. One wounded: Tyrone Blakeney. One—what do you want me to call you, Ms. Pratt?"

"Nell. How about, one person completely out of place there?"

"That'll do. One shooter, one driver. In a car that you and Tyrone tell us was checking you out before they started shooting."

"How is Tyrone, by the way?" I asked. Better late than never.

"Stable. Shot multiple times, but none of the bullets hit anything vital. Chapman wasn't so lucky. Anyway, Tyrone's talking, but he didn't say anything we didn't already know from you."

"He told you why we were there?"

"He did. Hopeless cause, but I guess somebody's got to try. You told me it was the woman who noticed the car first, right?"

"Yes. Tyrone was turned away, talking to me in the backseat. Cherisse saw the car on its second pass by us, and mentioned it, but Tyrone was too busy to look. The third time by was when they started shooting."

"Cherisse didn't recognize anyone? Or the car?"

"She didn't say. Only that she'd noticed the car passing us more than once. They were going pretty slowly, and it was clear they were looking at us. There was nothing else to see on that block."

"Did Chapman seem nervous?"

"Only after she'd seen the car a second time. Detective, what is this all about?"

Detective Hrivnak sighed. "Look, the department wants to close this case, call it a random shooting. I'm not so sure, but I don't have much to go on, and nothing that's going to change their minds. Not yet."

I knew the detective could be a bulldog when she wanted to find something, and she didn't take the easy way out. "Why are you not sure?"

"So far we haven't found any reason why anyone would want any of you dead, or at least out of commission or scared off. Of course, it's only been one day, but nothing jumps out. No attempt at robbery, right?"

I shook my head. "No. They could have stopped and grabbed wallets, purses, phones, whatever. They should know how long it would take the cops to show up, and they would have had time, right?" I hoped she didn't take that the wrong way, but I'd seen myself that the cops had been skeptical about the 911 call.

"Probably. So they didn't want your cash or phones or whatever, and they kind of messed up the car, so it wasn't so they could take that."

"This about drugs?" Marty said.

"It's a problem in that part of town, all right," Detective Hrivnak told her. "And gangs—Puerto Ricans, Irish, black,

71

Dominican, Polish, Asian. You name it, they're on the street dealing."

I was beginning to wonder why I worked in Philadelphia at all, if it was so dangerous. Ignorance was bliss, maybe, but I couldn't claim to be ignorant any longer. "Any evidence that the house we were looking at was a drug, er, den?"

"Nope—it was too far gone to support a lot of traffic. This one was pretty exposed, so nobody could go in and out easily. Although that could cut both ways—no one could sneak up on the house without being noticed. But there are plenty of other houses to use."

"Detective, what are you trying to tell us?" I finally asked.

"Unless it was some gang member proving himself, there's no reason for anyone who didn't know you to shoot at you. How old was the shooter?"

"Not a kid, if that's what you're asking. I guessed thirties, or maybe late twenties. Do you know what the weapon was?"

"What, you can't identify a make and model from twenty feet while it's firing at you?" she said snidely, then quickly corrected herself. "Sorry, that's not fair. I know you know guns, but I'll give you a pass this time. The slugs we removed from both victims were thirty-eight caliber."

"That's pretty common for street punks, isn't it?" I said.

"Yeah—it was nothing fancy. Not in the system, either— I had our lab check."

We all digested that information for a few seconds. Then I said, "Why'd you push to get the casings identified so quickly? I didn't think autopsies and forensic stuff happened so fast."

"Because you were there."

"What?" Marty and I said in unison.

Hrivnak's mouth twitched. "How many crimes you been involved in? Five, six? Maybe I'm superstitious, but I figure if you're involved, it ain't gonna be an easy case."

"I don't know whether to be horrified or flattered," I told her. "So what you're thinking is, there's some motive for this shooting that we aren't seeing—yet. What do you plan to do about it?"

"I do my job. I look at the victims. I look at other crime in that neighborhood. I look to see if anyone has an interest in that property, either seeing it stay up or fall down."

"And is there something you want me to do?"

"Yeah. Blakeney and Chapman brought you into this— you're the wild card, at least until we find some dirt on either of the other two. Look at the history and why you were there. I'll take care of the rest."

CHAPTER 8

We had little more to say to each other, so I signed the statement she had indeed brought with her, and handed Detective Hrivnak over to Eric to be escorted downstairs, after promising her that I'd contact her with any ideas I came up with, even if they seemed trivial. Then I went back into my office and dropped into my chair.

"Well, that was interesting," I said to Marty.

"Sure was. I do believe she trusts you now," Marty said.

"Enough to follow her gut, even if her bosses want this closed? I'm impressed. Do you agree with what she said?"

Marty didn't answer immediately, and she finally said, "I think so. I think we all agree that the guys in the car checking you out more than once is suspicious. Like maybe they were looking for somebody specific, not just any old body. Who else knew you were there?"

"Me, singular, or we, plural?"

"Whatever you know."

"Heck, I had no clue where we were going. No, I take that back: I had the address, but I had no idea where it was. I told Shelby to look into what we had on it, so she knew. But apart from that, we didn't even decide to go there until that morning. I told Eric I was going with Tyrone and Cherisse, and I told Shelby to look up any records she could find about the property, going back a ways. And that was it. You think Eric or Shelby told some drug thug to take me out?"

Marty stifled a smile. "Not hardly. So it doesn't sound like they were gunning for you, since they didn't know you'd be there. Unless, of course, the guys followed you—the plural you—from the Society to wherever you went. Which would mean they were following one of the other two. What do we know about them?"

"Not much. I met them both for the first time twenty-four hours ago. You said you'd met Cherisse—what do you know about her?"

"I met her, which is not the same as knowing her. There was some fuss when I inherited the family house when my father passed on, and I had to go to Licenses and Inspections to sort it out. I lucked out with Cherisse—she seemed to be the sharpest apple on that particular tree."

"How long ago was this? Because she looked like she was in her early thirties."

"Maybe three, four years ago? She was efficient—figured out what was wrong, fast, and fixed it. Best experience I've had, dealing with a City agency."

SHEILA CONNOLLY

"That matches what little I know about her. I haven't had a lot of interactions with the City. Are you hinting that she wasn't a typical City employee?"

Marty shrugged. "You said she was interested in this community redevelopment stuff? Maybe she figured working on the inside would be useful for that. Otherwise it's not usually a great springboard for a career, from what I've heard."

"Probably not, in most cases," I agreed. "I could see that Cherisse was using it as a way to get up close and personal with how the City works, and to see where the opportunities lay."

"Where'd she come from? Local?"

"I don't know. We never had a chance to talk about stuff like that. Let Hrivnak figure that part out." She had access to far more resources than I did.

"It could make a difference—you know, if she grew up in the city, or if she attended Temple or Penn here. Was she a poor kid looking to make a name for herself? Or was she a middle-class suburbanite who still thought she could save the world after college?"

"Are there any of those left?" I asked, feeling almost wistful.

"I don't know. I haven't met any lately, but I don't spend a lot of time with kids that age. Well, maybe Alice, or Lissa." Alice was a young intern, not a longtime staffer; Lissa was kind of a hired gun whom we turned to when we had a single project that needed research.

I nodded. "Alice may still cling to a few shreds of idealism, although she's pretty levelheaded. Lissa's been banged around a bit, so she's not as starry-eyed. They might know people who still cling to some idealism, though. Worth asking."

"You can do that if you want," Marty said. "I wish we knew more about Tyrone."

"I know what you mean," I said. "Cherisse didn't seem like the type that someone would try to kill. Tyrone has more ties to that neighborhood. And of the two of them, he seemed to take the lead, and not just because he was the man. More like he was the more passionate of the two. But I could see that they'd make a good pairing to get things done. He had the passion, and she had the expertise, as well as access to all of the property documents."

"That's for Hrivnak again. Ask her to send you whatever background they find on those two. And whatever organization Tyrone was representing," Marty said firmly.

Good thing we were starting off with Hrivnak on our side, for a change. "You know, this isn't going to get us very far."

"It's a start, isn't it?"

"Yes, but Hrivnak is better equipped to handle this than we are. What do we bring to this?"

"History," Marty replied quickly. "What we do is to find out what we can about that neighborhood, that block, that house. Who built it, owned it? Who left it to the Society? Maybe there's buried treasure under it. Or George Washington kept his mistress there. No—sounds like the building was built too late for that. Unless he buried that mistress under an earlier house on that lot. Or Martha murdered her and had her buried there."

SHEILA CONNOLLY

"Marty, this is ridiculous." Although I had to admit it was funny, and we needed a little humor right about then. "I will find out what I can about the site, but most likely it will turn out to be an ordinary street with ordinary row houses, where ordinary factory workers and their families lived until the factories went away for good."

"At least then you'll know and you can cross it off your list. Okay, let's take a step back. Why does anyone shoot at anyone else?"

This was one very odd conversation, but Marty and I seemed to have a fair number of those. "You mean ever? Well, there's anger, jealousy, hate. Money. Fear. Revenge. Am I missing anything?"

"Those are the biggies. Most things trace back to one of those, or a combination. Drug deals gone wrong—they come back to money, or maybe power. Maybe somebody wanted the property, or didn't want someone else to have it. Money again, maybe mixed with anger. Or fear. Like I said, if there's a body buried under the house, or walled up inside, maybe somebody doesn't want that found."

"Marty, the place is falling down, and the City plans to demolish it. That hypothetical body would be found no matter what. It would have been simpler if someone had just burned it to the ground. I'm sorry, but none of these ideas is really working for me."

"Give it time. If all else fails, you can go back to the random shooting theory. Would you like something else to distract you?"

Coming from Marty, that was always a dangerous question. "What?" I said cautiously.

"I was going to bring this up anyway, before yesterday happened, but now is just as good a time. The Oliver mansion is up for sale. You know the place?"

"I can't say that I do. What is it?"

"It's a late colonial house, built by a Loyalist around 1760, but he couldn't hold on to his property during the Revolutionary War—the local patriots got kind of pissed at him and burned his main house to the ground. The one that survived was built for his son. Then his heirs bought it back, in the nineteenth century, and they've lived in it continuously ever since. The last two descendants, a pair of maiden sisters, are in their late eighties now. Still mentally sharp, but they're not going to last forever. They want to make sure the old place doesn't end up as a shopping mall or condos, and they're looking for someone to take over in a custodial capacity. They'll give it away to the right organization, along with about eight generations of the furniture."

"Wow! Seriously?"

"For real. Interested?"

"I don't know how to begin to answer that. The Society is out of the real estate business, you know—or at least, we thought we were. We can't exactly pack up and move to wherever it is. Where is it?"

"Montgomery County. Not too far outside Philadelphia city limits."

"Okay, not convenient—our base is the city. I assume the gift is contingent upon keeping the property and maintaining it according to their guidelines?"

"Yup. You can't sell it, and you can't sell the

furniture—some of which is pretty nice, I might add—
and fill it with stuff from IKEA. They've got a damn good
lawyer, who's going to make sure it's in trust forever."

"Any money come with it?" I asked.

"Some. An endowment that might—stress that *might*—
be enough to cover taxes and insurance and keeping the
lights on. But I think it's safe to say that whoever gets it
will end up shelling out some cash along the way."

"Is it something that would attract tourists? Historians?"

"Maybe. If you marketed it right."

"Which would then require money and staff time.
Marty, what are you suggesting?"

"The sisters told me I should look around and find the
right person or institution. I'm offering you and the Society
right of first refusal. If you—we—don't want it, I understand, and no harm, no foul."

"I need to see it before I make any decisions." Hmm,
the last time I'd said that, I had come to regret it. Still, it
seemed unlikely that anyone out in Montgomery County
would be gunning for me.

"Of course. Tomorrow morning all right?"

Once again my life seemed to be spinning out of my
control, although this was decidedly more pleasant than
the last round. I considered. There was nothing on my
calendar of any particular urgency. A ride in the country
might be nice, although the weather and the landscape
were kind of uniformly gray and gloomy at this time of
year. At least in that case I could look at the place with a
jaundiced eye. If the lady heirs were now in their eighties,

there were probably any number of maintenance issues associated with the house that they hadn't dealt with lately, and it was important to take things like that into account. "Okay, I'll look at it. I doubt it makes sense for the Society, but at least we could put some feelers about for other prospects. You want me to drive?"

"Nah. Have Jimmy bring you into town and I'll take you from here."

"Do I need to dress up for these venerable ladies?"

"Don't wear blue jeans. You have pearls?"

"Yes, my grandmother's."

"Wear 'em. There aren't many people left who recognize the real thing." Marty stood up abruptly. "My work is done. I've got a date with Eliot tonight—maybe I'll run some of our ideas by him."

"Have a nice evening. And see you tomorrow morning?"

"Sure. I'll alert the sisters so they can polish the antique silver tea service."

After Marty had left, I stared stupidly at the pile of papers on my desk. Oh, right, the board reports. I decided they were the perfect antidote to murder and mayhem, so I dug in.

I was finished by late afternoon, feeling virtuous, when James called. "When do you want me to pick you up?"

"Anytime, I guess. You have any reason to stay late?"

"No. I'll be there at five thirty." He hung up quickly. Another call from the office—not exactly romantic, but that would have been rather out of place.

I couldn't think of anything to start, knowing I would

be leaving in half an hour, so I pulled out a pad and started making a list. For a long time I contemplated the blank sheet of paper. What did I need to know? I decided to start with motives for an apparently senseless shooting. I put "Random Act of Violence" at the top. It was necessary to include it, but it wasn't exactly helpful.

Next I added "Professional." What did I mean by that? The occupations of the victims? Do-gooder and City employee—I decided to leave myself off the list. Both working in a housing-related area, which was why they were together at the time. But that did not mean that they were killed because of that. Somebody else's profession? (A hit man who needed the work? No, that was ridiculous.) A developer who wanted the land? For what? It would still be a slum. Someone looking for a pipeline to government funds to put up subsidized housing for the poor? Maybe. Worth looking into? Maybe.

All right, now "Personal." Someone who hated Tyrone or Cherisse—or me. I thought I could eliminate myself, not because I had no enemies, but because the shooters could probably have hit me if they wanted to, or followed me and finished me off. Ergo, they hadn't wanted to kill me. Maybe scare me or drive me away from that area. The problem was, I didn't know enough about either Tyrone or Cherisse to imagine who in their lives might want them dead. Were they married? Seeing anyone? I thought I recalled Latoya mentioning that Tyrone had married. Were they now or had they ever held jobs that made enemies who cared enough to kill? Were they the secret children of a major drug lord and had betrayed him and he'd had to make an example of them? But both of them? Or two drug-lord fathers? Or didn't hit men care who else they took down? Did they get paid by the number of kills?

Nell, you are losing it. Leave it for tomorrow. I laid my pad neatly in the center of my desk, then claimed my coat. On the way out I said to Eric, "I'm leaving for the day. I'll be in tomorrow, but Marty and I are planning an excursion to Montgomery County, so I'll be out in the middle of the day. Anything else I need to know about?"

"You said to remind you about the board reports."

"Almost done. I want to give them a quick look in the morning, and then you can pretty them up and copy and mail them. See you tomorrow."

Down the hall, down the elevator, through the lobby (waving at Bob), out the door. I was early, and it was chilly, so I stood in the lee of one of the massive pillars and watched people go by on the street. Everything looked very ordinary. Close to rush hour, there were plenty of pedestrians, as well as a few cars. This street, this neighborhood, had always seemed reasonably safe to me, although I had to remind myself that a high-profile murder had taken place in the parking lot directly across the street, well before my time. The killer was still in jail, but his name popped up in *where are they now?* kind of op-ed pieces every now and then. How long ago had that been? Long before I was reading newspapers, I was sure. A black activist, a journalist, convicted of shooting a cop. He still had his supporters in the larger community. How much had changed in the last generation?

James's car glided to a stop at the curb, and I hurried down the steps and climbed in, leaving my dark thoughts behind.

CHAPTER 9

"How was your day, dear?" James said in a mock-ironic tone as he merged into traffic.

"Peachy-keen. Nobody shot at me."

"That's good to hear."

I pondered a moment as James navigated a particularly thorny intersection, then said, "Detective Hrivnak stopped by this morning."

"Really?" James said in a carefully neutral tone. "What did she want?"

"I think obliquely she was asking for our help. She isn't buying the random-shooting theory, but I gather her superiors want to close the case. I can see both sides of that." Although I did want to see those guys who had given me the scare of my life caught and punished somehow.

"Why does she think it wasn't random?"

"Because her gut tells her that that particular spot was

not a likely place for that kind of crime. There was no reason for those guys to go looking for someone to shoot *there*. There were plenty of other places with more potential victims, if they were looking to make a statement of some sort. Which leads her to think that maybe they were looking for one of us, and I'd like to eliminate myself from that list, because I haven't done anything to tick off any armed killers lately, and certainly not in that part of town."

"Hmm," James said noncommittally. "So she wants to look at Tyrone and Cherisse?"

"Yes, if she can."

"Why did she come to you? You didn't know either one of them, right?"

"No, I didn't, although Marty met Cherisse a while back, and Latoya once dated Tyrone. Small world, isn't it? Anyway, the police can look into their personal lives better than Marty and I can, but she asked if we could check out what was so important about that particular address and whether it might have anything to do with it."

"So Marty's involved, too?"

"Yes, and Hrivnak knows it. Marty happened to be in my office when she came calling. She talked to both of us." I glanced in his direction, but his right ear wasn't giving anything away. "You have a problem with that?"

He sighed quietly. "You and Marty in combination have a knack for finding trouble. I'm not saying it's your fault, either one of you, but it does keep happening."

"I know. Look, I'm not convinced we're going to find anything that's helpful, and we're going to be looking at the Society's documents, inside our nice, safe building.

But this has made me realize that I should know more about the neighborhoods outside of Center City and Society Hill. Even if they're disaster areas now, they were once important to the city."

"I admire the principle, Nell, but I'd prefer you didn't go tramping around those neighborhoods."

"Believe me, so would I! I'm not planning to organize guided tours for our patrons, or anything like that. Maybe a series of online articles for our website or newsletter, or a small pamphlet. Maybe we could get the city involved, and they could help distribute it. Or we could call it a public service. And you know we're going to nominate Eliot for the board slot, and he's the perfect person to help with this."

"Nell, you are remarkably resilient," James said. "You're actually planning to turn this shooting into a research opportunity for the Society, complete with publications."

Was that a criticism? I turned toward him as far as my seat belt would allow and said, "What, you think I should be wallowing in a puddle of tears? Would you be happier if I fell apart?"

"No, of course not. I only hope that you feel you *can* fall apart if you need to. I'll be there to pick up the pieces."

"Oh." Maybe I was in denial, trying to pretend the whole thing had never happened. And maybe it was unrealistic of me to believe that I would be "all better" after only one day. Or two. Or two hundred. "Thank you."

The rest of the ride home was quiet.

Over dinner I said, "I didn't tell you about Marty's latest proposal."

"Not crime solving, I hope?"

"No. Apparently there's a colonial estate in Montgomery County that's up for grabs, and she wondered if the Society would be interested in taking it on." I proceeded to explain what Marty had told me, but that didn't take long because I didn't have many details. "So I said I'd go see it with her tomorrow morning. I don't think it's a good fit for the Society, either practically or financially, but it sounds lovely and I'd be happy to see it, and either Marty or I should bring it to the board, if there's even a remote possibility that it could work out. Or a board member might know someone who might be interested."

"You should be safe enough in Montgomery County."

"I don't know about that, James. Isn't it hunting season?" I said, suppressing a smile.

"For deer, I believe. Are you worried about being mistaken for a deer?"

"While sipping tea in the parlor? Not really. But after yesterday I'm not going to take anything for granted."

We spent a quiet evening, with no shots fired. I noticed that James stayed just a bit closer to me than usual, which I thought was sweet. He might be a big, strong FBI agent, but he was worried about me. I was surprised at how good it felt to have somebody who would worry about me.

The next morning we drove into the city together, and James dropped me off at the Society. "You're spoiling me, you know," I told him as I collected my things before getting out of the car.

"I want to. If you want me to be rational, I could say that I go this way anyway, so it's merely practical to drop you off. But you may have noticed that I don't feel exactly rational at the moment."

"I do appreciate it, you know. You don't see any armed thugs loitering on the street, waiting for me?"

He actually scanned the scene in front of us. "No. But you know it's easy to conceal a weapon. Have fun with Marty, and don't commit to anything."

"Hey, don't tell me how to do my job!" I gave him a thorough kiss and climbed out of the passenger door, then hurried up the stairs. It was cold, I told myself, ignoring the fact that I felt all too exposed on the street, where almost anyone might be hiding a weapon.

Upstairs in my office, there were no surprises waiting— no Detective Hrivnak, no phone messages. I made myself a cup of coffee, then settled behind my desk and sorted through what I needed to do. Marty would arrive in an hour or less, and I should find out what I could about what I was going to be looking at, so I wouldn't embarrass myself. Realistically, as I had told Marty, there was no way the Society could take on a building, no matter how beautiful and historical it was. We didn't have the staff to manage it, nor the money to hire people to do it for us. It might have been more appropriate if it were in the city, but instead it was way out in the suburbs. I would be more than willing to direct some of the Society's staff time and cultural capital (if there was such a thing) to finding the right institution to take it, but the Society was not that institution. Still, Marty was merely doing what she had promised the sisters, and I was always happy to see a piece of history that I had missed. And there were plenty of those.

At ten of ten, Marty called from her car and said she was idling at the curb in front of the building. "You ready to go?"

"I am. No change in plans?"

"Nope. If they offer lunch, say yes, but it may be cucumber sandwiches and petit fours."

"I won't complain. Be right down!"

On the way out I told Eric where I was going and that I wasn't sure when I'd be back. I checked to see that I had my cell phone, and that it was set to vibrate. "You can call me if anything urgent comes up."

"What would you call *urgent* right now?" Eric asked.

"Well, maybe if Detective Hrivnak calls. James has my number, and Marty will be with me. I guess that's about all. Thanks, Eric."

I made my way downstairs and out to Marty's car.

"Everything good?" Marty asked as she pulled away from the curb.

"Just fine. Do I look like I don't think so?"

"No, you look normal. Maybe that's the problem—you get shot at, you should look . . . different."

"Well, I'm sorry I look too good. I promise you I'm quivering inside."

"I'm surprised Jimmy isn't glued to your side, as a self-appointed bodyguard."

Since Marty and James had grown up together, she knew him well. "I think he'd like to be, but he respects my independence. I'll let him comfort me later."

"I bet," Marty said with what looked like a smirk.

I ignored her innuendo. "Did you talk to Eliot?"

"I did. He's definitely on board with being on board, if you know what I mean."

"Good. He knows the vote is next week, right?"

"Yes. But we don't see any problems, do we?"

"Not that I know of. I'm looking forward to getting to know him better. Did you have a chance to talk about the neighborhoods project?"

"We talked about it a little, but let's save that for the ride home. I should fill you in on what we're going to see now."

"You know, you never told me why the Oliver sisters approached you about this. Anything I should know?"

"It's complicated."

"Marty, with you it's always complicated. Why'd they pick you as their, what, agent? Ambassador?"

"I had a school friend who lived out that way, and she introduced me to the sisters because she thought I'd be interested in the house—this was years ago. She told them about my role at the Society, and I guess we spent some time talking about what the Society does. Before you ask, they've never been members or donors. So when they decided to sell, they got in touch with me. I think they don't trust real estate agents, who are busy counting up the dollar signs. And their lawyer, in Center City, was a friend of my father's."

All the interconnections were typical for Marty. Heaven help me if I ever had to draw a diagram to explain her links to anything.

"Please remember, Marty, I haven't made any promises. You know the Society as well as or better than I do, and you know what our limitations are."

"Of course I do. But maybe together we can come up with some ideas for the place. It really is gorgeous, and mostly untouched."

"All right, fill me in." I settled back in my seat to listen.

Marty launched into a brisk summary of the house we were headed to see. "Traditional high-end colonial set in the midst of over fifty acres of land. Built in 1769, and it includes a carriage house and barn. Built for the son of a wealthy local family when he got married—and it was a real power marriage, to the daughter of one of the most prominent men in the Commonwealth. They did lots of entertaining—Ben Franklin stayed there now and then, before the Revolution. Typical layout, and most of the woodwork is original. Great staircase. As the story goes, they kept slaves in the attic, a long, *long* time ago. What else you want to know?"

"Have the ladies had any conversation with local officials?"

"I don't think so—not genteel enough for them, and they didn't want to get the lawyer involved, at least not yet. We might be able to walk them through the process to gift it to the town, but that's the last resort. Look, nothing has to be decided today. We're just chatting. Did I mention they want to give the furniture with it?"

"Yes, you did, yesterday. I will reserve judgment, but I won't make any promises to them. You said yesterday they were mentally alert?"

"Yup, sharp as tacks. You'll see."

After another half hour of driving, we pulled into a long driveway and arrived in front of a handsome colonial house. I made a quick visual inventory: central doorway with traditional portico on columns, flanked by two windows on either side. A carriage house with three bays, closed off by arched doors, lay behind the house on the right. The ground-floor windows had to be six feet high—no expense spared when the place was built. Two central brick chimneys indicated the fireplaces that had heated the rooms. From a quick perusal, I couldn't see any obvious signs of neglect or damage: the paint, while not new, was still sound, the roof had all its shingles, and the foundation stones were still well pointed. It was, simply, a beautiful example of the architecture of its time. But that didn't mean the Society could do anything with it.

Marty parked, and I followed her to the front door (whose hardware also appeared to be original). She rapped the large brass knocker firmly, and it took little time before we could hear the tap-tap of shoes—with heels, if I guessed correctly. The door was opened by a woman only a couple of inches shorter than I was, wearing a nice shirtwaist dress and, as I had deduced, low-heeled pumps. A string of pearls circled her neck, and her white hair was swept neatly up in a soft chignon. I hoped I would look anywhere near as good when I was approaching ninety.

She extended a hand, and I took it; her grip was strong. "I'm Phoebe Oliver, and you must be Nell Pratt. Thank you for coming all this way to see us. We don't get many visitors these days, I'm afraid—Penelope and I have outlived most of our peers, sadly. Please come in. Good to see you again, Martha."

"I'm always happy to see you, Phoebe." Marty and Phoebe exchanged a brief hug, and I wondered how well they knew each other.

"Would you like a cup of tea after your journey, Ms. Pratt, or would you prefer to see the house first?"

"Please, call me Nell. Frankly I'm itching to see the house. It's imposing, and your family appears to have taken good care of it."

"We can't take all the credit. I'm not sure how much Martha has told you, but our ancestor had it snatched from him a very long time ago because he chose the wrong side during the Revolution. It was our great-grandfather who managed to buy it back, shortly after his return from the Civil War, before too much had been changed. But you're right—it had been lovingly maintained in the interval, and there was little to do in the way of repairs. I will be happy to show you."

Marty and I followed her through a series of rooms, large and square, with wide-plank floors the color of honey, and simple paneling embellishing walls and fireplaces. I noted that there were radiators under most of the windows, so there had been some changes made over time, but those were not obtrusive. The rooms were furnished, but the furniture was a bit sparse. Still, each piece was of the correct period and was gleaming with the kind of polish that only time and care could provide. It was, without question, lovely.

We ended the tour downstairs in the dining room,

where a sumptuous tea was laid out on a mahogany table that could have seated a dozen people. Another elderly woman, clearly related to Phoebe, stood behind the spread, beaming. "I'm so glad you could come! I'm Phoebe's sister, Penelope. I'm sorry I didn't join you on the tour, but I was engaged in the kitchen, and I do have trouble with the stairs these days. Please sit down and serve yourselves."

The teapot was indeed silver, as were the matching sugar bowl and creamer. The plates, laden with goodies—yes, including finger sandwiches and small cakes, as Marty had predicted—were, to my semi-experienced eye, English bone china; the teacups were almost thin enough to see through, with handles the size of large spaghetti. I felt as though I had stepped back into another time, and I was glad I had worn my grandmother's pearls.

We made chitchat about people we all knew, about the county and the region, about the history that surrounded us, and it was all very pleasant. Then Phoebe, who was clearly the spokesperson for the duo, carefully set down her cup in its saucer and said, "now, shall we talk business?"

CHAPTER 10

Marty and I looked at each other, but I had the feeling the ball was in my court. "Phoebe, Penelope, what is it you're hoping to do with this house?"

"Keep it standing, and as close to its current, and, may I add, historical state as possible," Phoebe said quickly. Penelope nodded her agreement.

"And what do you think your options are?"

Phoebe regarded me steadily. "Ms. Pratt, we are neither stupid nor feeble-minded, even though we are women who grew up in a very different world, and we are unquestionably old. We were raised in this house, and we treated it as a house, rather than a museum. We scuffed the floors with our Mary Janes, and, yes, we even slid down the staircase railing a time or two. We knew the place was centuries old, but that didn't mean a lot to us then.

"Neither have we been shuttered in this place all our

lives, though we never married. I attended college and graduated, and we traveled to Europe together. Penelope lived in Boston for a time, and was once engaged. Yet somehow we always ended up back here. It was not exactly a deliberate choice, but we have not been unhappy. We were blessed with enough money to live out our days, with a bit left over. We've been lucky.

"Now we know we won't last much longer, and we accept that. Patience, Nell—I *am* going to answer your question. We are well aware that this is a valuable piece of real estate. We could, no doubt, find a private purchaser for it, one who would pay a lot of money for a place of this size, with a good deal of privacy. Movie stars, titans of industry, and the like."

I wondered if I saw a twinkle in Phoebe's eye. She seemed to be enjoying this.

"But there is no guarantee that such a buyer would keep the house as it is, or even keep it at all. He might tear it down and build what I believe they call a McMansion, or he might give it to some fringe church or sect, or turn it into a private medical clinic for substance abusers who can afford expensive treatment. We selfishly don't want that, and since it is ours to dispose of as we choose, we want to set the terms—terms that will survive even our deaths. A lot has happened in this house over two centuries. We want to honor that long history. Can you understand that?"

I nodded. "I can and do. After all, you know what I do: I manage a library and museum that seeks to preserve the past, so that later generations can enjoy it. I realize that this is not always a popular thing to do, and that many ordinary people think we're obsolete. So I am on your side, in principle. But the reality is, few institutions want to take on something like this. Say there's a way to create an endowed house museum, a nonprofit organization that would open it to the public on some regular schedule, because there has to be a public component to it. I don't know the details of your financial situation, but I'm not sure that anyone has the money to keep it just as it is forever. Any house needs care and tending, because houses seem to want to fall to pieces."

Phoebe smiled. "Do you live in an older home, Nell?"

"I do, one that's about a hundred years younger than this one. It's beautiful, but it's a constant battle to keep it that way. So you can't create a time warp or freeze it forever."

"We know that. What do you see as other alternatives?"

"This is not my area of expertise, but you could give it to an institution or to the county or the township, along with enough money to keep it going. They, too, will have to open it to the public in order to justify owning it and managing it and paying for its upkeep. Municipalities have to answer to their voters when it comes to budgets. And making it a public building will create wear and tear on it, particularly the interior."

"And your Society will not take on that responsibility?"

Hadn't Marty told her? Or was Phoebe just verifying that information? "We can't, I'm sorry to say. We're already stretched thin financially, as are many of our cultural colleagues. Take the Barnes Foundation, for example, because it's a similar case. Albert Barnes created a wonderful art collection in the nineteen twenties, and he wanted it preserved exactly as he had arranged it, in his home. He left the house and plenty of money to the foundation. His will allowed very limited access to the collection. Well, a few years ago that will was broken in a rather acrimonious and public lawsuit, and the collection was moved to Philadelphia, near other museums, so that vastly more people could enjoy the collection. And the fact that people *want* to see the art means that they will pay to see it, so the new arrangement generates income to sustain the building and its contents. I'm sure the man is turning over in his grave, but many more people have the opportunity to enjoy the art."

"But that would not apply in this case," Phoebe said. "What are you suggesting?"

"You're right—we can't just pick up your house and drop it in the middle of Fairmount Park, and its location is part of its historic identity. I cited that example because it shows that Barnes's vision for the future became obsolete, and a way was found to perpetuate it, in a somewhat different form. As for your house"—I looked briefly at Marty again, but she showed no inclination to jump in—"I have no idea what to suggest to you, because I only heard about this yesterday, and it's been kind of a difficult week so far."

"So I understand," Phoebe said, not unkindly. "But if I interpret events correctly, you were willing to venture out of, shall we say, your comfort zone because there are those who believe that even the lowliest row house is part of the city's past and is worth remembering."

Touché. I smiled at the sisters. "You're right. Look, I'm

on your side, really. I would love to help you find a way to work this out, to everyone's benefit. It's a big plus that money doesn't have to be the driving force in this decision. But right now I don't know where to start."

"That is perfectly understandable, my dear," Phoebe said. "We will be happy to give you some time to reflect, and to investigate the options. Just don't take *too* long."

I had the feeling we were being politely dismissed, but that didn't trouble me. Phoebe had given me a lot to think about.

Marty stood up first. "Phoebe, Penelope, thank you so much for giving us the tour, and for explaining so clearly what you want to do. I thought Nell needed to meet you and hear your thoughts, and I still believe she and the Society can help. And I can help her. Let us kick this around with each other, and with some of our colleagues, and see what we can come up with. We can't promise you anything, but we'll try."

"We can't ask for more than that, Martha dear. Can we, Penelope?"

"No, no, not more. We want to hear what you think. I'm sure you'll work hard for us." Penelope beamed at both of us, nodding all the while.

"Well, then," Phoebe said, "we should let you begin your drive back to the city. Thank you for taking the time to hear us out. Nell, it has been a pleasure to meet you."

"The pleasure is mine. I'll be in touch, I promise."

At the door we shook hands, or rather, Phoebe shook my hand, and Penelope pressed it gently, softly. She never stopped smiling. They closed the door behind us as we made our way to Marty's car. We sat down in it, but before Marty started the engine, she asked, "Well?"

"Well what?" I retorted. "They're delightful, like they've stepped out of another time. The house is beautiful. And I haven't the slightest idea what to do."

"Exactly," Marty said. "At least there are two of us in the same boat now." She started the car and pointed it down the long driveway. "But I have faith that we can figure something out."

I was glad she did, because I didn't. "You know, you were awfully quiet in there. Very unlike you," I told her as she headed back toward the city.

"I've heard the story, and I know the house. I wanted you to have their full attention."

"Those ladies are really something, aren't they? Phoebe in particular."

"They are. As you no doubt observed, Phoebe is the dominant sister—she's a couple of years older than Penelope. Penelope has been a follower all her life, but she's very sweet."

"You aren't by any chance related to them?" I had to ask: Marty seemed to be related to half the people in Pennsylvania and a few more in New Jersey.

"Not that I know of, but I think my grandfather had a fling with their mother, sometime around 1920."

"And you know this how?"

"Family stories. Some you tell at parties, some behind closed doors. Doesn't matter anyway now. So, I and the rest of my family don't want to step in, and you're telling me you, meaning the Society, can't."

"Yes, and you know why. We're holding our own now, but we can't even think about expanding."

"I get it. Just making sure we're on the same page. So now we beat the bushes to come up with another idea. Let's find some time to go over our donor and membership lists and figure out who we can approach."

"We?"

"Yes, we," Marty said sharply. "I know people, but you as president of the Society have some public clout. We may need both to get this done."

I mulled that over for a couple of miles. Then I said, "You know, what Phoebe said, kind of comparing what I was doing in Philadelphia and what they want to do with their estate, got me thinking. I didn't see it before, because a city slum and a suburban manor house seem on the surface to have little in common, but they are both part of local history. The Society works to preserve Pennsylvania history. So in a sense we have an obligation to both, unequal though they are. But the problem as I see it is, with limited resources, how do we pick and choose? We have to set priorities. And we have to think about which projects will be best for the Society in the long run. I'm sure there are people on the board who would say we should go for the estate, because that's the way a lot of older members see our mandate. Trying to stick our noses into City neighborhood development, past and present, quickly becomes political and is definitely controversial. But is it any less our responsibility?"

Marty kept her eyes on the road. "Good questions, Nell, and I don't have any quick answers. I've been involved with the Society one way or another most of my life. Even I have seen a lot of changes, and I'm not going to argue that we should preserve it just the way it is. We have the collections, and they're great. But history doesn't stop at any particular time—it just keeps going. The city is like a living thing, and it keeps changing, shifting. We can choose to hunker down and tend to our collections, or we can make an effort to shape the course of public understanding of what history actually is."

"Wow, Marty. I've never heard you say anything like that. Certainly not at board meetings."

"Hey, just because I devote most of my time to the Terwilliger collection doesn't mean I'm blind or clueless. I'm involved in other stuff in the city and beyond, and it's not all pretty. I think we have an opportunity to here to at least open up a discussion, and maybe to do some good. We don't have to make a decision today, but I think we have to stake out a public position pretty soon, especially after what happened to you. You have the public's attention for about two seconds; what're you going to do with it?"

This was turning out to be quite a week. Only two days earlier life had been peaceful and normal; since then I'd been shot at in a slum, been all but handed the keys of a colonial mansion, and was now faced with redefining the historic mission of the Society. I wanted to take a nap.

"Can I sleep on it? Please? I need to think about all of this. I agree that it's time to open this discussion, but can it wait until tomorrow?"

"I guess." Marty sighed dramatically. I checked to make sure she was smiling.

She dropped me back at the Society building, saying she was headed home. I trudged up the steps, waved at Bob, and made a beeline for my office. "Any messages, Eric?" I asked when I arrived at his desk.

"Plenty," he said, handing me a stack a half inch thick. "Mostly press, though. I said you were out of the office, which was true, and that you would get back to them, which I didn't assume was true."

"Thank you, Eric. In fact, I may want to talk to some of them, but I need to figure out which ones. I'll deal with that in the morning." Maybe the news cycle would have moved on by then, and my decision would be made for me.

The phone on Eric's desk rang again, and a moment later he stuck his head in. "It's that detective. You want to take it?"

"Yes, I guess. I'll pick up." I waited until Eric had shut the door to my office, then picked up the phone. "Detective Hrivnak, what can I do for you today?"

"Tyrone Blakeney wants to talk with you."

"Really? Why?"

"He didn't say. He said it was okay if I was there, too."

"When?"

"He's still in the hospital and he's in rocky shape but stable. I woulda gone over today, but the doctors say he's gotta rest some more—a couple of bullets came pretty close to some important parts of him. How about tomorrow morning? Want to meet me there, say, nine?"

"Uh, yeah, I guess that would work. In the lobby? Oh, which hospital?"

"Jefferson. See you then."

I sat back, confused. Why would Tyrone want to talk with me? With or without the police? But I couldn't think of any reason to turn down the request, and I was trying to keep the detective happy. So it looked like I should be there. At least it was near the Society.

I picked up the phone and hit James's number. When he answered, I said quickly, "Tyrone Blakeney wants to talk to me at the hospital tomorrow morning at nine. I can drive myself if that's a problem for you."

"No problem. Did he say why?"

"No. The request came from Detective Hrivnak, so I have no idea."

"Will you be ready to leave at five today?" he asked.

I checked the time: already past three, thanks to my excursion to Montgomery County. "Sure. See you then." We hung up.

I strolled out to Eric's desk. "I'll be out of the office for maybe a couple of hours in the morning tomorrow. Are we all set with the board reports?"

"Yes, ma'am. Signed, sealed, and delivered, as the saying goes. Want me to send a reminder to the board members?"

"Give 'em a couple of days after they've received the packet of materials and then nudge them, so they'll remember to read the reports. And I may have something to add to the agenda—I'll let you know." After I'd mulled over the "Save the Manor" project. Or did I mean "Save the Neighborhoods"?

CHAPTER 11

James arrived right on time. As I scrambled into the passenger seat of his car, I said, "You don't have to do this every day, you know. I can take the train."

"I know," he said.

When he didn't add anything, I told him, "I've been doing this for years, and I've never had any problems. Well, there are always drunks or homeless people in the subway tunnels, but I know how to avoid them, and they don't usually bother anybody."

"I'm sure," he said. And stopped again.

"So?" I demanded.

"I'm only trying to be supportive. Look at it as therapy for me, not you. I need to feel that I'm doing something to help."

"Oh. Well, if you put it like that. But if you have

work-related things you need to deal with late in the day, I can manage."

"Of course you can. Did it occur to you that I like to have someone to talk to during the drive? It's that or tune up some oldies and sing along, which means I get some really odd looks on the highway."

I tried to picture that. "I bet. If you stick headphones on, they'll think you're having an important conversation with someone. At least, until they get close enough to hear the bass line."

"I'll take that under advisement. So, how was your day?"

"Marty dragged me off to the country, remember? We visited the delightful Oliver sisters, who are living in an impressive colonial home in the wilds of Montgomery County."

"Ah, right—you told me about that. Does Martha have a plan?"

I was still surprised that she didn't. Was she bringing this up now only to distract me? "Not that she's shared with me. In fact, she was curiously silent. In a perfect world she'd probably find a way for the Society to adopt the building, but she knows we don't have the money to do that. Nor does she, personally. You think she could put together a collection of assorted Terwilligers and make them all ante up a share?"

"Frankly I don't think that's likely," James said. "The family fortunes are not what they once were. Plus her line—her father and grandfather—is the only one that took a serious interest in local history, so it would be a hard sell to the rest of them. What's the place like?"

"Preserved in amber. It's lovely, and very little has changed in the past two hundred-plus years, down to the pieces of furniture and maybe even some of the draperies. It would make a great house museum, but I don't know who would want to step up. The ladies are charming, and they served us a perfect tea. Which is why I'm starving— tea sandwiches and dainty cookies do not a meal make."

"I'm sure we can remedy that once we get home."

We managed to put a meal together, and it was only after we'd sat down to enjoy it that I said, "I told you on the phone that Tyrone Blakeney has asked to see me, but I'm still puzzled about why."

"The detective didn't explain why?"

"No, but you know she doesn't share more than she feels necessary."

"How's he doing? Is he critical or something?"

"No, she said he's stable, but he's still in the hospital. I suppose he could be considered lucky that he survived at all."

"Are you going to ask him if he has any ideas about who was shooting at you?"

"That's hardly my role, especially with a detective sitting right there. And I doubt he'd want to bare his heart to me even if she wasn't. It's more likely that he's looking to get some PR out of this event and needs my cooperation."

"You sound cynical. But it suggests that he believes his project is going forward, in spite of events."

"With or without him? Or Cherisse? I suppose it does. Would that be a bad thing?"

"You don't suppose he orchestrated all this as a publicity stunt?" James asked.

"James, someone was killed!" I erupted. "And Tyrone was badly wounded—it wasn't just for show." I'd seen the blood, so I knew.

James held up both hands. "Just asking. He might have asked the wrong person to stage it—somebody who's a lousy shot."

"I refuse to believe that. I'm going to wait and see what he has to say, and I'll make sure Detective Hrivnak sticks around to hear it."

"Good. What do *you* think about his project, shooting aside?"

"This all came up so fast that I haven't had time to do any research into it, or into any of the competing ideas. I know it's not a simple task to salvage a dying neighborhood. But then, nothing ever is in this city. In a way, the manor that Marty and I visited is kind of the flip side of the issue. It's undeniably historic, and it's beautiful. Say someone—it could be anyone, from the township to a museum to a private donor—had limited resources and could choose only one: How would he or she decide which? Who gets to declare one is more important and more worthy than the other?"

James chewed a mouthful of food, no doubt allowing himself some time to think. "That's not an easy question to answer, as I'm sure you realize. In fact, you and the Society are probably the best equipped to make that assessment, or at least make the case for one or the other." When I started to protest, he stopped me. "I know, there's no way the Society could take on either project, but who could? At least you're in the position to answer that, by identifying potential supporters. Or would you rather wash your hands of the whole thing? You could walk away from the North Philly project, you know, and nobody would think less of you, under the circumstances."

"Maybe. I'd look like an elitist coward if I went for the other one now. Thank goodness I don't have to decide anything right away."

The next morning James dropped me off in front of Jefferson University Hospital, but he refused to leave until he'd seen Detective Hrivnak arrive. "Let me know when you get back to the Society, will you?"

He really was worried about me, probably more so than I was. It was sweet but troubling. "I will," I told him as I climbed out of the car.

When I approached the watching detective, she said, "He babysitting you now?"

"He's worried. Does he have any reason to be, or should I tell him to back off?"

She shrugged silently, which didn't help at all.

I tried another tack. "Why does Tyrone want to talk to me? You've already interviewed him, right?"

"Of course, as soon as he could speak."

"Did he give you anything useful?"

"Not really. He claims he was so busy trying to convince you about his brilliant plan that he wasn't paying attention to what was happening on the street, even though Chapman was. Which was not too smart of him. He should know better—he grew up in that neighborhood."

I wasn't surprised. "Maybe that's why he's so committed to the project. And maybe he thought he was safe there. Cherisse was more anxious—I told you, she's the one who noticed the car. She's not from the neighborhood?"

"No, from out past Chester, but she went to Temple, so she knows the general area. She was a bit younger than Tyrone, so maybe her experience was different. Ready?"

"Yes, let's go. I really need to get back to work."

The last time I'd been in this hospital, it was when James had been injured, so it didn't hold happy memories for me. "Is there anything you want me to say, or not to say?"

Hrivnak was moving fast ahead of me. "Nope. I'm not expecting anything in particular, but he asked, so I'm delivering you."

"Is this an official interview?"

"Not necessarily. You want privacy?"

"No, not really. I'd rather you stayed. Remember, I don't know this man, and I have no idea what he wants or what he's going to say. I doubt it would be anything too personal."

"No problem," the detective replied. "Here we are."

We walked into a double room, with one empty bed. Tyrone occupied the one closer to the window. He looked remarkably good for someone with some nasty holes in him. He was dozing when we approached, but opened his eyes when he heard us.

"Ms. Pratt, thanks for coming. I wasn't sure you would." He nodded toward Hrivnak. "Detective."

Was the formality for the detective's benefit? "Call me Nell, please. After what you and I have been through together, we should be on a first-name basis, don't you think? I was sorry to hear about Cherisse, but I'm glad you're okay."

"I'll live. Yes, it's a shame about Cherisse—she was really a big help in managing the interface between my group and the City. It was through her efforts that we turned up your Society's connection. You would not believe the state of record keeping at city hall."

"I can guess. I know how hard it is to keep track of our own materials, and we're a lot smaller than Philadelphia. Look, Tyrone, I don't want to take up too much of your time, and you need your rest, so let's get to the point. Why did you ask to see me?"

He glanced at Hrivnak. "This off the record, Detective?"

Hrivnak was leaning silently against the wall. "Sure, if you want. Unless you plan to point a finger at someone in particular."

"Just so we're clear. Ms. Pratt—Nell—first I want to apologize for dragging you into something that nearly got you killed. I swear, I had no idea that there was anything dangerous about the place. You've seen it—there's nothing there. That building, the one you own, isn't worth anything to anyone, including my group. For us it's just a symbol, and a good visual for the press. But in itself it's worthless."

"So why was anyone shooting at us?"

"I don't know, swear to God. I've been thinking on this for two days now. I grew up in that neighborhood, and I still know some folk there. I can't think of a single one who'd want to do me harm, much less go after anyone with me."

"What about new gangs?" Hrivnak demanded. "You up on all of them?"

"Well, not exactly. I haven't lived there for a while, and I know things change, sometimes pretty fast. But you still have to ask, why go after us? We weren't doing any harm to anybody. We aren't looking to take anything away from anybody, because there's nothing left to take."

I glanced at the detective, but she didn't seem to have anything to add. "You're saying you don't think the shooting is related to anyone from the neighborhood, right?" I asked. Tyrone nodded. "So what about outside the neighborhood? You tell me you're trying to save the spirit of the neighborhood, its history—but are you the only group who wants to do that? Are there any developers who want a piece of it, who want the land, never mind the house? Or anyone who's trying to drive off the competition?"

Tyrone looked at me like I'd sprouted a second head. I had to wonder what the heck he had been expecting from a museum director. "I, uh, I'd have to think about that, maybe ask around the community. It's a possibility."

"You do that, Mr. Blakeney," Detective Hrivnak chimed in. "If Nell here hadn't asked those questions, I would have. Look, my captain would like nothing better than to shut this case down. You want to keep it open, and find out who tried to kill you and did kill Cherisse, you'd better give me something to work with. You do want to solve this thing, don't you, Mr. Blakeney?"

"Of course, Detective. I want to help. Let me talk to my people, see if they've heard any rumors. Are you talking to anybody at the City?"

"Yeah." Hrivnak didn't elaborate.

I couldn't think of any more questions to ask, and Tyrone looked like he was flagging. "Listen, Tyrone, if you and your group decide to go forward with this project, I'll be happy to put together a history of the neighborhood, or any particular property. We can talk about it when you're back on your feet."

"That's more than generous, Nell, and I appreciate it. I'll let you know. You have any more questions, Detective?"

"Not right now," Detective Hrivnak said, giving nothing away. "Feel better. Let's go, Nell."

We walked back out into the corridor, then turned toward the elevators. "Do you believe he's on the up and up, Detective?" I asked when we were out of earshot.

"Maybe," she said, pushing the elevator button. "He's got no record, but not many people escape that neighborhood without a few secrets. We've given him something to chew on."

"Are you looking at Cherisse's department at the City?" I said as we entered the elevator.

"Wow, you don't give up easily, do you?"

"No, I don't. Someone shot at me. I didn't like it. I'd like to find out why, and even if I don't, I'd like it to matter.

That's all. We've worked together in the past, and I respect your abilities. I want to help if I can."

"I'll keep that in mind, Nell. Yeah, we're checking out the City, but this little property of yours is like a flea speck to them. I can't imagine anyone there would care, unless they want back taxes or something. You want a lift back to your place, or is your boyfriend waiting?"

"I can walk, Detective—Meredith." It might take a while before I could walk along city streets, even the familiar ones, without looking over my shoulder, but I had to start sometime.

CHAPTER 12

On my way to my office, I stopped by Shelby's office and flopped into a chair across from her desk.

"Hey, lady," she greeted me. "You just getting in? You taking—what do they call it?—bankers' hours?"

"Nope, I was calling upon my fellow victim Tyrone at the hospital. He asked to see me, mostly to apologize, I think. My friend Meredith the Detective escorted me."

"Oh, so now you're buddies with the lady cop?"

"Sort of. Her superiors want to close the case, call it a random shooting, but that doesn't feel right to her."

"Interesting. You agree with her?"

"Maybe. I don't disagree. There's something odd about the whole thing. Why us? Why then? Why there?"

"Speaking of the 'there,'" Shelby said, "I pulled what pitifully few files I could find about the property transfer. Nineteen seventeen, it was. At least at the time it was still part of a row. The donor who left it to the Society in his will had bought it as an investment property, and it was kind of puny compared to his estate, the rest of which he left to his family, apart from a few other bequests. Maybe he knew it would be a pain in the butt for his heirs to get rid of so he passed it off to us."

"Was he an axe murderer? A bootlegger?" I asked hopefully. Maybe there would be a way to spin this event somehow.

"What, you think there's a body or a cache of something valuable? Nope, he was a rather dull and ordinary citizen with some money, period. In case you're wondering, there are no descendants left to quibble about it. Sad to say, it's all ours. Have you called our lawyer yet?"

"No, I've been a bit busy. Maybe I'm afraid to ask the lawyer because I won't like what she tells me. Anyway, Marty dragged me out to the burbs yesterday to look at a colonial manor house that's going for free to the right person or organization—which basically boils down to one that will leave it exactly as is, forever."

"Interesting. Is it a dump?"

"On the contrary, it's lovely, and in reasonably good shape. Let me ask you a hypothetical question, as a development person: How would you go about finding someone who wants it?"

"Could they live in it, like a resident caretaker?"

"Maybe. I didn't think to ask that. They might have to live in the slave quarters in the attic, though."

"I think there are some places in Fairmount Park that operate like that. Or how about this: if a college or university took it over, they could offer it to visiting faculty or honored guests, as long as they were careful with it. But the college would have to be somewhere near the house for that to make sense."

"That's a thought," I said, impressed. "Could you keep thinking about it and jot down any other ideas you have? I'm still trying to decide if it's worth taking to the board, or if it would just be a distraction."

"That I can do. I can be creative, right?"

"Sure, as long as nothing in the building changes physically."

"On a completely unrelated subject, how's Mr. Agent Man handling things?"

I sighed. "You mean, people on the street trying to kill me? He's being unusually attentive. I think he feels guilty that he can't protect me, even though he knows it's impossible unless he locks me in the basement. But it's kind of shaken him up. As it has me, of course."

"I think it sounds sweet—shows you how he really feels about you. Does he have any opinions about the shooting?"

"Not that he's told me. He did say the only way he could take part in the investigation was if this turned out to be a hate crime. I can't see that happening. And yes, I appreciate that he worries about me. I'm not quite sure how to deal with that—we're both pretty independent."

"Nell, you don't have to be so independent any more, get it? Let him beat his chest and take care of his woman. Anyway, are there no angry white supremacists in Philadelphia for him to hunt down?"

"Plenty of angry people of all colors, but I think the supremacists are outnumbered."

"It only takes one with a gun."

"All too true." I stood up. "I'd better get to work—I haven't even seen Eric yet this morning. If it's still morning."

"It is—barely. Shoo!" Shelby said, smiling.

Down the hall I greeted Eric. "Shelby says it's still morning, so good morning. Have I missed anything?"

"No, ma'am. Even the press calls have died down—must be some other crisis going on."

"At least I'm not in the middle of it. Could you get the Society's lawyer on the phone, please?"

"Sure will."

I'd barely had time to take off my coat and sit down when Eric called out, "Ms. Gould is on the line!"

"Thanks, Eric," I replied, then picked up. "Hi, Courtney?" Courtney Gould was a bright young thing at a venerable old law firm in Center City, one that we'd been using for generations. But she knew her stuff, and I was pretty sure she'd act more quickly than her predecessor would have—he'd finally retired at eighty-seven.

"Nell, are you all right?" Courtney said quickly. "I saw the newscast. You must have been terrified. What on earth were you doing in that neighborhood?"

"Looking at a piece of property that we thought we'd gotten rid of a long time ago. Apparently somebody messed up the paperwork in 1917 or shortly after that. Can you look into it and see what our liabilities and our options are? Like, do we still own it, or can we wash our hands of it?"

"Sure, no problem. Just give me the details and I'll get to work on it. Sooner rather than later, I assume?"

"Well, now that it's public knowledge, I think we need to resolve it quickly."

"I take it the City is involved?" Courtney asked.

"How did you guess? And now, of course, they're short-handed, since they've lost Cherisse Chapman. Do what you can and get back to me, will you? I'll e-mail you the particulars. And before you ask, we have nothing in our records that will help—we've checked. I hope you have more there. As far as we can tell, the Society acknowl-edged the bequest with a nice thank-you note to the family, but there's nothing about its sale in our records."

"Of course. And I'm glad you're all right. You want the firm to send you flowers?"

"I'd rather have chocolates, but that's not really neces-sary. Thanks for the thought."

"I'll get back to you ASAP," Courtney said and hung up. I amused myself for a moment trying to imagine what the law firm could have put on the card with the flowers. *So glad you're not dead*?

So now back to work, if I could remember what I'd been working on only three days earlier. Board packet: done and out the door. "Eric?" I called out again.

He poked his head in the door. "Need something? Coffee?"

"Actually, coffee sounds good—I haven't had my morn-ing ration. But I wanted to check if there's been any feedback from board members about the info packet you sent."

"Not a peep. I'll get that coffee." Eric disappeared down the hall.

I wasn't surprised. Normally our board didn't look at the information we sent them—which could be substantial—until the afternoon before the meeting, and then they skimmed it. It didn't worry me: nothing we had sent out this time around was controversial, including Eliot's nomination for the board, and I'd heard no objections about that.

But that reminded me . . . if I wanted to move forward on this neighborhood history project (still an *if*), I should talk to Eliot and pick his scholarly brain. I should have some sort of proposal in hand in time for the board meeting, even if I didn't end up moving forward with it. When Eric returned, bearing a cup of hot coffee, I said, "Thank you! Can you get me Eliot Miller on the line?"

"The professor? Sure."

"Oh, and is there anything else on my schedule for today?"

"Nope. I think people are giving you plenty of space, after what happened. You are okay, aren't you?"

"Better than expected, but thank you for worrying, Eric."

Eric had Eliot for me in thirty seconds, so I picked up. "Eliot, I'm glad I caught you! I have no idea what your course schedule is."

"Nell, how are you? I have nothing scheduled before midafternoon. Marty has been keeping me updated on events, but I didn't want to intrude. Is this call about Society business?"

"Yes and no. It's not about your board nomination, but it *is* about what happened this week. Marty must have told you that we still seem to own that wretched piece of property in North Philadelphia?"

"She did. You haven't learned otherwise?"

"No, and I guess I don't expect to. I've asked our attorney to check into where things went wrong and what we should do about it. But I have to say, meeting Tyrone Blakeney and Cherisse Chapman, and seeing the area, was a real eye-opener for me."

"I take it you've stayed out of that part of town before now?" Eliot asked.

"Yes, although based only on rumor and what I've read. Unfortunately that part of town lives up—or should I say down?—to its reputation. But now I wonder if we've been shirking our responsibility to the city's history by cherry-picking the best parts and ignoring the rest."

"Understandably, if so—that's what your visitors want. What is it you'd like from me?"

"I have this very vague idea that the Society could do something about the city's fallen neighborhoods, based on the documents and items in our collections. Okay, call it white guilt if you want, but I feel we should make an effort. And I could use your expertise to fill in the gaps in my own education. Can we get together?"

"Sure. Lunch?"

"What, today?" I sputtered. "Well, sure, I guess."

"Anybody else you want to include?"

"Like Marty, you mean? I'd rather we do this one-on-one. If the idea doesn't pan out, then I haven't wasted anybody else's time. If we decide it's viable, then of course she'll be included. Is that okay? She's not the jealous-harpy type, is she? She knows I'm taken."

Eliot laughed heartily. "I wouldn't call her that. Where would you like to meet?"

"Someplace with booths, so we can talk. You have any ideas?"

He mentioned a place that lay halfway between the Society and his office at Penn, and we agreed on one o'clock. I sipped my coffee and tried to figure out what questions I should ask the expert.

———

We arrived at the restaurant at the same time, and Eliot guided me to a comfortable booth at the back. I'd met him several times before, usually with Marty, and he had impressed me with his quick intelligence—and his sense of humor, which in the case of academics didn't always go hand in hand with expertise. I could see why Marty was smitten with him. Still, with a couple of failed marriages behind her, she was proceeding cautiously.

"You're looking well," Eliot began once we were seated, "especially considering the circumstances."

"Thank you, I think. My ducking reflexes are working very well."

Once we had perused the menus and ordered, Eliot began, "You said on the phone that you wanted to talk about a neighborhoods project? After an encounter like yours, most people would run the other direction and never look back."

"I feel some of that, but visiting that part of North Philadelphia was a revelation to me. It's so easy to stay in my nice safe part of the city and forget that the other parts even exist. But if I'm going to be a responsible historian, and the custodian of the Society, I can't—or shouldn't—do that. You know the Society and you know the city and its history, so you're the best person I can ask: What can we do?"

"I'm glad you came to me, Nell. Where do you want me to start?"

"Would you mind explaining just what your area of expertise is, and how it fits in the academic universe? I've read your résumé, of course, and it's in the board packet, but you'll have to translate some parts of it for me. It's been a long time since I studied anything academic."

"Of course. Penn offers an interdisciplinary program within the College of Arts and Sciences, at both the under-graduate and graduate level. That means we can draw on faculty members across the university, and also reach out to others in the city. The subjects in which we offer classes range from urban industry to race relations to poverty and public policy, and also include such things as architecture and class, music and art. We encourage independent study projects involving a wide spectrum of subjects."

"Wow. In a way I'm jealous—I wish I'd known about such things when I was in college. I was an English major, which doesn't help a whole lot in my current position."

"I'm sure the grammar in the documents you send out is impeccable," Eliot said, struggling to keep a straight face.

"Thanks a lot. So, given what Penn offers, what do you think the Society can do that would fill a niche?"

"Are you planning an exhibit?" he asked.

"No, we don't do that anymore. I was thinking of a booklet, or a series of small studies of the different neighborhoods, showing how they've evolved and changed over time, that could be combined as a single booklet at some future date. That we can support with our own collections."

Eliot nodded. "That sounds appropriate, and manageable with your resources and staffing. My department might be able to arrange an internship, if you need the help."

"And of course we already have Lissa, although we've been keeping her busy anyway. She's been a great asset."

"I'm glad to hear that. Lissa is a very hard worker, and she knows her material well. But do allow her time to finish her degree work."

"Of course—I don't want to hold her back. So, to return to this concept, is it appropriate to start with North Philadelphia? I'm asking not only because of my own experience there, but because it's so close to all the nicer parts of the city, the ones that tourists visit, but it feels like it could be on another planet."

"I think starting there makes sense, and it would be historically appropriate. What's your time frame?"

"I have no idea, since I just came up with this. I haven't really talked to the rest of the staff, and I don't know the details of what we have in the collections." If this was going to go forward, I needed to involve Latoya ASAP, I reminded myself. "But there's another piece, and I don't know if or where it fits: What's happening right now? Who is looking at this problem, and what solutions or plans have they put forward? And are they all on the same page, or are they fighting with each other?"

"And willing to shoot someone to further their plans? A very interesting question, Nell. And one for which I have no quick answer. I study the history and the policy. The people who are trying to reclaim the neighborhoods for ordinary people rather than gangs are on a different page."

"You mentioned something about policy. Can you find me a quick survey of what's going on, and who is involved in it, in the city government and independently?"

Eliot laughed. "You don't ask much, do you? Let me ask around among my colleagues. I'm not sure this has been set down in writing, but I'm sure they'll know who the players are. Find yourself a friend at the City. Talk to Tyrone, if he's willing. In an ideal world there should be no conflict of interest among these groups, but this is Philadelphia."

"I know what you mean," I told him. We talked for a bit longer, and then we left the restaurant to go back to our respective jobs. I had a lot to think about, but I was still determined to do something about the problem, if I could.

CHAPTER 13

By the time James picked me up after work on Thursday—three days after an unknown someone could have killed me—I had to acknowledge that I was still rattled. Oh, I was trying to put on a good front: going to work on time every day and looking busy; handing out variations on *oh, shucks, I'm just fine, thank you very much* to well-wishers; and pretending everything was normal. The reality was, I was not fine and things were not normal. Only I didn't know what to do about it. Denial wasn't working, although I had no idea what the standard timetable for denial to take effect was. Should I try therapy? A long vacation on a beach with James?

Speaking of James, he wasn't pushing me to do anything in particular. Part of me was happy with that. After all, I was a big girl and I could take care of myself. Another part of me was pissed: the little girl inside me was having a tantrum and crying for help—that I didn't know how to ask for. What was I going to do? Just wait it out? How long would that take?

"Nell?" James's voice interrupted my internal dialogue.

"What?" I snapped, then backtracked. "Sorry, I didn't mean to bite your head off."

"Are you all right?"

"Yes. No. I don't know. Take your pick."

"Something wrong at work?" he asked carefully.

"No, work is fine. Work is the easy part. Except this whole mess had got me wondering if we've been seeing the world through rose-colored glasses for the past century or so." I turned to face him, as far as my seat belt would allow. "I was an English major, remember? I never took more than the intro art history class. I never did graduate work in business management, or the theory of arts administration. I kind of backed into my current position, as you saw. Before that I was writing impassioned, grammatically correct letters asking people for money, or grant proposals, either of which was certainly a better fit with my skills. But things happened so fast and so oddly that I never had time to think through what I was doing, or wanted to do with the position." *Breathe, Nell, breathe.*

"And now something has changed?" James asked.

"Yes. Maybe. Look, don't get me wrong. I love the Society and its collections. It's a privilege to have access to them up close and personal, and it's also a privilege to make them available to the public, all the while preserving them. That works for me. But there's never enough money to do it right, and frankly, there's no way to change that, unless some multitrillionaire shows up and gives us a blank check. We make tough decisions all the time: Can we do that? Should we not do that or put it off for another year or decade? And I'm supposed to be guiding that process."

"You're not alone in this. What about the board?"

"What about them?" I replied. "Nice people, mostly older men, who think that at this point in their lives they should give something back to the city or the cultural community. I applaud that. But for the most part, we meet a handful of times a year. I send them a stack of documents an inch thick before each meeting—reports, proposals, statistics—and half of them don't even read those documents. Some of them have their own agendas, or their own pet projects, and will make a case for those rather than looking at the bigger picture. I understand all that. It's typical of our kind of institution."

"But?"

"Who is the Society responsible to? The board? The self-selected membership? Researchers? Or the general public, who sees very little of any of what we have to offer?"

James didn't reply immediately, and I had run out of steam. Finally he said, "Nell, you've been through a traumatic experience, maybe even a life-altering one. But you can't fix everything, and certainly not overnight."

"You're saying I shouldn't try?"

"Of course you should try. But give yourself a little time, and think through what you *can* do, under the circumstances. Reality being what it is."

I knew he was right, but I was impatient. "You've been

shot at, right? And I know all too well that you've been stabbed. Did any of that change you?"

"Over time, yes. I carry a weapon at all times, as you know. I seldom draw that weapon, and when I do, I don't do it lightly. Nor do my colleagues, I hope. I appreciate the value of life, my own and other people's. My work is to keep the world, or my small corner of it, safer and more honest, I guess you'd say. What's yours?"

I didn't answer quickly, because his question deserved a serious answer. "To keep history alive. To help other people see the past and how it is part of their lives now and why it matters."

James nodded. "And that's a worthy goal. Do you want to stop doing that?"

"No, not really. But I guess after seeing North Philly, I feel like we've been polishing up and showing off only the pretty stuff, not the whole package."

"Let me ask you this: Who's going to pay the entrance fee to look at slums? Abandoned factories? The history of gangs?"

I slumped back in my seat. "Well, that's the problem. We give people what they want to see, or we give them what we as administrators have been indoctrinated to believe is what they *should* see. But there's so much more out there!"

"If it means that much to you, Nell, then come up with a plan. Figure out how to sell the idea to your board, even if it takes adding a bit of sugar to make them swallow it."

"Hmm," I said. Then I started to think. In so many

parts of Philadelphia, the past had been a whole lot nicer than the present, but there weren't many people around now who remembered that. It might be tricky to present that particular past in a way that didn't underscore how badly things had gone wrong since, or paint the current situation as hopeless. It couldn't be: the city and its citizens couldn't just put a torch to it all and walk away. There had to be a solution, or at least one to work toward. And we at the Society had ammunition, if we chose to use it. I reached out and laid a hand on James's arm. "Thank you."

"Anytime."

By the time we got home, I was calmer. "Listen, can we do something tonight that doesn't involve thinking? Like play Scrabble or watch a silly movie? No more earth-shattering concepts?"

"Of course. You want to go out to eat?"

"Not really—I think decent food would be wasted on me right now. And I don't want to get drunk. I just want to unwind and let my subconscious do the dirty work for me."

"I might have some ideas," James said drily.

"I bet you do." I smiled at him.

We followed my own prescription to the letter. We threw together a random meal and watched something that made us both laugh, and then we went upstairs and found other, equally satisfying things to do. Then I treated myself to a long bubble bath in our deep claw-foot tub, feeling relaxed and content. I couldn't change the world, but I could change a little piece of it. It might take some time, but then again, it might work eventually, with patience and persistence. And it was definitely worth trying.

———————

The next morning I awoke feeling refreshed and focused, a pleasant change. James was already downstairs in the kitchen, so I stretched and plumped my pillows and tried to organize my day in my head. I had no plan—yet—but I had a plan for a plan. I wanted to call my staff together and see what they'd found about Philadelphia neighborhoods and what we, as a collecting institution, could do to present them in a reasonably favorable light. I knew the employees had widely varied backgrounds and interests, not to mention access to different parts of the collections, so I would be interested to see what they came up with. I wouldn't worry about seeking donors or outside support until I had an idea firmly in hand, and there was no deadline. If the city's neighborhoods had been crumbling for more than half a century, then a couple more weeks wouldn't make a lot of difference.

Cherisse's death was still a dark spot in my mind. Since I hadn't heard anything from Detective Hrivnak, I assumed there was nothing new. Maybe there never would be. Or maybe I could go over to Cherisse's office and poke a stick into a few holes and see what crawled out—what people said about her. Had she had any enemies at work? Outside of work? Obviously I knew nothing about her personal life; would her colleagues? *Who do you think you are, Nell—Nancy Drew?* that annoying responsible grown-up voice inside said. I listened, but I knew I had a legitimate reason to visit the Licenses and Inspections offices, even if I wasn't going to go through channels and wait three months for an appointment: the Society still owned a property in North Philadelphia. I had every right to ask about that property—its current status and how to resolve its ownership going forward.

I got out of bed, dressed quickly, and went down the back stairs, to find James ready for work, lacking only his jacket (and his weapon) as he sipped coffee and scanned the headlines of the *Inquirer*.

He looked up when I entered the kitchen. "You're looking better," he said.

"I feel better, sir. Your ministrations are very therapeutic. Thank you. Is there more of that?" I nodded toward his cup.

"Of course. And you're welcome. Anything on your plate for today?"

"The usual."

"No word from the detective?"

"Nope. Even if she can keep her foot wedged in the door to keep this case open, I'm sure her higher-ups want her to give it low priority. What will be, will be."

"A sensible approach."

"I thought so," I said cheerily, and helped myself to coffee.

―――――

Eric beat me to work, so as soon as I had greeted him I said, "Can you send out a quick e-mail and ask everyone to meet me in the downstairs boardroom? Nothing urgent—don't let them think there's a crisis!—but I wanted to throw out an idea and see what people think. Say, nine fifteen?"

"Should I plan to be there, too?" Eric asked.

"Of course. You're a relative newcomer, both to the Society and to the city, and because of that your perspective might be helpful. I promise I'll keep it short. Why don't I go get myself some coffee while you do that?"

"Yes, ma'am," Eric said, and turned to his keyboard.

No sooner had I sat down at my desk with my coffee than Marty Terwilliger appeared and sat down. Ah, sweet normality! "Good morning to you," I greeted her. "Haven't seen much of you since Wednesday."

"I want to talk about the Oliver place," Marty said.

"So do I. Look, I've called an impromptu all-hands staff meeting in about fifteen minutes, and actually, that property might fit into the discussion. You can come along and explain what's going on there."

"Okay," Marty said cautiously. "You seem awfully upbeat this morning. Happy pills?"

"No, nothing like that. I guess I'm coming to terms with what happened earlier this week, and now I'm trying to find a way to use it for good. If someone is going to shoot at me, I want it to mean something, and this was kind of a wake-up call."

"You aren't planning to quit or anything?" Marty asked, looking anxious.

"Nope, I'm planning to dig in. You'll see."

Marty and I were downstairs waiting when the staff trickled in shortly after nine. They looked uniformly bewildered at being there on such short notice, for the second time in a week. I smiled at them all, trying to put them at ease. When most people had arrived, I figured I should get started.

"Good morning, everyone. Before you panic, there's no bad news. First, I wanted to thank you all for being so supportive this week. I guess I was more upset than I wanted to admit, and you helped me keep it together. I have to say, the whole thing has given me a new perspective on how the Society should operate, and I want to enlist you to help."

"Didn't we already talk about this on Tuesday?" Ben asked. "We haven't had a lot of time to hunt up anything."

"Yes, we did, Ben, but I'm hoping to focus our efforts so we don't waste time and energy. And there's another project that Marty described to me after I talked with you that sheds a different light on it."

In as few words as possible I reviewed my epiphany about the dead or dying neighborhoods of Philadelphia: why Tyrone and Cherisse had asked me to come with them, what I'd seen, and why I thought the Society had some sort of responsibility to do what we could to help things change. After I'd finished my summary, I said, "I know some of you haven't been here very long. And I'm sure you're all aware how hard it is to change the direction of a venerable institution like ours. Kind of like turning the *Titanic*."

A few people laughed at my attempt at a joke, so I pressed on. "As I said, Marty brought to my attention a different project, the acquisition and maintenance of a colonial estate outside the city limits. We visited there on Wednesday, and I'll admit it's beautiful, and in surprisingly good condition. And it's exactly the kind of opportunity our traditional members and supporters would expect us to pursue. But is it the right thing to do?"

Shelby spoke up. "Nell, I'm not sure I follow. What's your point?"

I surveyed my staff. Some of the people around the table I'd worked with for a decade now. They were all here because they cared about history—they probably could be making more money somewhere else. They were smart and hardworking, and I wanted them to see what I was seeing now, after Monday's events had ripped the blinders from my eyes. "Look, everyone. I've just started thinking about this, so there's nothing like a plan in place. Even the board doesn't know about it, except for Marty here. I'm laying this out for you now because I want to know what you think. If you tell me I'm way off course, I'll accept that. I need your help and cooperation to make either idea work."

Latoya spoke for the first time. "Let me see if I have this right. You're saying we have a choice right now. Either we direct our resources toward this Save the Neighborhoods concept, or toward the Save the Mansion idea? I assume we don't have the capability to do both."

"I think that's what it comes down to, Latoya. Both are deserving projects, no question. I don't have facts and figures about what either would require, but I think what matters right now is what we as a staff think we *should* be doing. We talk and write about preserving history, but which history? The long and ongoing evolution of one of the nation's great cities, even when it includes slums and crime and decay, or the maintenance of a beautiful and demonstrably historic home of a single rich family at a particular point in the past? Which is more important? Which fits the Society's mission better?"

My passionate speech was greeted with silence. I wasn't surprised: it had taken me days to arrive at my current viewpoint, and I couldn't expect staff members to have an immediate response.

I smiled at them. "I'm sorry that I dumped all this on you all at once. It's been a hard week for me, and I'm looking at things differently now, and I think it's important to share it with you. We don't need to make any decisions right now. There's no timetable or agenda, and I haven't promised anything to anyone. But I want us all to think about what I've said. Talk about it with each other. What is it we believe the Society is and should be? That's a pretty fundamental question, but one we need to look at."

Latoya spoke again. "How will the board react?"

I turned to her. "To either of these ideas? A fair question, and I have no idea. I don't want to take this to them until there's some sort of plan or proposal. I could use the excuse that it's too late to include it in next week's meeting agenda, but I'd like them to start thinking about these things, too. I may give them a verbal summary, like I've just given you. Hey, if neither one works out, no harm, no foul. But it seems to me that these two projects both reflect our institutional mission and how we see history. I welcome your input. That's all I've got for now. Thank you for listening."

Everyone stood, looking uncertain. Some wandered out. Shelby came over and said, "Hey, you don't mess around."

"Think I scared them all?"

"Well, maybe the ones who like to get up in the morning and go to a safe, predictable job. But I for one think you're right: it's something we as an organization need to think about now and then. Maybe we'll all go back to sleep for another century, but at least you tried. Let me know when I have to rewrite all my boilerplate letters, will you?"

"Of course, Shelby," I said, and she left as well.

Marty and I were left alone. "You sure you know what you're doing, Nell?" she asked.

"Nope. But I feel like I have to try."

"Then I'll back you. Don't say anything to the board just yet. I might have some ideas . . ."

"You always do. So let's get to work!"

CHAPTER 14

Marty too disappeared to do whatever it was she did. I patted myself on the back. I had started one ball rolling, or one hare running, or something. I had faith in my staff—they were a smart, creative bunch, and I was sure they would come up with some new ideas.

I was pondering what to do next when I realized Latoya was standing in the doorway. "A moment, Nell?" she asked.

"Sure. Is this about what I said at the meeting? Please, sit down." I was a bit puzzled: Latoya seldom came to me, and our relationship was cordial at best. Maybe I'd struck a chord? Or she was going to tell me I was crazy?

She sat. I sensed she was choosing her words carefully. "Aren't you suggesting a rather political problem to take on?"

"You mean external politics, in the case of the

neighborhoods project? Yes and no. Yes, in that any meaningful change to the underlying problems will have to come from city government, maybe even with federal funding, and definitely with the help of community-based organizations, and certainly all those are political. What I see the Society doing is assembling the documentation, artifacts, images, or whatever we have here for each target neighborhood and making those resources available to whoever we believe will do the most good. I see that as a part of our mission, one aspect that we've kind of neglected." Maybe I was treading on risky ground. After all, I could easily be labeled a suburban bleeding-heart liberal, and maybe I had no right to try to push the Society in my direction. I really wasn't sure where Latoya stood. I knew her academic interests were directed to the Pennsylvania Abolition Society, whose papers resided in the Society's collections. In fact, when Latoya had first been hired, she had negotiated a four-day week to allow her to pursue her own research using those documents. But I had no idea whether her current participation was more active than that, and I had never asked. I waited to see what she'd say.

She tilted her head at me. "We've never really talked about personal issues, have we? I know only what staff gossip tells me about your home life, and I have no clue what your political or religious orientation might be. I believe you're a fair and honest person, and a reasonably good administrator, but up to this point you've never really stepped up and articulated a philosophy for this place that you're responsible for."

I was careful in my answer. "I think that's a fair

assessment, and I don't know much more about you on a personal level. Look, this week I've had a wake-up call. I'm still processing it, but what came through to me loud and clear is that we've been ignoring a large chunk of history, and that doesn't seem right. Because that history, at least for the city, nearly cost me my life this week. Okay, maybe that's melodramatic, but being shot at in a slum I'd never even seen, no more than a mile from here, got me thinking. I was shocked at how much I didn't know about the city, and that's my own fault. Do I think I can change the course of this place? Hardly. But I want to try. Do you have an opinion? Because I'll listen."

"Because I'm black?" she said, then retreated quickly. "Sorry, that was uncalled for. You've never shown any discrimination toward anyone. But you have to admit it is a factor in Philadelphia and its history."

"Of course it is, and the Society should acknowledge that. You can certainly make a contribution, because you probably know more about the relevant records than anyone else in this building. If you're interested."

She looked at me squarely. "That's something I have to think about, Nell. I like my job. I also like keeping my research separate from my job, even though they both take place in this building. I'm not sure I want to upset that balance, but having said that, I'm not sure I feel that way only because I don't like change. So, like you, I want time to think."

"Fair enough. But if we move forward on this, I would value your help."

"Thank you, Nell."

As she stood up to leave, I added quickly, "One more thing: Tyrone. I don't mean to tread on your personal life, but can you tell me if he's an honest man? A good man?"

Latoya wavered. "I can't say that I know the man he's become. But he was always very committed to what he believed in, and he wanted to do good. I think one of the things that drove us apart was the intensity of his commitment. I was always more restrained, more rational. But even now I wouldn't believe that he is involved in anything suspect. Is that what you want to know?"

"I think so. I don't know him well, but I had the same impression. Thank you."

I watched her leave, but I stayed in my chair. Was I going off the rails? Had the shooting completely upset my equilibrium? And worse, clouded my professional judgment? At least I'd reached out for opinions from my colleagues. If I was wrong, they'd rein me in, I hoped.

Now what? It occurred to me that a visit to Cherisse's City department might give me some more insight into the problem with the property—and into Cherisse's character. I had some legitimate questions. Cherisse had come to see me about the Society's property. I wanted to know how she'd come across it and what we could or should do about it, from the City's perspective. Then I could compare that to our lawyer's opinion.

They couldn't turn me away, could they? After all, I had seen Cherisse die. That should give me some leverage. And it seemed highly unlikely that Licenses and Inspections had sent a hit man to take us out, all over one pathetic building. So I would go take on city hall, or more specifically, the

Municipal Services Building, where all the business actually got done.

I went back to my office and gathered my things for the short trek over to the Municipal Services Building, more often known as the MSB. I had looked up the pertinent information, so I knew where I was headed once I was in the building. Whether they'd let me past the desk was another question. I was hoping that the name Cherisse Chapman would get me in. Maybe I was on a fool's errand, but I was still too wired to sit in my office and do paperwork.

"Eric, I'm going over to the City offices to see if I can find out anything about our North Philadelphia property. I should be back in time for lunch."

"Duly noted, Nell. Nice day for a walk."

"That it is." I set off, armed with no more than the address of our orphaned property. My strategy was minimal: mention Cherisse, talk to anyone who had worked with her, and as a distant third, see what the status of the property was in the queue. It wouldn't surprise me if whoever was in the office refused to jump me to the head of the line, and I wouldn't blame them. On the other hand, I was something of a public figure myself, and I wasn't there to complain about something, which probably put me in the minority.

The walk took no more than ten minutes. Bless James for his solicitude, but I kind of liked walking from the train station to work, and I was pretty sure I needed the exercise. The MSB stood on the far side of city hall, a tall, gray rectilinear building that was all windows, shaped like dominos. Its only distinguishing feature was the large gold eagle over the entrance. I went under the eagle and found myself in front of a large reception desk. Everyone was so security-minded these days! But better safe than sorry, especially when a government was involved.

"Excuse me?" I said to the man in uniform behind the console. "I need to speak to someone in Licenses and Inspections about Cherisse Chapman?"

"She's, uh, no longer with the department," he said, looking uncomfortable.

"Yes, I'm quite aware of that, since I was with her when . . . it happened. I only wanted to talk to someone about something she was working on for me." Which was actually true.

The man gave me a once-over and decided I was not threatening. "Eleventh floor. Sign in, please. And I'll need to look in your purse."

I signed while he riffled through my bag to make sure I had no weapons or explosive devices. Then he handed it back to me and waved me toward the elevators. On the way to the eleventh floor, I tried to remember whether I'd been in this building before. I had some vague memory of a meeting about City grant applications, although I couldn't remember what department had been involved. In any case, it had been years earlier. When the doors opened, I glanced around. While the exterior of the building presented a brave face to the public, the interior working offices looked like any other office space—messy. There was a department name on the glass door, but beyond that stretched half a floor's worth of battered old desks, filing cabinets, and Bankers Boxes. There were people behind most of the desks, and many of them were women. I stood wavering in the doorway until someone finally noticed me and called out, "Can I help you?"

I took that as an invitation to move farther into the room. Up close she looked closer to thirty than twenty, and she hadn't bothered with makeup. Her clothes were best described as *business nondescript.*

"I hope so," I told her, smiling. "I wanted to ask about something that Cherisse Chapman was working on?"

The woman's face fell. "Oh, well, she's not here anymore."

"I'm afraid I know that," I said. "I'm Nell Pratt."

The woman's eyes widened. "Oh, right, you're the one . . . How terrible for you. And what a shame. Nobody's touched her stuff yet. Well, maybe there was a policeman here who took anything personal. Not that there was much. She wasn't into pictures and souvenirs. Oh, please sit down. Can I get you some coffee or anything?"

"Coffee would be good. Is there someplace we could sit that isn't such a goldfish bowl?"

"Oh, right, sure. There's a table in the break room. Follow me."

I followed her around a corner and down a windowless hall, until she turned into a dingy room with a table and a couple of plastic chairs. A counter with a sink in the middle held coffee supplies, and there was a small refrigerator that I assume was intended for employee lunches.

"Sit, please." She waved vaguely at the table.

I sat. "I'm sorry, I didn't catch your name?"

"Oh, sorry—again. I'm just so flustered. I'm Melanie Saggiomo. I hadn't known Cherisse for long, and then, boom, she was gone! Black or creamer? It's the powdered stuff."

"Black is fine." I waited until she had managed to put together a cup of coffee and set it in front of me, along with some sugar packets and a plastic stirrer. "Thank you."

"Is there something I can help you with?"

"Well, I'm not sure where to start. You see, Cherisse and Tyrone Blakeney came to see me on Monday because of a property that the Pennsylvania Antiquarian Society apparently owns, although we thought we'd sold it decades ago. We went out together to see the place, and you know what happened after that. But I spent only a couple of hours with Cherisse, and we never even discussed how she identified the ownership, or what we need to do now. Maybe you can help me?"

"Well, I can tell you about the program, but I'd have to track down the file for any other details."

"That's all right. Anything you can give me would be a plus." I sipped the bad coffee and tried to look expectant.

"Are you aware of the Vacant Property Strategy?" When I looked blank, Melanie hurried on. "Of course you're not. I don't know why you would be. Well, about five years ago the City created a new initiative within our department, with the goal of doing something about the vacant properties around the city. It's been working well; we've managed to inspect nearly half of them, and we're trying to force the owners to register them as vacant—which means they acknowledge responsibility for them, for the record—or sell them, or rehabilitate them. We've managed to work with the courts, so we have some leverage—the owners can no longer just ignore us, and that's been pretty successful too—the department has brought in more than six hundred thousand dollars in licenses and permits in just the last year."

"So what was Cherisse doing?"

"She was hired a year or two ago when the department staffed up to handle the initiative. She was really into it, almost like it was a crusade, not just a day job. That's probably how she found your property."

"So why did she come to see me, rather than just sending a notice of some sort? Did she do that with everyone she tracked down?"

"No. Wait—Tyrone was with her, right? They were working together—he's part of some kind of neighborhood group in North Philly, and that's the area she was focusing on most recently. I gather he's got some big plans, and I think she was trying to help him with the paperwork so he could consolidate some of the abandoned properties, make the neighborhood more appealing to potential developers."

"That seems logical. I feel so guilty—maybe that doesn't make sense, but if someone hadn't messed up the paperwork long ago, we wouldn't have been there on Monday."

"It's not your fault!" Melanie hurried to reassure me.

"I know, but still, I feel bad. What was she like?"

Melanie once again looked uncomfortable, if only briefly. "She was a hard worker—always in early, and stayed late."

"No husband or kids waiting at home for her?"

"No, although I think she was seeing someone. Anyway, she was real careful with her paperwork—she made sure it was correct *and* she turned it in quickly, which is not always true around here."

"Was she from here? Did she have family in the city?"

Melanie shrugged. "I don't really know. Cherisse wasn't a group kind of person, if you know what I mean. She was nice, and she said hi and stuff, but she didn't hang out with anyone in particular. She didn't buddy up to anyone here, not even our boss. She wasn't a suck-up. Mostly she kept to herself. It was hard to complain about her, because she was doing a really good job."

I nodded. "When we were together, in that neighborhood, she seemed really committed to what she and Tyrone were doing. I don't know anything about him, either. Has he worked with a lot of people in this department?"

"Not me. But I know he's been working hard on clearing the titles to a lot of these properties so he can move forward."

"He's not an investor, is he?"

Melanie shook her head. "No, and he's not working with the big developers, either. I think he just really cares about that neighborhood. He's a lot better with people than Cherisse was. Maybe that's why they made a good team. Sorry, that's really about all I know."

"I appreciate your telling me. Now, what do I need to do with the property we apparently still own?"

"Why don't I take a look at Cherisse's desk and see if she left anything about it?"

"That would be really helpful," I told her as I followed her out into the big room. Melanie headed for a desk that looked like a fish out of water in the room: while there were still files and documents stacked up, they were all carefully labeled and aligned and sorted into categories in a tiered rack. There was a single container with pens and pencils, and a middle-aged phone, but not much else on the desk.

"What did you say the address was?" Melanie asked.

I told her, and she riffled through one of the stacks from the middle of the rack—presumably the "pending" category.

"Oh, yeah, here it is. I can't let it leave the building, but I can make copies for you. You got a lawyer?"

"Of course, but as president I like to keep on top of things. And our lawyer charges by the hour, so the more I can take care of, the more money we'll save."

"I hear you. I'll just be a minute." Melanie grabbed up the file and headed for a copy machine on the other side of the room.

I looked around the room, trying to match the number of people working—and they all looked busy—with the tens of thousands of properties that needed attention. It was still mind-boggling to me. What a terrible waste that someone like Cherisse, who was eager and committed, should be wiped out for no reason, when she was only doing her job. Not that I'd learned anything more about Cherisse with this visit: quiet, competent, kept to herself. Nothing there to guide me. I knew I hadn't been the target. Had she? Or had Tyrone? Or no one at all?

Melanie returned with a neat stack of photocopies. "Here you go! Thanks for stopping by—we don't see many of the owners here. Mostly they want to disappear and we have to hunt for them."

"Thank you for your information. I'll try to get this sorted out quickly and take at least one file off your stack. Oh, let me know if there's any kind of service for Cherisse, will you? I'd like at least to acknowledge her."

"Sure. You have a card?" I handed her my business card, and she said, "Thanks. I'll be in touch if I hear anything."

I exited the building, smiling at the guard at the desk, and walked out into the plaza in front. What now? I had no idea.

CHAPTER 15

Still a nice day. I strolled across City Hall Plaza, taking my time. The city hall building itself was amazing. William Penn had set the open space in the middle of what would become a major city; he had called it Centre Square. I was sure he had never envisioned this massive wedding cake of a building plunked down right in the center of it. One of the largest municipal buildings in the world. Tallest masonry building. Supporting walls twenty-two feet thick. It was roughly the same age as the Society building, although they bore no resemblance to each other. I'd been walking past it for years, and it still never failed to impress me.

I picked up a sandwich on the way back, carefully avoiding thinking about what to do next. Luckily when I returned to the Society, the answer provided itself, in the form of Detective Hrivnak. She did not look happy, but then, she seldom did. "Were you looking for me, Detective?"

"No, I'm here to look up the history of the Hrivnaks," she all but snarled. "Of course I'm here to see you. Got a minute?"

"Sure. Upstairs?"

"Nah, that room in the corner will be fine." She turned on her heel and marched toward it, and I had no choice but to follow. I shut the door behind me.

"What's up?"

"Nothing, is what. This investigation is going nowhere, and I've been told to wrap it up. There's a whole list of more important crimes lined up, and my boss thinks this is a waste of time. I can't say that I blame him—a lot of crime happens in that neighborhood, and we can't follow up on everything. Don't hold that against us."

"I don't. I know it's a problem—too few cops, too much ground to cover, too much violence. No money to hire more cops. You have to pick and choose."

"You got it."

I wondered if this was just a courtesy call, or if she was trying to send me a message. "You know, we still own that property, at least at the moment. Now that our title has been established, we can't just walk away." I carefully left aside that someone had died in front of that property—in front of me.

"Join the club. Let your lawyer take care of it and dump it as fast as you can."

Was that bitterness I was hearing? "That has been my

plan, so far. But the more I think about it, the more I wonder if there's anything the Society can do."

"Oh, jeez, you're not going to stick yourself in the middle of another mess, are you?"

"I don't plan to. Look, until this week I never paid any attention to the housing and property issues in the city, even though maybe I should have, since I've worked in the city for years. And now I'm horrified." When Hrivnak started to protest, I raised a hand to stop her. "Yes, I know, typical liberal white guilt. But I can't just crawl back into my nice, safe elitist hole here and ignore it now."

"You want to join the force?"

Was that actually humor from the detective? "No, not exactly. But if there are agencies or groups who are trying to reclaim their neighborhoods, the Society can help by giving them the history of the way things were, when those neighborhoods were thriving. Pictures, letters, newspaper clippings—the kind of stuff that makes a place seem real to other people, when all they see now is a gang battle zone."

Detective Hrivnak sat back in her chair and studied my face. "Nell, you are a piece of work. Somebody tries to kill you, and you turn it into a do-gooder opportunity."

"Is that wrong?" I challenged her.

She slumped. "No, I guess not, as long as you do it from your nice, safe building here. Don't go wandering around drug turf."

"Believe me, I won't. The history is here in this building. Look, do you mind if I get in touch with Tyrone? Might as well start with his group, his neighborhood. Our neighborhood."

"I guess. You know any local journalists?"

"I can probably find some—I know there are a few who come in now and then to go through our archives looking for pictures. Why?"

"Get one on your side, get him interested. No offense, but anything that comes out of this place isn't going to attract a big audience, and you don't have a heck of a lot of members. Now, a smart guy with a local paper—or even a blog—will reach more people."

"I see your point. We need a voice that people will listen to."

"Exactly. Just don't stir up any trouble while you're at it. Don't pick a hothead who wants to make a name for himself."

"I understand, Detective—Meredith. I will look into it. But I still want to start with Tyrone. He's out of the hospital, I assume?"

"Yeah, since yesterday."

"You have an address for him? Home? Office?"

Hrivnak reached into her pocket, pulled out a card, and scribbled something on the back, then handed it to me. "Here."

"Thanks. Before you go, did you do any background on him before your boss shut you down?"

"Some. Local boy makes good—born in North Philly and dragged himself up and out. Still knows some people there. Good community organizer."

"Any of those people hold a grudge against him, that he got out when they didn't?"

"We never got that far. Don't you go looking!"

"Detective, I doubt that anyone in that neighborhood would talk to me." I certainly didn't feel like attracting any more gunfire.

"You got that right. We good?"

"I hope so. I promise I will do my best to stay out of trouble, and I don't plan to go anywhere near that neighborhood again."

"Amen." The detective stood up. "Well, that's all I wanted to say. Good luck with your project."

I thought she sounded skeptical. "You don't think it can help?"

"People have tried before. You might as well give it a shot."

That was probably as close to her blessing as I was going to get. I escorted her out of the building and went up to my office to eat my sandwich and think.

As I passed his desk, Eric said, "We've got RSVPs from three board members, and nos from two. Is that about normal?"

"Probably. We need a quorum to vote Eliot in, but apart from that there are no big issues on the table." Unless I got this neighborhoods project whipped together by next week, but that was unlikely, and I didn't want to rush it and blow my chances. "I'm going to eat my lunch now. I think I'll get some coffee first. You want anything?"

"No, ma'am—I'm good, thanks."

Still restless, I wandered down the hall to the staff room. There I found Latoya helping herself to coffee. She was the only one there, since it was still early for lunch. "Latoya, you knew Tyrone. Can you tell me anything more about his background? Education, experience, that kind of thing? I'd like to talk to him about this neighborhoods project, but I don't know much about the community development organizations around the city. Is he effective at what he does? Or haven't you kept up with his activities?"

Latoya looked surprisingly uncertain, and I wondered if she had something to say. Finally she said, "Come to my office."

I followed her down the hall, and we turned right before we reached my end. I didn't want to jump to any conclusions: Was she being private, or did she have something on Tyrone? When we reached her office, she set down her coffee and gestured at a chair. "Please, sit."

"Is there a problem?" I asked cautiously.

Latoya appeared startled. "What? Oh, no. I just don't like to broadcast my personal business to the entire staff, but in this case, you have a legitimate reason for asking. I didn't grow up around here—I was raised outside of Pittsburgh and came to Philadelphia for college. I liked the area, so I stayed on and got a master's degree. Tyrone was a couple of years ahead of me at Penn, but he was—how should I put this?—a high-profile figure on campus, even then."

"Was that good or bad?"

"Good, in general. He was an activist, but not an angry one, if that makes sense to you. He had his causes, and he worked hard to bring attention to them. Saving his old neighborhood was one of those causes, even then, and apparently the one that stuck. He made it out, but he felt he owed the place something."

"Does he do it professionally now? I mean, how does he support himself? A nonprofit in that part of town can't pay much, if anything."

"You're getting ahead of my story, Nell," Latoya chided. I shut up; I wanted her to keep talking. "As you might guess, Tyrone was charismatic. Charming. Interesting. He came from a world that I knew nothing about. He could have downplayed his origins, but he chose not to. As I think I told you, he doesn't do this for egotistical purposes—he's a true believer. In any case, we kept crossing paths, and eventually we started seeing each other."

I could easily visualize that: cool, reserved Latoya and outgoing, rapid-fire Tyrone. They would have been a complementary pairing. "But it didn't last?" I prompted.

"No, but we parted as friends. I'm not sure I've seen him in the past five years—we run in different circles, I guess you'd say. It was something of a shock when someone shot at him this week—I'd heard nothing but positive things about his activities."

"I don't mean to pry, but you can understand my curiosity—I'd still like to know if he might have been the target of the shooting. From what you've said, it doesn't sound like it, but he could have changed since you knew him well. Can you tell me anything about his personal life? Partner, kids, where he lives?"

"I know only a few details. I believe he's married, to a woman he met when the City issued municipal bonds to support the Vacant Property Initiative a few years ago. I think she's a banker, but I've never met her. I wouldn't know about children. As for where he lives, I have no information."

"Wait a sec," I said, and pulled the detective's card out of my pocket. "Here's his address." I handed it to her across the desk.

She read it and nodded as though it meant something to her. "Do you know that area?" she asked. When I shook my head she said, "It's what I'd call a compromise neighborhood—on the brink of gentrification, safe, with some nice older homes if you're willing to put a little effort and money into them. His professional wife would have no reason to apologize for the address, but Tyrone wouldn't have to feel defensive of turning his back on his origins, if that seems logical to you."

"I think it does. That's an interesting comment. At least he hasn't moved out to the suburbs. So it's his wife's income that supports them?"

"That would be my guess, although I have no direct knowledge." Latoya was always careful about accuracy. "Is that of any help to you?"

"To be honest, yes and no. What you're telling me is that there is no obvious reason—that you know of—why anyone would take a potshot at him when he's in his childhood neighborhood, which he is still trying to help."

Latoya nodded. "Yes, I think it's fair to say that. Are you still clinging to the belief that it was *not* a random drive-by shooting?"

"I'm trying, but so far I'm not finding much support for that idea. Still, it just doesn't feel right."

"Don't make it too personal, Nell—the shooting is just a reflection of the kind of neighborhood that it's become."

"I know. I understand. I just don't like it." I stood up.

"Thanks for filling me in. If I should happen to see Tyrone again, should I mention you or would you rather I didn't?"

"If I come up, fine."

Back in my office with my coffee I finally had a chance to eat my sandwich. The random-drive-by theory was looking better and better. Still, I felt compelled to talk with Tyrone again. We might not have any answers to the shooting between us, but his neighborhood could be the subject of the Society's first neighborhood profile, with his help and that of his organization. It could serve as a model for any others. And he could help me shape the plan.

CHAPTER 16

I finished my sandwich, then reached for my phone. I should strike while the iron was hot, which translated to, find out now whether this idea has any chance of working, sooner rather than later, before I and other people devoted a lot of time to it. Speaking with Tyrone was a good place to start, if he was up to it—after all, he'd been shot just this week and couldn't possibly be fully recovered. I had never wanted to find out how many times or where he'd been hit, but at least I knew he had been alert and talking to me earlier in the week. If he was home recuperating, I could see him there, if he didn't object. If he didn't feel he could handle it, I'd just have to wait. As I had told my staff, there was no deadline for my idea. The city wasn't going to change quickly, and its problems were not going to go away.

Before I could change my mind, I called the number

that the detective had scribbled on the card. On the third ring, a man answered. "Tyrone? Is that you?" I asked.

"Yeah. Who's this?"

"It's Nell Pratt. From Monday?" Wow, that sounded dumb.

"Oh, Nell, I didn't recognize your voice. How you doing?"

"I'm fine. I'm more worried about you. You got out of the hospital yesterday?"

"Yeah, they let me out. I'm okay, but they gave me a list of stuff I'm not supposed to do, and most everything I want to do is on it."

"Is anyone there to take care of you?"

"No, but I don't need help to just sit and stare at the television. I tried reading, but I kept falling asleep and then I had to read the same page over again. Did you need something?"

"It's not urgent, but this whole . . . episode got me thinking that maybe the Society hasn't done enough to, well, represent the whole of the city, including the run-down parts."

"You've seen it," he said bitterly. "What's to represent?"

Maybe he had a right to be bitter. He'd been trying to do something good, and he'd gotten shot for his efforts. "What the neighborhoods used to be, not what they are now."

A moment of silence. "Go on," Tyrone finally said.

"I was thinking about whether the Society could put together some neighborhood profiles that groups like yours could use to promote your vision of redevelopment. Using old pictures and stories, advertising, things like that, from our collections."

When Tyrone spoke again, his tone was warmer. "I like it. You thinking of starting with North Philly?"

"Well, since we've got the public's attention"—for about a minute, at least—"it seems like a good place to start. When you're feeling up to it, can we get together and talk about it?"

"You free now? Because I'm going crazy sitting here staring at the walls."

"Only if you're feeling strong enough."

"Don't worry about me—I've survived worse. You know where I live?"

"The detective told me. You really want me to come over now?"

"Yes. My last painkillers have just kicked in, and they'll last maybe four hours tops, and then I'll fall asleep. Now's good."

"Then I'll be there."

It occurred to me that it might be a good idea to call James, since I assumed he expected to give me a ride home, and I wasn't sure where I'd be at quitting time. As near as I could tell, Tyrone lived in a neighborhood not far from the Art Museum, but I didn't know the streets there well. I called James's office number.

"Morrison," he said absently.

"Pratt," I shot back.

"Oh, hi, Nell—I wasn't expecting you to call. Problem?"

"No. I wanted to let you know that I'm going to go over to Tyrone Blakeney's home to talk to him about this neighborhood project."

My statement resulted in a long silence from him. "You sure that's a good idea? Where's he live?"

I told him the address. "That's safe enough, don't you think?"

"I suppose. You want me to pick you up there?"

"I'm not sure how long I'll be there. I wanted to get things started, but he's just out of the hospital and on medication, so he may fade quickly. Why don't I call you when I know my plans?"

"All right. Later, then. Take care." He hung up, all business.

I felt vaguely dissatisfied. In effect I had dutifully asked James's permission to go to this place, and he had grudgingly said yes. I resented having had to ask, although given that there was a crime involved and no one was sure whether Tyrone had been the target, there might be some risk attached. But how could I go on with my life looking over my shoulder all the time? I thought it would pass, but how long would that take?

I gathered up my things and told Eric, "I'm going to go talk to Tyrone Blakeney now."

"Isn't he the man . . . ?" Eric asked anxiously.

"Yes, he's the one. He's out of the hospital and home now, and I wanted to discuss what the Society might be able to do to help him and his organization. I don't know how long I'll be gone, because I don't know how much he can take, so I may or may not be back before the end of the day. Oh, and I've alerted the FBI of my whereabouts, so they shouldn't be calling."

Eric suppressed a smile. "Got it, ma'am. Be safe."

I went downstairs, then walked over to Broad Street to catch a cab at the hotel there. Tyrone's address was too far to walk and too short a distance to take the subway, so a cab it was. It took only fifteen minutes to arrive at his home. It was, as Latoya had suggested, a pleasant neighborhood, shabby but not grubby—the houses looked well cared for, and the streets were clean and free of trash. Tyrone's door had a shiny brass knocker, which I used, and then I heard him call out, "Door's open." It said something about a neighborhood when you could leave your door unlocked. I let myself in.

"Tyrone? It's Nell Pratt," I called out once I was inside.

"Here," he answered. I followed his voice to the living room on the right.

"You're looking better than the last time I saw you," I told him, "and I'm not just saying that to be polite. How're you feeling?"

"Grateful, I guess. None of the bullets hit anything that mattered. It looked a lot worse than it was."

There had been a *lot* of blood. I quashed that memory quickly. "It did look bad, not that I have a lot of experience in that area. I'm sorry about Cherisse. She seemed really invested in what she was doing."

"She was. She was making a difference. So, I'd offer you something to drink, but that would mean I'd have to get up."

I waved off his offer. "Don't worry about it—I didn't come all the way over here for a cup of tea. You want me to jump right in?"

"Please. Have a seat."

I sat. "After seeing that neighborhood with you and realizing we—by that I mean the Society—have a stake in the place, I started wondering if there was something proactive we could do to help local efforts to clean up the neighborhoods and maybe make them viable again." I went on to tell him the thoughts I'd had so far, explain what we had in our collections that might be useful, and mentioned that I'd asked my staff to look for materials that were relevant. Tyrone listened without comment until I was finished. "Well?"

"I think it's great. You know, neighborhood organizations get kind of caught up in what they're doing in the moment, without ever seeing a bigger picture. Mostly they're struggling to survive, so you can't blame them, but what you're suggesting could broaden our reach and put things in perspective for the public. Especially since, like you said, nobody remembers the way it was. People need to be reminded."

"I'm glad you feel that way. I don't know what I can promise, because I'm not the person in charge of managing projects like this, and we don't do exhibits anymore. But I think I can sell it to the board and the staff, as long as none of our other programs suffer. Listen, one thing I was wondering—do you have any journalists, in print or online, on your side? We could use some public outreach, and the Society has kind of a limited appeal. I don't think our newsletter would reach the people you need."

"Let me think on it—I might have some ideas. I should be back at work by next week, and I can ask around. But I like the way you're thinking."

"Well, being shot at was a wake-up call, and I want to make it matter. I don't think I've met your wife—I understand she's in banking?"

"Investment banking—you know, bonds and stuff."

"Do you think her company would have any information in their files? Demographics and that sort of thing? I understand that she was involved in the mayor's initiative a few years back."

"Yeah, she was. That bond issue raised a lot of money. Most of it's been spent, but it hasn't been wasted, which is more than you can say for a lot of City funds. That's how we met, across the table."

"So you've been doing this for a while? How would you grade your efforts?"

"A solid B, maybe. There's a lot that needs to be done, and it won't happen quickly, but we need people who can stay the course. Like me."

He hadn't complained, but I thought Tyrone looked tired. "Well, that's all I had to say. Nothing works fast at our place, either, but I wanted to know that you thought it was a good idea before I took it any further. I'm still thinking it through and getting a handle on what resources we have."

"Nell, I truly appreciate what you're trying to do, after what happened. Most people would want to put it behind them."

"Well, maybe this is my way of working through it." I stood up. "Look, I'll let you get some rest now. We can talk next week, all right?"

"Great, and thanks again. You can see yourself out, right?"

"Sure, no problem."

Outside on the pavement I checked my watch: close to four o'clock. What was I supposed to do with an empty hour?

I decided to walk. I did need the exercise, and the fresh air, and the time to sort out my thoughts. I might as well head over to FBI headquarters and meet James there. If he was still busy, I could find myself a cup of coffee and sit and contemplate Independence Hall or the Liberty Bell. I could even shop at the stores of the Gallery along the way—I seemed to recall that it had been the result of an earlier city redevelopment project, and it had changed the face of Market Street in Center City. Or I could stop at the Reading Terminal Market, one of my all-time favorite places in Philadelphia, and pick up some stuff for dinner, since I knew I had a ride home. I tended to overshop when I was in that place, which made it hard to haul everything back on the train. Come to think of it, the whole Convention Center complex had been another public project, although the City had created a separate authority to manage the financing—Mitchell Wakeman, whose largesse was supporting the renovations at the Society, after I'd cleared the way for his favorite construction project in Chester County, had played a major part in that project. All in all, the buildings along Market Street demonstrated that a mix of public and private financing could make a real difference in a city. Now I needed to convince the citizens that the neighborhoods were worth investing in as well.

It was a fairly long walk, but I found myself pleasantly

tired by the time I arrived at the market. I allowed myself some time to ramble through the crowded aisles, admiring the rich variety of vegetables and fruits and fish and meat and so much more, trying to decide what I was in the mood for. I smiled at the young Amish women in traditional caps behind the counters. I ogled the absurd chocolate figures— really, noses?—before I looped back to the vegetable corner and stocked up on glorious clusters of fresh mushrooms, and herbs, and staples.

Halfway through I called James. "Hey, there," I greeted him.

"You ready to go home?"

"Not yet. I'm at the Reading Terminal and I wondered if there was anything in particular you wanted to eat. Meat? Fish?"

"Get some of everything," he said, and I could hear the smile in his voice.

"My exact idea. I should be over at your place in about fifteen minutes, if you want to meet out front."

"See you then."

When we had hung up, I went back in search of dinner. And dessert. Life was looking up.

CHAPTER 17

I found myself a seat on a bench in front of the building that housed FBI headquarters, overlooking Independence Mall, and arrayed my bags around me. I was definitely an upscale bag lady. Most people were busy catching trains and buses and eager to make their way home this Friday evening, and I amused myself with watching them.

Independence Mall had a checkered history. Independence Hall had obviously been there for a long time, but the empty green space in front of it had once been filled with other buildings—it had never been intended as a grand vista. That idea came later.

The park had been created in the 1950s—a venture supported by both the City and the state—and sadly, some of the early buildings, like what little had been left of George Washington's "White House," for a decade or more the temporary national capital—had fallen to the wrecking ball, razed in favor of green grass. Maybe that should make me feel better: even high-end history could be overlooked by those with later, different agendas. Besides, people would rather look at pretty vistas and tidy monuments than rubble foundations and what was left of outhouses. And where George Washington had kept a full staff of slaves. Funny how the history of history changed over time.

"Is there room for me?" I looked up to see James. "This looks like you're stocking up for a siege."

"Not exactly. But there's stuff at the Terminal Market that I really like, that I can't get anywhere else. I splurged. Are we ready to go?"

"We are. You want me to carry some of this stuff?"

"Please." I followed James to where he parked his car, and we loaded up the trunk. At this time of year it was easy to get out of the city, unlike summer, when it seemed that half the population of the eastern end of the state decided to head for the Shore, all at the same time. They never learned.

Once we had arrived on the highway, James asked, "How is Blakeney?"

"Better than I expected, I have to say, for someone who was shot multiple times only a few days ago."

"What's that part of town like?"

"You should know better than I do—you lived over there for years, didn't you?"

"Yes, but I didn't walk around much, and I didn't know the individual streets."

"Walking is the best way to get to know an area," I

told him. "Anyway, his street, and the others I saw, were kind of genteel shabby. I'm inferring that his wife makes the money, since she works for one of those big-name investment banks, but that he would only compromise his principles so far. He'd have trouble being effective at what he does if he'd gone for a big house in a snobby neighborhood, no matter where the money's coming from. That kind of address alone would undermine his credibility."

"Good point. What did he think of your idea?"

"I think he liked it. I didn't push hard, but I do want to keep moving forward on it. I did ask him if he had any friendly journalists in his back pocket—we would need some publicity."

"You're excited by this whole thing." It was a statement, not a question.

"Yes, I am. Not just because of what happened this week, but because it feels like the right thing to do. Don't get me wrong—I love the work I do, and I love spending time with all our documents and artifacts. Sometimes it seems that there's this whole separate culture that doesn't leave the same kind of trail, but still deserves to be seen. And we can make it visible. It would be a good thing."

"I can't argue with that," James said.

I appreciated his support. I only hoped the board would be as willing. "Good. Tomorrow I want to dig into the mishmash of City agencies and see who does what, just so I understand it. I don't want to waste time and energy talking to the wrong people or reinventing the wheel. And then I should check the boards of those against our membership list, although our people tend not to be political. Oh, I'm sorry—was there something you wanted to do this weekend?" I still wasn't used to having to incorporate another person into my weekend planning.

James didn't look particularly perturbed. "Nothing specific. How about this: You spend tomorrow researching and laying out your battle strategy, and then on Sunday we do something completely unrelated to either of our jobs?"

"I would like that, if we can figure out something that fits. Maybe a movie? As long as it doesn't involve anything historical or guns."

"That could work."

We had a lovely dinner that involved a lot of chopping of fresh vegetables and opening a new bottle of wine, and then retreated upstairs for other traditional pastimes.

———

The next morning I still believed that my neighborhoods idea held water—or maybe I meant held air, if this was my trial balloon. Hey, I was off duty: I could muddle metaphors all I wanted. I clambered out of bed, pulled on some comfortable sweats, and wandered down to the kitchen, where there was coffee waiting, bless James. He was sitting at the kitchen table, his rarely worn reading glasses perched on his nose, reading a section of the paper by the light streaming in from a window. How had I gotten so lucky?

"Morning," he said, then went back to the paper.

"The same to you. Nice day. Did we ever get leaf rakes? Or a yard service?"

"No and no. Do you like to rake?"

"For about five minutes. I will hazard a guess that it will take more than five minutes to clear our yard." Which, if I recalled the papers we'd signed, was about half an acre.

"I think that is a fair estimate. We will have to find a service."

"I'll be online shortly—I can take a quick look. Although I have no idea what the this might cost."

"I don't, either. We'll ask."

I poured a cup of coffee for myself and set about making toast. "Do you happen to have met any of our neighbors? I can't say I've even seen them, although when all the leaves are gone they might be more visible. There aren't any retired Mafia dons or bank robbers on the block, are there?"

"Not to my knowledge," James replied. "I haven't heard any kids around, either, so I'm guessing they're middle-aged and up. I do believe there are Peppers down the street, though."

"As in Old Philadelphia Peppers? Bankers and lawyers?"

"Yes, those."

"Good to know." I buttered my toast. They were probably on the Society's contributors list, although that wasn't always the best way to introduce myself. *Hi, you sent us a nice check recently. Good to meet you.* Maybe, if we crossed paths, I could start with asking them what they knew about the history of our shared neighborhood.

After breakfast I settled myself in front of my laptop at the dining room table with a fresh cup of coffee and prepared to untangle the swamp that made up Philadelphia's attempt to solve the slum/housing problems. It wasn't easy. There were at least five municipal landholding agencies involved, and I wasn't sure if anybody could sort out where their jurisdictions stopped and started. The City's Redevelopment Authority seemed to be the oldest, dating back to 1945, but it appeared to be on the wane. It had been formed to assemble parcels of lands, but that had become more difficult as laws had changed, and what had been a staff of more than three hundred in the 1980s had shrunk to barely more than sixty now. Sad to see, because they had had a good record in creating affordable housing and working with nonprofits to make it happen.

It was easy to get depressed just reading the history of some of these agencies. The City owned a lot of so-called surplus properties—but most of them were vacant lots, and the rest had long since been abandoned when the owners had found it would cost more to repair the places than they were worth to anyone. The Industrial Development Corporation had been founded in the 1950s, to foster public-private developments to provide financing programs for home buyers. There was a Housing Trust Fund that raised money for affordable housing development, home repairs and homelessness prevention (I wasn't sure what that meant). There was a Community Development Corporation Tax Credit Program that provided money directly to the community development corporations—was that what Tyrone's agency was? There was the Neighborhood Transformation Initiative, created by former Mayor John Street more than a decade ago to issue bonds through the PRA, which had a fair track record but had almost exhausted its funding. Wasn't that the program that Tyrone had said his wife had helped to create? And then there was Licenses and Inspections's own Vacant Property Strategy, launched only a few years ago. I'd been in their offices, and they looked swamped.

I sat back and shook my head to clear it. So many agencies, so little coordination among them all. So many programs with potential, even with funding, created with such high hopes, now overwhelmed. One study I came across said that all these blighted properties cost the City more than twenty million dollars per year just to maintain, if you figured in police and fire protection, pest control, and waste cleanup. And all those City personnel had to do their jobs while ducking bullets. All that money just to try to prevent things from getting worse, not make improvements.

So what did little old me, with my little nonprofit museum with a minuscule budget, think I could do about it? Should we all just plan to write history to say, *and then Philadelphia went under, sunk beneath the weight of abandoned properties that bred crime and filth and pestilence*? I was doing a great job of depressing myself, but I hadn't come up with any solutions.

Then Marty called. "You busy?"

"Me personally, or both of us?"

"Whichever."

"Then the answer is, yes and no. I've been looking at half a century of redevelopment efforts in the city of Philadelphia, and I don't like what I see. But I'm just about done with that. Did you want something?"

"So you've been wallowing in the slums. What about the Oliver place?"

"To be honest, I've been thinking about it, but not as much as the neighborhoods project. Has something changed?"

"I didn't give you the whole story before, but Penelope—the younger sister—isn't doing well, health-wise."

"I'm sorry to hear that," I said. Not that I was surprised; she'd seemed more frail than her older sister when we'd had tea with them.

"So you can understand that they'd like to get this whole thing resolved while they still have some options."

"I can see that, but I haven't come up with a solution. How about you?" Marty knew everybody in the five-county area, including New Jersey, and their entire family tree, which often intersected with hers. If she couldn't come up with a buyer or manager or whatever, I couldn't begin to hope to. And this one wasn't even about the money.

"I've got some ideas, but nothing I'm ready to talk about. Want to get together for dinner tonight and kick it around?"

"Can James come play, too?"

"If he has to. I'm still not used to you having to check in with someone."

"Get used to it. Besides, he provides a different perspective, which can't hurt."

"If you say so. I'll come over around six, okay?"

"I guess." I couldn't argue that I had other plans.

Marty hung up, and I wandered off to find James. "Marty has invited herself to dinner," I announced when I located him moving boxes around in one of the unused rooms on the second floor that would be a bedroom if it had a bed and no boxes.

"Okay," he said cautiously. "Is that a bad thing?"

"She wants to talk about the Oliver house and what to do with it. And probably all the other stuff, although she didn't admit that."

"You need me there?"

"I'd like you to be there, but that might be selfish of me. My head is still in the slums, and I have no brilliant ideas about what to do with an elegant mansion in the country."

"They're two sides of the same coin, aren't they?" James said, leaning against a stack of boxes. "On the one hand, you have an area no one wants to live in, with no houses worth living in, where you risk your life walking down the street. On the other hand, you have a house built and furnished with the finest that money could buy in 1760-something or whatever, in a safe, pretty area, only nobody wants it—or not for the right reasons, from your perspective."

"Well, I don't want to condemn it to be razed for a mall," I said. "It might be better to put the mall in the city, from the citizens' point of view. Not the developers', though, I fear."

"You're probably right. Isn't there some quid pro quo?"

"What do you mean?"

"Is there nothing that requires a developer who wants to make big bucks off a high-end property like the Oliver house to invest equally in a disadvantaged area?"

"Different jurisdictions, I'd guess. The city is an entity unto itself—it's both a city and a county, as I'm sure you know—and it may have its own guidelines, written or unwritten. Out in the wilds, it's not as clear-cut."

"Are you worrying about funding? Permitting? Approval from the local municipalities?"

"Sure, all of the above. Even if a city or town can't or won't ante up any money—which, to its credit, Philadelphia has done—they still have the right to approve or reject projects."

"What about coming at it from the developers' side?" James asked.

"They're in business to make money."

"But your buddy Wakeman has principles—you saw that in Chester County," James pointed out. "His project wasn't just about the bottom line."

"But he's a special case," I protested. "And I think we're square, since he funded our current renovation, so I can't exactly call in a favor."

"All right. So Marty just wants to kick this around?"

"I don't think she has a plan, if that's what you're asking. Maybe we should include Eliot?"

"If she'd wanted him here, she would have invited him," James said. "Or invited us to her place. Or something."

"Trouble in paradise, do you think?"

"No, I do not, and don't go looking for trouble."

"Yes, dear," I said demurely. "What are we having for dinner?"

CHAPTER 18

Marty arrived on time. James opened the front door to her. "It's a pleasure to see you, Martha," he said solemnly. I could barely hear them from the kitchen, where I was still chopping things.

Marty snorted. "Yeah, right. I invited myself. You didn't say no, so here I am."

"Well, come in anyway," James told her, smiling. "We're going to eat in the kitchen."

"Suits me." Marty walked past him and headed for the kitchen. "I brought peace offerings," she said to me, handing me a bottle of wine and what was unmistakably a pastry box. She knew me well.

"Thank you. You weren't disrupting any plans, you know. I spent most of the day trying to figure out who runs what in Philadelphia housing and neighborhood development, and then I tried to explain it all to James. How'd I do, James?"

"As well as can be expected, given that you're dealing with Philadelphia," he said. "I'll open the wine."

"Smart man," I told him as I sautéed onions. "So, Marty, did you merely want to see our smiling faces, or did you have something you wanted to talk about?"

"Both, of course. But mainly the Oliver house."

I swallowed a sigh. "I haven't really had time to think about it. As I told you, I've been digging into what I'm calling the neighborhoods project. And I guess that means that I think it's the more important problem."

"That's what I figured. Don't worry, I get it. I know you talked with Eliot about it, and he's a great resource. By the way, he approves of what you're trying to do. I'm probably in a better position to work on the Oliver situation. I've been going over our donor lists, and I've come up with a few ideas. I hope. I told you on the phone, Penelope Oliver is not well, and she'd really like to see a solution in place before she passes."

"I can't blame her, and I hate to disappoint a dying woman. What've you got?"

"Edward Perkins."

"Edward . . . oh, you mean Alice's uncle. Why him, out of all our members?"

Marty started ticking off points on her fingers. "Because he's been a good supporter of the Society for years. Because he's got lots of money, although that's not enough by itself—and no, he doesn't want to buy the Oliver place himself. Because he knows a lot of people, and he can be persuasive—you hired Alice, didn't you? Because he loves history of all kinds—he's not prejudiced about the big, bad city. Heck, he still has a gorgeous town house off Rittenhouse Square, although he doesn't spend as much time there as he used to. You want more?"

"Uh, no, I get the picture. But what are you suggesting?"

"I don't know yet. But he's the best person I can think of to start with. And he knows how to get things done, quietly."

Edward Perkins was, in fact, the ideal member/donor/supporter. He didn't throw his weight around, but he was often a steadying presence at meetings. While he was not on the board—not for lack of invitations!—he knew those who were and how to sway them. Hiring his niece Alice, which he had suggested, had not been a hardship. She was a bright, capable young woman. I had no expectations that she would remain at the Society for long, but she was more than pulling her weight while she was with us. If he counted our hiring her as an intern as a favor, all the better—but we probably would have hired her anyway.

I was turning over possibilities in my mind when Marty interrupted. "You going to talk to your pal Wakeman?"

"I don't know. James kind of hinted at the same thing. I hadn't planned to because he's already done us a huge favor. But I'm not going to approach him before I come up with a concrete plan—one that will make financial sense to him. He's a practical man, and he's going to want specifics."

"Fair enough. You talk with Tyrone?"

"I did." I added tomatoes to the sizzling pan on the

stove and turned down the heat, then started opening jars and sniffing spices to see what appealed to me.

"What's your take on him?"

"As a person? As a community planner?" I wondered if I should share Latoya's comments with Marty, and decided to stick to generalities.

"Whatever you think is important. You're the one proposing to work with him."

"I think he's smart, and he's committed to what he's doing. He's not in it for the money—but his wife makes plenty of that—or for the personal glory. He came from North Philly, and he wants to give back. I think we can work together."

"Wow, that's quite a summary after spending, what, an hour or two with him," Marty said.

For some reason that annoyed me. "You don't think I'm a good judge of character? Or do you know something about him that I don't?"

Marty sensed my annoyance and raised both hands. "Hey, I didn't mean anything. I guess I'm used to you being more cautious."

"Well, maybe I had some of that knocked out of me this week. Life is short—why wait? Either he's a good guy or he isn't. As far as involving the Society, I'm doing my homework first, before committing our resources. Is that all right with you?" I had to wonder why I sounded so testy.

"Peace. Jimmy, help me out here."

Jimmy had managed to stay out of the discussion so far, but he couldn't ignore Marty's direct appeal. "Who, me?" he said in mock innocence. "I trust Nell's judgment.

Although I will state for the record that I'm not happy with her putting herself at risk."

I put the lid on the skillet before turning to face them both. "Where the heck is the risk? And are you saying that I should wrap myself up in cotton wool and stay in my office forever? Calling my minions to do my bidding when I want to see a particular document? I'm not that fragile, you know, so I get to decide what I want to do. I can't imagine anyone would want to hurt me." Still, the image of bullets smashing through car windows and blood spattering was hard to erase. But that wasn't about me—was it? I took a deep breath. "I apologize. I guess I'm still on edge. But I do think this is important, and I think Tyrone and I are on the same page. Can we talk about something else now? Read any good books lately, Marty?"

Marty and James exchanged a glance, but the talk turned to safer topics. We frittered away the rest of the evening enjoying each other's company, carefully avoiding any sensitive issues. Marty left about ten, and James went through the front of the house, locking up, turning off lights. When he came back, he poured what was left of Marty's bottle of wine into our glasses. "Martha is not going to let go of this Oliver house thing, you know."

"Yes, I know. She is tenacious, and I think she feels an obligation to the family. But if she wants to take the lead in sorting that out and let me handle the other thing, that works out just fine. Damn, the board meeting is next week, and I doubt that we'll have either plan ready to present to them."

"I think *plan* might be an exaggeration at this point," James noted.

"I know, I know. There is pressure of a sort for the Oliver house that we can't control—Penelope's health. I liked both the sisters, and I'd love to be able to come up with a solution for them, but I don't know if I can, and certainly not quickly. As for the other, it's not a new problem, so nobody is expecting a quick fix. Where the Society could fit still isn't completely clear to me. Tyrone did say he'd be back at work next week. He claims he's up to it."

"They raise tough kids in the Badlands."

"So it seems."

James drained his glass. "I'll do the dishes in the morning. You ready to go upstairs?"

"I do believe I am."

CHAPTER 19

Sunday I had really hoped that we could do normal, ordinary couple-ish things, pretend we weren't a gun-toting FBI agent and a museum president who had recently been the possible target of a murder attempt. It didn't take me long to realize that I was too wired (even before coffee) to spend a day lolling around the house and relaxing. Recuperating. Whatever. I could set my body down in a chair, but I couldn't stop my brain from spinning. Maybe it was a normal response to the past week's near disaster, but that didn't make it any easier to deal with.

"Nell, you have now gotten up and sat down again six times since we came into this room," James said in a neutral voice. "Is something wrong?"

"Of course something's wrong. I can't stop replaying what happened in my head, and all the what-ifs that came after that," I said, sounding petty even to myself. I held up a hand before he could protest. "No, it's nothing you have done. You have been my rock, my tower of strength, my knight in shining armor—pick whatever term you like. The problem is me—I'm just not handling this well. I need some distraction."

"Like what?" James asked.

"I have no idea! What is the FBI's prescribed antidote to near-death experiences?"

"Apart from filling out all the paperwork?" he replied with a smile. "Counseling? It's always recommended, but few people take advantage of it. You want to do something physical?"

"It's cold outside," I muttered, completely unreasonably.

"Go to a gym?"

"I hate gyms. They're boring. And before you suggest it, I can't think of a current movie that would distract me."

"A shooting range?"

I cocked my head at him. He had never suggested that before, and it was kind of a touchy question, based on my personal history with weapons, which he knew well. "Interesting idea, but not quite right."

"I'm running out of ideas. An art museum? Historical site? Drive across New Jersey and look at the ocean? Drive to Baltimore and look at some other city's slums?"

"You really are scraping the barrel," I commented. "And before you mention it, we don't need any more furniture at the moment, so that's out. We could look at curtains for this place, now that the leaves are gone, but I think that would drive me nuts with or without these other problems. We might end up having to live with expensive valances with green frogs, just because I wasn't thinking straight. I can't sit still to read a book, or even a magazine."

"We did once raise the question of bowling," James said.

I stared at him, then burst out laughing. "You're right, we did. Actually that's not a bad idea. It involves throwing heavy things to knock down other things, which is probably a metaphor for something. It's loud. And nobody pays attention to you. Do you know of any bowling alleys?"

"You could Google them. How far do you want to go?"

"Let's not cross any state lines."

James went to the computer on the dining room table and booted it up. After a few minutes I came over and looked over his shoulder. "Who knew there was a ranking for Philadelphia-area bowling alleys?" I said. "At least it looks like the sport is thriving."

"It does."

After a few minutes of comparing pros and cons, we settled on one that looked midsized and not too far. "Are you sure this is what you want to do?" James asked.

"Yes," I said with conviction. Anything to get out of the house—and out of my head.

I discovered after we'd bowled a couple of games that we had somehow arrived at the right choice. It was a pleasant, mindless diversion that involved a modest level of physical exertion, and it was loud and bright and distracting on multiple levels. James beat me in the first game, but I rallied and beat him in the second. "One more?" I asked.

"Can you handle losing again?"

"Bring it on!" I told him.

By the end of the afternoon, I'd beaten James again (although I suspected that he'd let me win), and I was pleasantly tired. As we drove home, I said, "Thank you."

"For what?"

"For understanding. For being patient with me. For figuring out exactly what I needed. You know, you're pretty good at this relationship thing." After the words came out of my mouth, I realized that we might be treading on dangerous ground: we had never really talked about prior relationships, beyond the bare outlines. Nor had I wanted to dig into our pasts. I'd been married, it hadn't worked out, we'd parted friends, end of story. James had never been married (which always mystified me), but it was clear that he must have had one or more serious relationships in his past, which showed in how he was treating me. It couldn't be spontaneous. If it was, how on earth had he remained single so long? But I wasn't going to ask. I wouldn't even ask Marty. Whatever our individual histories, it was up to us to decide what and how much to share. What we had right now was working—why rock the boat? Now, if we could only manage to avoid crimes, solo or shared . . .

"You're quiet," James said as he pulled into our driveway. For once there was no one waiting for us to sandbag us with demands.

"Just thinking how wonderful you are," I replied.

"Thank you. I try. How does pizza sound?"

"Heavenly. Will you do the ordering?"

"I'm not sure my fingers are all functioning after that

workout, but I'll do my best. You bowl a mean game, lady."

"Fruit of my misspent youth—I was on my high school bowling team. Mostly for the cupcakes from the bakery next door to the alley. I'll open the wine while you call."

———————

Monday I felt almost normal, and enthusiastic about my new neighborhoods project. I knew full well that a lot of good ideas never panned out, but I was eager to give this one a try. I accepted James's offer of a ride to the city only because I wanted to be at my office bright and early so I could set down my thoughts and see if anyone else had come up with any. Oddly enough, there was someone waiting in the shadow of the stone pillars—a woman I didn't recognize. While she didn't look threatening, I stopped for a moment to look her over. She was tall, slender, well dressed, and black.

I was not going to let myself be intimidated by strangers on my own ground. "Can I help you?" I called out, as I started up the steps.

"You can if you're Nell Pratt," she said, without smiling.

"I am. And you are?"

"Vee Blakeney. I'm Tyrone's wife. Vee is short for Veronica. I wanted to speak with you about what you talked about with him on Friday."

Was this good or bad? Should I trust her? What the heck—she didn't look exactly menacing, and I was pretty sure that she wouldn't spoil the sleek lines of her expensive handbag with anything as clunky as a gun. "Sure. Let me unlock the door and we can talk."

I did, relieved to see Bob behind the desk. Vee followed me in.

"Mornin', Nell," Bob said. "This lady with you?"

"She wants to talk with me, yes. We'll be in the old boardroom. Unless you're desperate for a coffee fix?" I asked the woman.

"Thanks for offering, but I haven't much time. I'm on my way to work, but I hoped I'd catch you here first. I'm sorry I didn't call, but I decided only this morning, and I didn't want to disturb you at home."

"It's not a problem. Follow me," I said, walking past the grand staircase to the room behind it. Inside I gestured her toward a chair, then sat catty-corner to her. "What can I do for you?"

I was hoping she wasn't about to read me the riot act about bothering her poor wounded husband, but instead she surprised me. "Tyrone described the project you suggested, and I think it's a smart idea. I believe he mentioned I was part of the team that put together the bond issue for the Neighborhood Transformation Initiative that John Street pushed for when he was mayor?"

"He did, and I've read about it as well. I was thinking of contacting you, although I don't know if you have any current involvement. I thought it would be a good benchmark to get your take on the situation then, what it took to persuade the City that issuing municipal bonds to provide the money was a good idea, and what results you've seen."

"I was thinking along the same lines." She reached into

her sleek messenger bag—the days of briefcases were long past, but I'd guessed her leather bag would sport a discreet designer label—and pulled out a thick portfolio. "I had some copies made of the parts that I thought would interest you—you know, the summaries, the appeals, the testimony before city council, that sort of thing." She handed it to me.

It was a hefty package. "Thank you! This is amazing, and I'll look forward to reading it. Can I ask you for some personal feedback? You don't have to answer if you don't want to—I have no idea what your involvement was."

"It was a while ago, and I was a very junior associate. As I recall it, I spent most of my time making stacks of photocopies and carrying them to meetings. I assume you want the parts that didn't get written down?"

"If you can share them. You know, the off-the-record deals that people cut, the horse-trading, the behind-the-scenes stuff. How much time can you spare?"

She studied me, and I wondered if she was trying to judge my sincerity. "I can give you the outlines. You know John Street?"

"I know *of* him. I've only been in Philadelphia a decade, so I don't know his early history with the city. I have done some reading about the Neighborhood Transformation Initiative, though. It sounds as though it really mattered to him. Did he have a personal stake in it?"

"He wasn't raised in Philadelphia, but he spent quite a few years on city council. He was no angel, but I think he saw the program as a way to put his stamp on things. Of course, there was some controversy about his plan to tear down deteriorated properties without regard to their historic significance—I'm sure you can appreciate that—but the bond issue went through. He might have had a few issues outside of his role as mayor, but he was elected for a second term. And he was never charged with a crime."

I almost smiled at what Vee was *not* saying about the man and his tenure. But after a decade, I was used to Philadelphia politics and how things worked. "Has the program been a success, in your opinion?"

"I think so, by most standards. At least the money didn't go straight into the pockets of fat-cat developers. Property values in the city went up, and some new housing was created."

"Could it happen again?" I asked.

"Not likely, or not at the moment. You've seen the state of some parts of the city—there's still a lot to be done, but those areas are so dangerous now that no one wants to touch them. It's a shame."

"Someone told me that you grew up in North Philadelphia."

I could swear her eyes grew colder. "I did. I got out." She didn't elaborate.

Apparently that subject was off-limits. Was Tyrone also off-limits? "But your husband is still involved in the neighborhood."

"He is." She glanced at her watch. "I should be going. I'll leave the documents with you—maybe you can pull some language from them that would be useful."

"Thank you for bringing them by. I can't tell you where the Society may take this, but I want to explore all the angles before I give up. Do you think a collaboration between the City or another agency and the Society could work?"

"It couldn't hurt, and if it doesn't, all you've invested in this place is time. And I get where you're coming from: if you want your Society to survive, you'll need to look relevant in the present, not just the past."

"I agree," I said, then stood up. "Thank you for your time. I'll see you out. And give my regards to Tyrone—it was very kind of him to talk to me, under the circumstances. Did he really go back to work today?"

"He did. He's a hard man to keep down." We'd reached the front door. "It was nice meeting you, Nell. Let me know if you need any other information."

I carried the thick portfolio up to my office, wondering what had been included. Whenever the City did anything involving money, a lot of paperwork was generated, both official and unofficial. Had this bond issue gone through because enough people believed it was a good idea and the right thing to do? Had the force of the mayor's personality been enough to push it through, in his first term? Had there been developers lurking in the wings with their hands out? And did any of that mean that saving the city's neighborhoods was a hopeless idea now, more than a decade later?

At least I knew one person who could answer one of the questions: I put in a call to Mitchell Wakeman, Philadelphia regional developer extraordinaire.

CHAPTER 20

I was surprised that Wakeman called me back within an hour: this was one busy man, and we didn't exactly know each other well. But I had done him a huge favor earlier in the year, by clearing the way for a project that was dear to his heart, one that went beyond money. He knew about causes. Still, I felt mildly embarrassed because he had already done so much for the Society.

"Nell—glad you're not dead," he said. Abrupt as always.

"Why, thank you, Mitchell. How kind of you to notice."

He made a huffing noise that might have been a laugh. "What do you want now?"

"I want to save the neighborhoods of Philadelphia. No, that's sort of a joke, so let me ask for something simpler. As a hypothetical, what would it take to get regional developers—or, heck, any developers—on board with a neighborhood initiative in the city?"

"You're not asking me to get involved, are you?"

"No, I wouldn't do that—you've done enough. And I've already figured out that such a project could be toxic to anybody. This is purely hypothetical. What would it take to get them to step up and find a way to help, uh, distressed neighborhoods?"

He thought for a few moments. I waited. Finally he said, "Money, of course. You've got to show that they'd at least break even. Or if they lose money, that they'll get some other city project that'll make up for it. Yeah, that's kind of hard to arrange, at least publicly. But doing it because it's the noble thing to do isn't going to cut it."

"Understood. Anything else?"

"Get the press behind the project. Make the developers look good."

"Already working on that. What else?"

"They won't bite off more than they can chew. If they make big promises and can't deliver, they'll look like fools. Never a good idea. Keep the project—or the first one, if you're thinking long-term—a manageable size that can be completed in a reasonable amount of time."

"Does that mean looking for a small, hungry developer or group, or a big one that wants to add a dash of prestige or public service to its portfolio?"

"Could go either way. If somebody wants to put together a group, to spread the risk, make sure they play well together. We don't want them squabbling in public or holding things up."

Like I could do that: he was the only developer I knew on a personal basis. "Can you give me names of companies that would be interested, potentially? I know I can go through the phone book, but you know these people and what they're really like."

A longer pause this time. "Let me think about that. What're you doing in the middle of this, anyway?"

"The Society still owns a property in North Philadelphia. That's why I was there last Monday."

"Huh. Most people would walk away and not look back."

"I can't, Mitchell. Not now; not after what happened."

Mitchell Wakeman was silent for a few moments. Finally he said, "I'll get back to you. Good talking with you—stay out of the line of fire, will you?" He hung up.

I wasn't offended by his abruptness. Mitchell Wakeman might lack a few social graces, and he didn't tolerate fools, but he was smart, connected, and one of the all-around good guys. And if he said he'd get back to me, he would.

After I'd replaced the phone, I looked up to see Alice Price standing in my doorway, looking uncharacteristically hesitant. "Eric said you were free?" she ventured.

"I am. Come in, sit down. What's up? You're leaving? You've gotten a job running a major museum in some exotic foreign country?" Alice was one of the brightest interns we had ever had, at least as long as I'd been with the Society. She had graduated from college but was taking some time off to consider her options, and we were lucky that she had decided to do it under our roof. But I knew that once she made up her mind she'd be gone.

Alice laughed as she sat down. "That's how you see me? I'm flattered. But no to both of those, at least for the moment. I'll let you know if things change. Right now I want to talk about Uncle Edward."

I was surprised, yet not, since it was Uncle Edward who had suggested her for the job. "I could play dumb and ask you why, but I'm pretty sure you'd see through that. Has Marty talked to you about the Oliver house?"

"I've talked to her. I think we're on the same page, no matter who started it. But can we take a step back and talk about that other thing you proposed? Let me see if I've got this right: you want the Society to engage in an ongoing research project to assemble evidence of the lost neighborhoods of Philadelphia as they once were."

"In a nutshell, yes." I stopped and waited, because I was sure she had more.

"I'm sure you've reviewed all the efforts in the past to save or revitalize those neighborhoods."

"Let's say I'm a quick study, after last week. I've done some research, yes."

Alice nodded her head. "I can see that what happened might give you a more personal stake in the matter. I'm glad you're all right."

"Thank you. So am I. So why have you come to me now?"

"You asked for input from the staff, and that's why I'm here. I don't mean to offend you, but it seems to me that addressing this problem requires more than research, more than money, more than goodwill on the part of a lot of well-meaning people."

"Yes, I agree. Are you leading up to something?"

"Marty and I talked briefly about all of this. She was being very cautious, I guess you could say, but we both think that Uncle Edward could play a part in this."

I sighed. "There are so many ways to respond to that statement, Alice. Let's start at the beginning. We hired you because Edward Perkins hinted there might be some financial benefit if we did. I hope you know that if you had been a galloping idiot we would not have hired you, under any circumstances. But you're not, and you have been a real asset to the Society, and if you were to leave tomorrow I'd write a glowing letter of recommendation to anyone who asks. And, as I'm sure you know, your uncle kept his part in the unstated bargain and made a nice contribution to the Society. Our mutual slates are clean, so to speak. He has always been a good member here, and I wouldn't presume to ask anything out of the ordinary from him."

"I understand. But what if there was an arrangement that would benefit everyone involved?"

"How do you define *everyone*?"

"Uncle Edward, the Society, the City, the development community, and probably a few others I haven't thought of yet."

"Why are you bringing this to me? Or rather, why you rather than your uncle?"

"As you may have noticed, Uncle Edward is rather fond of me."

I knew that Edward Perkins had no children of his own,

and that he had taken a special interest in Alice's future. But I had no idea what kind of influence Alice could wield over him, nor did I want to ask her to use it. "Alice, I don't want you to sweet-talk your uncle into something based on his affection for you."

"Nell, my uncle is a shrewd man, and he's not a pushover. He wouldn't do anything just because I asked, not without thoroughly investigating the idea. And he has been known to say no, even to me. But if there was a good idea that he was not aware of, and if I presented it to him in the right light, I'm sure he would consider it. The answer might still be no, but he will have given it some thought first."

"And you want to approach him about this neighborhoods project?" I asked.

"I think I can. But only if you approve. I know he's supported the Society in the past, in a variety of ways, but this particular subject might not appeal to him."

"You're a lot younger than he is. Do you think this makes sense?"

She nodded. "I do. The Society is a great institution, but it hasn't exactly moved with the times. It would help you if you looked more, well, relevant in the twenty-first century."

I sighed. She was right, and what she was saying was what I had already said to myself, one way or another. "You haven't talked to your uncle about this yet?"

"No, not yet. I wanted to talk to you first. I didn't want to overstep."

"When were you planning to approach him?"

"Soon, I think. Uncle Edward is not getting any younger."

I thought for a moment. It seemed vaguely distasteful to encourage Alice to approach her uncle Edward. Such an approach should come from me, or from the board. But Alice had come to me and volunteered, and I knew he would listen to her. "Alice, you scare me. You sure you aren't a forty-year-old in a twenty-five-year-old body?"

"My mother keeps saying that. No, I'm just smart. And observant. I know that scares some people. But I'm here at the Society now, and I'm happy to volunteer whatever capabilities I have to help."

"Thank you for offering, Alice." I fought an urge to hug her—I guess I was still overemotional. "I wish I could say I had a plan, but I've only been thinking about this for a week, you know. And I don't want to offend your uncle. He's been more than generous with us."

"I can make it clear that approaching him was my own idea, which is true. And I can tell him to talk with you. I'll go away now and let you think—I won't say anything unless you approve. Thank you for listening." Alice stood up.

"Alice, I'm the one who should be thanking you. You are an amazing young woman."

Alice just smiled, and left quickly. And, per her instructions, I sat and thought. Tyrone and his wife were on board (I needed to read what she'd given me). I had talked to Wakeman about the construction aspect of the problem, and he might possibly come up with some cooperative developers (it was too much to hope that he'd put his own company in the mix). Alice thought her uncle might consider financial support; did that mean that Marty and I should set up a meeting with him quickly? I ought to talk to Marty about what we should or could ask for—she knew him better than I did.

Could we have something like a proposal cobbled together in time for the board meeting this week? Unlikely. Maybe I should touch base with Eliot again, although obviously Marty had already spoken with him. I wanted to draw a flowchart, showing who knew what and whom and how they could help. Should I go after someone at the City? Who had been Cherisse's boss, and did I know him or her? Did Marty or Eliot? Or should I throw caution to the wind and tackle the mayor? I didn't know him personally, but maybe some board members did.

Could I go home yet? I felt like I'd done a full day's work, and it wasn't even lunchtime. As if my list weren't already long enough, the phone rang, and Eric announced, "It's your detective."

"Thanks, Eric." I took a breath. I had no idea what she wanted. If she was going to tell me she was definitely off the case, I wouldn't be surprised. I picked up the phone.

"Detective, how are you today?"

"We've got the shooter."

That I hadn't expected. "What? Who? How?" I sputtered.

"Local street thug, too dumb to dump the weapon. Used it in another shooting, but he didn't get away this time."

"Is he, uh, dead?"

"You kidding? You read the papers, watch the news? We of the city police are very careful to avoid killing any suspects, although we may injure them a bit. Our suspect is now chained to a hospital bed and has demanded a lawyer."

"Is he known to the police?"

"Only in a general way. We have not yet determined why he would have shot at the three of you on the street last week."

That sounded like it came from a departmental press release, not Meredith Hrivnak. "Maybe it was a case of mistaken identity? Does Tyrone resemble any known drug dealers? Or does he have a brother in a gang?"

"Nope, Tyrone's clean. We'll see what the guy we arrested tells his lawyer. Thought you'd like to know."

"Thank you. So I don't need to come by and identify him?"

"Nope, we don't need you."

Should I be insulted? No, I decided. "Oh, have you told Tyrone yet?"

"Yeah, I called him first. He claims he doesn't know the guy."

"Do you believe him?"

"Don't have any reason not to. We'll do a background check on the kid, but a heck of a lot of people pass through that neighborhood, and most of the time they don't leave a trail. He could be local, or not."

"Well, thanks again. It makes me feel better to know he's off the street."

"You're welcome." The detective hung up. I seemed to be talking to a lot of people who rationed their words. At least it was efficient.

I thought for a moment about calling James and decided against it. He couldn't obtain any more information about the arrest, and I wouldn't ask him to anyway. I'd tell him when I saw him later.

Maybe it was time to talk to Shelby again, and find out what we had in our files about Edward Perkins. I knew in a general way where he ranked among our supporters, but I didn't have the details at my fingertips, and I hadn't needed them when we hired Alice. I had been honest with her: she was a smart young woman and would no doubt have her pick of jobs when she left us, as I was sure she would. I might as well make use of her kind offer while I could.

I headed out of my office and down the hall, where I found Shelby scrabbling among piles of paper on her desk. She looked up when I walked in and said, "Oh, thank goodness! Please say you're giving me an excuse to stop doing this?" She waved at all the papers.

"What are you doing?"

"Trying to write a summary of the project funded by the last federal grant we received. I doubt you remember it—we got it about five years ago, and now we have to do a final accounting or they'll never, ever give us money again. Hence the paperwork."

I dropped into a chair across from her. "That's the

government for you. My request is simpler, and no doubt will give you a great sense of accomplishment so you can go back to this other thing."

"I am at your disposal," Shelby said.

"Edward Perkins," I said.

"Ah," Shelby said sagely. "What do you need?"

"Aren't you going to ask why I'm looking at him?"

"I think I can guess. His name is on a lot of the lists that I see. Besides, I've already talked to Marty about him."

That startled me. "What? Why?"

"You don't know? She didn't say. She just wanted a quick snapshot of his financials, and his contributions history."

Now I was confused. Alice had told me that she had come to me first. Was Marty already thinking along the same lines? "Have you done it yet?"

"Ha! No, I've been doing my job here, but I'll get right on it."

I leaned forward and lowered my voice. "Detective Meredith says they've caught the shooter."

"Well, hey, that's good news. Isn't it?"

"I suppose. I hope she'll find out whether this was random or whether there was a reason for the shooting."

"Well, lady, I don't see you as a threat to drug traffickers in North Philadelphia, so I can't imagine it's personal."

"I agree. It's just one of those things that feels unfinished. I'm not ready to file it away and forget it. How long will it take to get a quick profile on Mr. Perkins?"

"You want financial status, domiciles, friends, other affiliations, the whole nine yards?"

"If you please, ma'am."

"I should have it by the end of the day."

"Thanks, Shelby."

CHAPTER 21

I wasn't surprised when Marty walked into my office shortly after lunch. Sometimes things seemed to pick up speed of their own accord, and Marty was just keeping up the cosmic pace.

"We're meeting Edward Perkins tomorrow morning," she said bluntly.

"About what?" I asked. "By the way, thanks for clearing it with me first."

"Eric said you were free," she retorted. "That's the time Edward had available."

"Hang on—is this because of what you and Alice talked about?"

Marty looked a little guilty. "Oh, well, I guess I might have said something to Alice. She talked to you?"

I was beginning to feel like I had wandered into

somebody else's comedy routine. "Let's start over. Why are we talking to Edward Perkins tomorrow?"

"About the Oliver house, of course," she said. "What else?"

"You've talked to him about this?" I asked, trying to sort through the scenarios.

"No, but I asked if we could have an hour of his time. You have a problem with that?"

"I guess not." After all, I had a whole day to figure out what we were supposed to talk about—which project, and how much money. "As it happens, I've asked Shelby for his dossier, and she told me you did, too. She said she'd have it by the end of the day. Are you going to fill me in on what I need to know? Is he now or was he ever employed, or is he retired, or does he live off family wealth?"

"Nell, actually you don't need a whole lot of information, and he's pretty much an open book. One of the last of the Titans, you might say."

"Marty, I don't want to walk in cold." Especially if I didn't know what I was pitching. "I prefer to be prepared. I've met the man, but I can't say I know him."

"What do you think you know?"

I mentally reviewed what I had gleaned so far. "Never married. Solid philanthropist, and gives to all the predictable causes and institutions. Has a soft spot for his niece Alice, maybe because he's never had kids of his own. He's got money. Where'd it come from?"

"You've hit the high points. The money came from

both sides of his family—steel on one side, banking on the other. All on the up and up—no skeletons in his closets, or bodies buried anywhere. He really is old-school, and I wish we had a lot more like him."

"How did you come to know him?"

"Family connections that go way back." Marty didn't elaborate. I didn't really need to know; I knew enough about Marty's family to know that the links were complex and extensive.

"You on a first-name basis?" I asked, mostly out of curiosity.

"When I was a kid, he was Uncle Eddie, but that doesn't mean he's a pushover. He's a smart man when it comes to managing his money, which is why he still has most of it. He's getting up there in years, obviously, and he's looking to solidify his legacy."

"He's not leaving a chunk to the Society, is he?" I had to ask, although I didn't expect it.

"Nope. But he's got some other ideas, although I don't have all the details."

"For the Oliver house?"

"Yes. By the way, there's one thing that you might want to know: he was once engaged to Penelope Oliver."

"What? You didn't think this was worth mentioning before this? That puts things in a whole new light."

"I suppose. It certainly means he might be willing to work something out for the sisters."

With a personal connection like that, it seemed foolish to approach him about the neighborhoods project. I hoped Alice wouldn't be disappointed.

I sighed, although either Marty didn't notice or chose to ignore me. "Where are we meeting?"

"His house, just off Rittenhouse Square."

That should be nice to see, at least—it was a beautiful neighborhood. "Should you and I meet here? Or at your place?"

"I'm closer. Have Jimmy drop you off at my house and we can walk over. Meeting's at ten."

"Got it. You don't mind if I read Shelby's file, though, do you?"

"Knock yourself out. Anything else going on?"

"Detective Hrivnak says the police have the man who shot at us, and he's in custody. They picked him up for another crime, but he used the same weapon."

"Huh. He said anything yet?"

"Nope. He asked for a lawyer right away—maybe he's been through this before. But I'd guess that Hrivnak wasn't finished with him yet."

"I'm still surprised she cares about this case. Maybe she actually likes you."

"Could be. I'm not going to argue, and I'd certainly like to know what really happened, and why."

"Yeah, but you may never find out. Let's focus on moving forward. You ready for the board meeting?"

"I keep trying to blot it out of my mind, but at least the members have had all the info they could want—and you should know that, since Eric mailed it to you last week. Wait—is that why you're moving so fast on the Oliver property thing? So you can take it to the board?"

"Maybe. The board won't meet again until after New

Year's, and who knows how poor Penelope will be faring by then?"

"Does it really matter if the Society doesn't take part in facilitating this thing, whatever it turns out to be?"

Marty faced me squarely. "Nell, there's a possibility that we can do a good thing here. It matches the Society's mission. Yes, it may require commitments of time and effort, and yes, even money. We have a great opportunity here, and I don't want to miss the chance because we're being too cautious. Things move fast these days. Nothing ventured, nothing gained."

That, coming from Marty, was passionate. "Don't forget that we're voting on Eliot for the board this meeting. Everything good there?" I wasn't sure whether I was asking professionally or personally, but I'd let her choose.

"We're good. And we'll be talking with him after we meet with Edward."

"About?"

"You'll see."

It was clear that Marty was planning something. It was also clear that she wasn't going to share it with me, at least not until tomorrow. There was nothing to be gained by prying now. "I will look forward to it."

Shelby delivered the information on Edward Perkins about four o'clock, and sat waiting while I skimmed it. I made comments as I read. "Wow, he's older than I thought, considering that Alice is his niece. Or should I say grand-niece? Three houses—town, country, and shore. Memberships in the right clubs—I guess we can't ask how often he shows up there. Collects . . . Georgian silver?" I looked up at Shelby.

"Yup. My guess is that he inherited a lot of it, but he adds bits and pieces when they come to market."

"One other little piece of information you should add to the file: he was once engaged to Penelope Oliver."

Shelby's eyes lighted up. "One of the sisters who own the Oliver house? Well, that means something, although I couldn't quite say what. I wonder if they parted amicably."

"Marty did not choose to share that with me, if she knows. But neither party has ever married, for what that's worth."

I went back to reading until I finished what she had given me, then sat back in my chair. "I wish we could clone him. He's the perfect member."

"I know what you mean. He seems like an all-around good guy—with money. And he likes us."

"Exactly. Marty and I are meeting with him tomorrow morning."

"Ooh, do tell! About this Oliver property?"

"Yes. Marty's hatching something, but she won't say what. Still, I have to trust her—she pulls some amazing things out of her hat."

"We're lucky to have her here. You think any of the next generation will care as much?"

"About history? Or supporting nonprofits? I won't hold my breath. What's your daughter think?" Shelby's daughter had gotten married just around the time I'd hired Shelby.

"She's too much caught up in her own life right now. I hope I laid the groundwork for historic appreciation, but we probably won't know for quite a while."

"Seems odd to mourn the passing of the past, if you know what I mean," I said.

"I hear you. Anything else you need from me? Because that government report is due this week, and they ask for the weirdest information!"

"Go! And thank you for this stuff—I'll try to put it to good use."

"Bring home the bacon, lady," Shelby said as she went out the door.

And then it was time to meet James downstairs. Where had the day gone?

I was waiting on the steps when he pulled up, and I got in quickly to avoid holding up traffic. "Hello."

"Hello." He focused on getting us out of the worst of city traffic before speaking again. "How was your day?"

"Busy, although I barely left my desk. Hrivnak called—she said they made an arrest for another crime, but it turned out the gun the guy used was the one that shot Cherisse, so they've got the shooter. What're the odds of that?"

"It is a bit surprising. I suppose he never thought about tossing the gun, or maybe trading it for another."

"Based on my extensive experience," I said wryly, "most criminals are not very smart. Anyway, the detective said he was known to them, so it's not his first crime. I suppose a lot of people in those neighborhoods, particularly drug dealers, feel kind of invincible. I know if I were a cop, I wouldn't want to venture in there, not without plenty of backup. Oh, before I forget, Marty and I have an appointment in the morning, so could you drop me at her place?"

"No problem. Something I need to know about?"

"Nope, just Society business. She's plotting something, but she won't say what. Oh, and remember I have the board meeting on Thursday after work, so I suppose I should drive in that day."

"Fine." James glanced at me briefly. "You'll park in the lot across the street?"

"You mean the one with bright lights and a twenty-four-hour guard and surveillance cameras? Yes, I will. Safe enough for you?"

"It will have to do."

"Is there any way to find out what the police learn from the guy they arrested?"

"Are you asking me to find out?"

I backed off quickly. "No, you know I wouldn't do that. Heck, I'd probably have better luck with Hrivnak than you would right now."

"Exactly," James said. "You can leave me out of it."

We arrived home quickly, and after changing into comfortable clothes, set about making dinner, or at least an approximation of a meal. Good thing we weren't hung up on the conventions of polite society. I could probably quote chapter and verse from Emily Post, the doyenne of cultural arbiters of the early twentieth century (I needed how many forks? Placed in what order?), but I didn't want to live it.

Halfway through the meal, I started musing, mostly to myself. "You know, now they have a man in custody, and his possession of the weapon kind of points to him as the shooter."

"I'd say the odds are about eighty-five percent," James agreed.

"So if there's a decision tree or something here, then this is a fork: either this truly was random, or he knew one or another of us in that car, or knew *of* us and where to find us, thanks to someone else fingering us."

"Are you going somewhere with this, Nell?" James asked.

"Well, if we set aside the random branch, then we arrive quickly at another fork: either the guy had something personal against one or us, or someone who did paid him to shoot at us."

"Okay," James said cautiously. "How far do you plan to take this?"

"I'm just thinking out loud. I could talk to myself, but that looks a little odd."

"Fine. Proceed, but keep it short, please."

"Right. Fork A of branch B: the guy didn't know me, but he might have known either Tyrone or Cherisse. Fork B of branch B: someone wants one of us dead, and in this case it could be me."

"Theoretically," James said. "But could you possibly have done something to make someone that angry?"

"I doubt it, although every time the Society raises its dues, which are ridiculously low, quite a few people get angry. Angry enough to kill? I don't think so, but researchers can be a bit maniacal. Okay, let's set that aside. Which leaves us with Tyrone and Cherisse. The police have checked them out, and while I don't have the details, I gather they passed muster—no dark past or seamy associates. He grew up in North Philly; she was a suburban girl. He's a community activist; she was a City employee. They met through a shared interest in neighborhood revitalization. While there could be an individual who got hot under the collar about what one or the other of them wanted to do with their abandoned or derelict property, it seems more likely to me that a person with a beef would get in their face on the spot, not hire a hit man. And the economic side of that equation doesn't work; sure, that person would lose the property, but the property isn't worth anything anyway and probably has a lot of back taxes and such attached. If it's their favorite drug house, there are plenty more empty ones to choose from."

"Nell, do you have a point?" James asked.

"I think so," I said, and was surprised; I had thought I was just spitballing. "Nobody had a professional reason to shoot at either one of them, unless maybe there's someone in Tyrone's organization who wants to play a bigger role. But killing someone seems kind of extreme, just to move up the ladder of a struggling nonprofit. Which leaves only one alternative: it was personal."

James pushed his plate away and leaned back in his chair. "Say that it is. Don't you think Hrivnak has looked into that?"

"Maybe, but not very hard—her higher-ups won't let her. The case is closed, more or less."

"And what are you going to do about it?"

"Nothing. It's not my job. I don't have the skills or the right connections, certainly not in that part of town. Or the time, for that matter. I'm juggling a couple of major projects that came out of nowhere, and there's a board meeting this week. I only wanted to sort out my own thinking. And you're a good sounding board."

"Thank you. Is there any cake left?"

We adjourned to the parlor and the television with our cake.

CHAPTER 22

The next morning I dressed with particular care. Silly, maybe, but I knew that Edward Perkins was in a position to do something for the Society, or at least for the Oliver sisters, and I didn't want to offend him by appearing too casual, as if I wasn't taking him seriously. In my position, I figured I couldn't go wrong overdressing a bit, while underdressing might kill a deal. It was all about appearances.

On the way toward the city, I reminded James that he was dropping me off at Marty's house. "We'll walk from there to Edward Perkins's house, and then I'll head over to the Society."

"Got it," he said, watching the road. "Anything else on the calendar?"

"Last-minute prep for the board meeting tomorrow, I guess. Nothing else scheduled, but these days things keep popping up unexpectedly. I'll call you when I know where I'll be at the end of the day."

"Sounds good to me."

"You know, you are far too accommodating," I told him. "Don't you have any major crises you have to handle? Can you really just walk away from your desk at five o'clock every day? That's not the way television shows portray the FBI—you're all supposed to be racing off to a fresh murder or a terrorist attack."

A corner of James's mouth went up. "Since when have television writers gotten much of anything right? Yes, things come up. Recently I guess I've been given what you might call special consideration, after what happened. But it's not necessary, and I assume it will end soon enough. In the meantime, I've gotten a lot of paperwork done."

"How exciting," I said, and it came out a bit snarky.

"Nell," James began, sounding exasperated, "I just want to be sure you're not at risk. Your detective friend may have identified the shooter, but as you suggested last night, what if he was working for someone else? That person might try again."

"To hurt me? That's ridiculous. You really think a drug-dealing thug would come into Center City just to go after me?"

"Allow me to worry about you, will you? Would you rather I didn't?"

"I'm sorry," I said in a small voice. "I'm used to looking out for myself. I don't want to be any bother to anyone else."

I think he smiled. "In case you haven't noticed, I don't do anything I don't want to do. Well, maybe for Martha, now and then. But I want to look out for you, if you'll let me."

"I will. But only if you'll let me worry about you when you're back on full duty chasing dangerous people with weapons."

"Fair enough. Here we are." He slid into a parking place outside of Marty's town house.

I unbuckled my seat belt, turned, and pulled him closer for a kiss, one that lasted quite a while. "Thank you," I said. "For caring. For watching my back. I'll try to get used to it."

"Do that. Call me later."

After he'd pulled away, I turned to find Marty leaning against her doorjamb with a smile on her face. "Nice way to start the day."

"I thought so. Am I coming in?"

"Yeah, sure. We've got time. Edward's place is only a ten-minute walk away. Coffee?"

"Always."

Marty stood aside to let me into her home, and I walked down the long hallway to the big room at the back. She took a quick detour to the kitchen area, set off by walls that didn't extend to the ceiling, and then joined me carrying two mugs of coffee. "Sit," she said, after handing me one of them.

She settled in a chair opposite me. "You read your materials?"

"I did, yesterday. I always do my homework. Even as a kid."

"Suck-up," Marty said, but with a smile. "Any questions?"

"Not about the facts. Who's taking the lead today, Edward or us?"

"He hinted that he has a plan he'd like to lay out. I don't have the details, but it sounds promising. And for some reason Eliot's part of it."

That I hadn't expected. "Really? He hasn't said anything to you about it?"

"No. The man is the soul of discretion. But he may be deferring to Edward, and as you may have noticed, a strong will and a full wallet will get you almost anywhere you want to go."

"Amen," I said. I knew I didn't qualify on the wallet front; where did I fall on strength of will? But I didn't need it today: I was going to listen to Edward Perkins.

Marty and I chatted while we finished our coffee, and then disappeared and returned wearing a handsome, colorful jacket that I hadn't seen before. She'd dressed up, too. "Nice," I said.

"Thanks. You ready?"

"Sure."

We strolled the few blocks to a quiet street near Rittenhouse Square. I loved walking these neighborhoods (I had to remind myself there was no point in comparing them to the sad slums not far north of where we stood—that was a different universe entirely): they were old and well maintained and beautiful. Edward Perkins's town house was no exception. It was not ostentatiously large, but it was exquisite. Marty rapped briskly with the no doubt antique brass knocker, and I was surprised when Alice opened the door.

"Good morning, Nell, Marty," she said cheerfully. "Uncle Edward is waiting for you. Follow me."

She turned before we could ask any questions, and led us past a handsome staircase, to what must have been the back parlor according to the original floor plan. I tried to stay focused, although I really wanted to study the moldings and woodwork. When we entered the room through a graceful arch, Edward Perkins stood. Next to him stood Eliot Miller. I resisted the urge to turn to Marty to see what her reaction was. Eliot smiled broadly at both of us, and I guessed that Marty hadn't been expecting him, either.

"Welcome to my home, Nell. Or perhaps I should say my city home? Martha, nice to see you again," Edward said graciously, then added, "Please, have a seat. May I offer you some refreshment?"

"Thank you, but no, Mr. Perkins," I said. Much more coffee and I'd have to ask to tour the plumbing facilities, although I did have some curiosity about how they'd fitted them in here. Marty shook her head as well.

"Edward, please. Very well, then. Let us begin."

We all sat. Alice took a straight-backed chair outside of our circle. We waited for Edward to begin whatever it was he wanted to say.

He did not keep us waiting. "My lovely niece Alice has been telling me very nice things about the Society since she began working there."

"I'm pleased to hear that," I told him. "She's been a great asset to us. I'd love to have more interns like her."

"I'm happy to know that. And I do hope you've recovered from your unfortunate experience last week?"

"I think so. It was disturbing, to say the least, but I can't allow myself to take it personally."

"Goodness, no, Nell. Let us hope that the nonprofit world does not have to stoop to violence to achieve its goals." He rubbed his hands together. "Well, I know that we're all busy people, so I will get to the point. I have been made aware that the Oliver sisters, Phoebe and Penelope, would like to divest themselves of their lovely house, but it is their fond hope that they can preserve it in some way—in form and in substance. I have had the privilege of knowing them for most of our lives. They are not foolish women, and they recognize that the modern world places some demands on any institution, so it is unlikely that their home could be preserved forever, and they are willing to make allowances for some discreet modern modifications. But their existing resources are not sufficient to guarantee its maintenance in perpetuity, so they turned to me for assistance and counsel. And I think we have arrived at a plan that could work. Will you hear me out?"

"Of course," I told him. "I'm flattered that you've included me in this discussion, but I'm not sure I see what role the Society can play."

"Patience, my dear. All things will be made clear. The Oliver house lies only a few miles from Utopia College. Are you familiar with it?"

I shook my head. "I can't say that I am."

"You might have known it under its earlier name,

Badger College. The change came about a couple of decades ago. It's a small undergraduate liberal arts college with an excellent teaching staff, which is not easy to maintain in this day and age. It is also the college that Penelope Oliver attended when I first knew her. Unfortunately she was forced to withdraw after a bout of diphtheria before completing a degree. But she always retained an affection for the place."

Edward settled himself more comfortably in his brocade-covered wing chair. "I am proposing to make a gift to the college, with the restriction that the funds be used to acquire the Oliver home. This will not be onerous for them. The location of the house is convenient to the campus, and they are in sore need of room to expand. And there are precedents—for example, the Benjamin West House, which Swarthmore College purchased many years ago and has put to good use, all the while preserving its historical attributes."

I managed to find my voice. "That is an extraordinarily generous offer, Mr. Perkins. Have the Oliver sisters agreed to this?"

"Oh, yes. They are willing to accept the transaction, as long as the building is maintained in something like its original form—not turned into a computer center or fraternity house or the like. I will ensure that my gift is adequate to provide for the care of the building, and that the funds cannot be diverted to other purposes. Phoebe, Penelope, and I have discussed this proposal, and they are willing to accept some modifications to the building, as long as they are done tastefully. They realize that the world has changed, and that they cannot control the future, so I think we have achieved a satisfactory compromise. They in turn will retire to their summer home, which is smaller and better suited to their current needs. Do you have any questions?" He sat back, looking quite pleased with himself.

I felt as though a weight had been lifted from my shoulders: I would not have to choose between projects. It was a lovely house, but I could see no way for the Society to take it on. This way, the Oliver sisters would get their wish, and a college would reap the rewards. "I think it's an excellent solution, Mr. Perkins."

"There is another component to this transaction, Nell," Edward added, his eyes twinkling. "The Oliver sisters are in possession of the documents of many generations of their family, regarding not only the house but the family's social and commercial activities in and around Philadelphia. They would like to make a gift of these papers to the Society, and perhaps provide some funding for the cataloging of them, something they themselves have never been equipped to do. Would your institution be interested in that collection?"

I wanted to ask somebody to pinch me, to make sure I was really hearing this. "We would be delighted to accept such a gift, and we would be honored to provide stewardship. But surely Utopia College has some interest in it?"

Edward shook his head. "No, their interests lie elsewhere. The college would appreciate it if you provided a summary or copies of the information that pertains to the house itself, for their own records, but they do not wish to accept responsibility for the collection. They feel the Society would be better suited as custodian of the Oliver family name."

"Then if they are willing, we accept." Maybe I should run it by the board first, but I'd bet they'd be happy. And if I didn't convince them, Marty would. I looked briefly at her, and I swear she looked gobsmacked, which was a rare state for Marty Terwilliger. Edward had pulled a fast one on her?

And then I realized that Eliot Miller was still in the room and hadn't yet said a word, just sat quietly with a Cheshire cat smile. And Marty was staring at him, eyebrows raised.

There was apparently more to come.

CHAPTER 23

Edward Perkins did not fail to notice our glances. "As you may have surmised, my story isn't finished quite yet. Would you like some refreshment now? Coffee? Tea?"

Much as I hankered to see Edward's collection of Georgian silver, I thought it might be more important to find out what other schemes he had come up with. "Thank you, but I think we'd like to know more about why you've brought us all here."

"Of course. There is another component to the Oliver transaction—its complement, you might say. This scenario involves the house in which we now sit. It has belonged to the Perkins family for generations, but at this point in my life I have no need for more than one home. I plan to move to my house in the country, if this scheme succeeds. My intention is to sell this house to my alma mater, the University of Pennsylvania, for less than its full market value. They have been looking for a suitable home for a proposed Center for Urban Transformation, and they feel that this building would suit their needs admirably, inasmuch as it is close but not too close to the main campus, and large enough but not too large for the anticipated staff. And, of course, it has a certain historical cachet, which is appropriate."

He paused, and I guessed it was for dramatic effect. "Professor Eliot has agreed to assume the directorship of this new institution."

That explained Eliot's presence at this gathering. I am proud to say that my jaw did not drop at this news. I glanced briefly at Marty and wondered how much she had known.

Edward went on, "I ask only that the university consider naming this new creation the Perkins Center. I think they can accommodate my vanity in exchange for this building, and they seem more than willing. The purchase price I have suggested to the university is not insubstantial. It is this sale that will provide the funds for my gift to Utopia College, which will make possible their purchase of the Oliver house."

I struggled to wrap my head around the complexities of this arrangement. Edward Perkins was far shrewder than I had ever given him credit for. He no doubt had worked out how to benefit from substantial charitable contributions while making everyone happy—the Oliver sisters, Utopia College, Penn, and even me. The man was one of a kind.

"Nell, the wheels are already in motion, and I ask only

that you keep this information to yourselves until the details are finalized. I'll let you know when you can release the news. And please feel free to contact me if you have any further questions."

"Of course, Mr. Perkins. And I must add, this is a wonderful and generous opportunity for all concerned."

Eliot finally spoke. "Marty, I'm sorry I couldn't share this with you, but Edward requested that I keep it secret while he negotiated."

"Yeah, whatever," Marty mumbled. I could see that she was miffed, and she and Eliot would no doubt have some heated discussions later.

"However," Eliot resumed, looking at all of us in turn, "there is another element of this arrangement that you need to know about. The university possesses excellent archival resources about the city and its history, and I have reason to know that those at the Society complement them. I'd like to see the Society take an advisory role in the Perkins Center, working alongside me and our staff to capture the history of Philadelphia's neighborhoods—*all* its neighborhoods, including those that have fallen on hard times. Perhaps a seat on the board of the new organization, if anyone on your staff might be interested."

I assumed that *wow* and *gosh* and *holy cow* were not appropriate responses under the circumstances. "That would be wonderful," I said sincerely. Would there be any money involved for the Society? This was not the time to ask, nor did it really matter: it would give the Society added visibility in the local community, and drag us into the twentieth century, if not quite into the twenty-first.

And that would give us a better shot at surviving in the longer term. And it would provide support for our new neighborhoods project. It was the best of all possible worlds, and I was stunned.

Edward stood up. "Well, that is all I wished to say. I know you all have other pressing obligations, so I'll let you go. My attorneys will keep you apprised of our progress, but they assure me that the basic elements will be finalized before the end of the year."

The rest of us stood as well, and I stepped forward. "Edward, I don't know what to say. This is an extraordinary arrangement, and I'm honored that the Society will be a part of it."

He smiled at me. "Nell, I believe that our local history should be preserved and protected, now and in the future. That is why I have been a Society member for many years, and I believe your organization should continue to play a role in this process. Under your guidance, and that of your board, you have earned the right to a seat at the table."

"Then I can only say thank you. I hope we can live up to your faith in us."

"I'm sure you will."

We muddled through good-byes after shaking hands all around with Edward. Alice and I stood on the front stoop while Marty and Eliot exchanged a few private words in the vestibule before joining us.

My head was spinning. Had I really heard what I thought I had? The nonprofit landscape of greater Philadelphia had just changed before my eyes, and the Society was going to be part of it. *Whee!*

I turned to Alice. "Were you your uncle's mole at the Society?"

"No," she said. "But I did tell him I thought the Society was doing an excellent job, despite limited resources and funding. And he listened."

"Well, whatever role you played, thank you. Is he going to want us to name something after him? Because we will."

Alice waved a hand at that idea. "No, this is not about his ego, or his legacy—well, maybe the Penn part. He wants to do the right thing. In doing it this way, he helps everyone—the university, the Society, the college, and the Oliver sisters. It's a quadruple-win situation."

"It certainly is."

Marty joined us, and we started walking toward the Society. The crowded sidewalks gave us little opportunity to talk about the extraordinary meeting we had just left. I didn't mind; I was trying to process the implications of Edward Perkins's amazing generosity. I thought possibly Latoya would welcome the chance to serve on the board of the new institute; she had a long-standing interest in abolitionist history in the city, and she was deeply immersed in the collections management side of things, having worked for years with the Society's collections. As long as this possible new role didn't take too much time away from her Society responsibilities, of course. Alice could handle the Oliver collection—she had already proved more than qualified, and also willing to ask for help when she knew she needed it. It was unclear how much time that process would take, but since her salary was effectively being paid by her great-uncle at the moment, it didn't really matter. Maybe it would keep her around longer than originally planned. I often wished more intelligent young people like Alice would fall in love with history and its artifacts, but places like the Society were seldom at the top of the list when new college graduates went job hunting.

Alice peeled off to the cataloging room when we arrived at the Society, and Marty followed me to my office and dropped into a chair, while I collected messages from Eric.

"Good meeting, Nell?" he asked, as he sorted through phone messages.

"Amazing, actually, but I can't talk about it just yet. Have I missed anything important?"

"Two calls you might want to return. One from your detective, the other from a Vee Blakeney at a bank. The rest can wait."

"Thanks, Eric."

I went into my office and fell into my chair, feeling a bit like Alice in Wonderland after she had fallen down the rabbit hole. The view was not the same as it had been the day before. I looked down at my messages. Hrivnak's said *Call*—typically terse.

"What's up?" Marty asked. As usual, she had followed me into my office without asking.

"Our detective wants me to call. Give me a minute." I punched in her number and waited until she answered. "This is Nell Pratt—you called earlier?"

"Oh, yeah, right. We got lucky. You know that shooter? He cut a deal: he fingered the guy that sent him after you guys last week, in exchange for a reduced charge on the gun possession and general mayhem on the other offense. The name Raheem Hill mean anything to you?"

"I can't say that it does. Should it?"

"Seems like this Hill character paid our shooter to do the deed. Not a heck of a lot—he works cheap. He was probably looking to score points with his gang."

"Who are these people?" I said, more to myself than to the detective.

"Raheem's a midlevel dealer. The shooter is lower down the food chain. Raheem says to jump, he jumps. Only now he's given Raheem up, which isn't good for our boy in custody."

"I don't suppose anybody has explained why Raheem wanted him to shoot at us?"

"Nope. He didn't ask; he just did what he was told. But it wasn't a mix-up—he made sure he had the right car."

"I figured that much, since he drove by more than once. Well, I suppose that's more than we knew before. Thanks for letting me know."

"No problem," Detective Hrivnak said, and hung up.

"What?" Marty asked, staring at me.

"The shooter was paid by his drug-dealing boss to shoot at us. Damn, I didn't think to ask whether he was told to shoot to kill or just scare us off." I knew he had scared me. Was Tyrone unwelcome there now? Was he involved in something outside of our community efforts that we didn't know about? And what about Cherisse? She didn't share Tyrone's history with the neighborhood, but had the police looked past her squeaky-clean suburban credentials?

I hit speed dial and got the detective back on the line. "Did you ask Tyrone if he knew Raheem?"

"Yeah, of course. He said he knew *about* him, but he couldn't remember ever going face-to-face with him."

"One more thing: Was the shooter supposed to kill anyone, or just send a message?"

There was a moment of silence on the other end. Then the detective said, "The way he put it, he was just gonna shoot up the car. If anyone got hit, too bad. But he didn't say anything about killing someone on purpose. That all you've got?"

"For now. Thanks." This time we both hung up at the same time.

"And?" Marty asked. She seemed to be enjoying herself.

"Tyrone didn't know Raheem, or so he says. Hrivnak didn't think to ask if this was supposed to be a killing. Tell me this: Why would anybody hire someone to shoot at someone else if he didn't know him?"

"If you think I understand the way a drug dealer's mind works, you're definitely misguided," Marty told me. Then she changed the subject. "So, what do you think about Edward's plan?"

"I think it's amazing. Can he make it happen?"

"I think so. He's made plenty of friends over the years, and very few enemies. When he promises something, he delivers. And he doesn't do it for his own glory. Too bad there aren't more like him."

"I agree. Did Eliot fill you in beforehand?"

"He talked about the institute, early on when Penn first brought it up—these things take time to plan. He did *not* talk about Edward's plan for supporting it."

"And now you're pissed at him?" I asked.

"Yes. No. Well, maybe. He could have told me *something*. I do know how and when to keep my mouth shut."

"Does this Perkins Institute mean Eliot will be too busy for the Society board?"

"I don't think so. And maybe I don't care—he committed to that a while back, and I'm going to hold him to it. Besides, the two roles dovetail so nicely."

"No conflict of interest?"

"I'd call it collegiality. Stop worrying, Nell. It'll work out, and if it doesn't, *something* good will come of it."

"That is an understatement. I want to elevate Edward Perkins to sainthood. Maybe Shelby knows how to make that happen. Admit it, Marty—this is an amazing outcome. I bet you're just mad because it happened without you."

"Maybe," Marty mumbled, avoiding my gaze.

"I've got one more call to make. You want to have lunch?"

"Nope. I've got to check up on what Rich has gotten done and see how this collections shuffling is going."

"Go on, then." I figured she wanted to crawl into the stacks and lick her wounds, but even she couldn't argue with the excellent outcome. When Marty had left, I picked up the phone and called Vee. A secretary answered in plummy tones and reluctantly put me through when I identified myself. "Hi, Vee. You called earlier?"

"Yes, I did, Nell, and thanks for calling back. There's something I'd like to discuss with you—I would have mentioned it earlier, but I wanted to clear it with the partners before I started spreading the word around. And I'd rather not do it over the phone. Unfortunately I'm jammed up for most of the day. Could you come by my office around four?" She rattled off the Center City address, which I recognized.

"I think that works for me. I'll let you know if anything changes. See you later."

One more enigmatic phone call. Interesting. Was I really out of the loop on all fronts? What kind of hush-hush project could she be involved in that would interest me? I guess I'd have to wait and see.

All this walking around the city had left me hungry, so I went down the hall and stuck my head into Shelby's office. "You want to grab a sandwich?" I noticed her desk was appreciably clearer than it had been the day before.

"Sure. I've just about wrapped up this grant report, so I can celebrate with a ham on rye."

"You do know how to live!" I waited as she gathered up her bag and jacket, and we walked out of the building together, and down to our usual sandwich place on the next block. We ordered, then found ourselves a table next to the window.

"Thanks for that information on Edward Perkins."

"Oh, that's right—you were meeting with him this morning. How'd that go?"

"Very, very well. There are some interesting things in the works, but I can't talk about them yet. But let me say that the Society will benefit mightily. Not necessarily with money, but with prestige and visibility, which might ultimately lead to more money."

"Well, that's nice to hear. Did the information help?"

"Yes, it helped to confirm that Mr. Perkins is a man of his word and has the resources to back it up. That's rare these days."

Our sandwiches arrived, and we settled down to eat. Halfway through my sandwich, I commented, "I had another odd call this morning, from Vee Blakeney. You know her?"

"Can't say I recognize the name. Who is she?"

"She's Tyrone Blakeney's wife, and she's a hotshot investment banker at a big firm here in the city."

"What do you think she wants with you?"

"I haven't a clue. It sounds like another mysterious project. I have to say, we must be doing something right, because at least people are looking to include the Society in their hush-hush projects. You can take some of the credit for that, getting our name out there."

Shelby smiled. "What about you? You've been in the paper plenty recently."

"Yes, but usually for the wrong reasons. I'm not sure how crime solving fits in with high finance or community development. But I'm more than willing to listen to other people's ideas."

"Well, here's to us!" Shelby and I clinked our bottles of iced tea.

After lunch I returned to my office and let Eric know

that I'd be leaving for a meeting at about quarter to four. Then I called James.

He answered with his professional voice. It occurred to me that I'd never seen his office at the FBI. Did he occupy a desk in a bullpen situation, or did he have his own office with a door that closed? Was there anyone who could overhear his conversations? Or were they all being recorded? "James Morrison. Oh, Nell, hi. Something up?"

"Three things." I could be businesslike, too. "One, the meeting with Mr. Perkins was great, and I'll fill you in later. Two, Detective Hrivnak told me that a drug dealer named Raheem Hill paid one of his flunkies to shoot at the car last week. And three, I'm meeting Tyrone Blakeney's wife, Vee, at her office at four to discuss something she wouldn't reveal to me over the phone. Can you meet me there?"

"Five thirty work for you? Give me the address and I'll park somewhere and meet you downstairs."

"That's fine." I told him where to find me coming out of the building. "See you then."

The FBI listeners would have nothing to giggle about after *that* romantic conversation.

At quarter to four I gathered up my things again, said good-bye to Eric, and set off for Vee Blakeney's office. It was located in one of the high-rises that lined Market Street on the other side of City Hall. I was certainly getting some exercise this way, but it felt good. When I reached the building I had to check the listings in the lobby: Vee worked for Dillingham Harrington, one of those firms that had resulted from multiple mergers of the old-guard firms after the financial ups and downs of the past decade or more. I didn't pay much attention to who was who these days, since I had nothing that vaguely resembled an investment, unless you counted my half of the Chestnut Hill house. And the Society had been using the same small, local bank for decades.

The building was gleaming, the elevator was swift and silent, and the lobby of Vee's firm was quietly impressive. I introduced myself to the receptionist, who announced my presence through her discreet earpiece/phone, and a minute later Vee came down a hallway to meet me.

"Thank you for coming on such short notice. I know that Tyrone appreciated your stopping by the hospital to see him."

"I wanted to be sure he was all right. I was a bit surprised he left the hospital so quickly, with his injuries."

Vee smiled. "I think he was trying to prove he was stronger than he actually is. Some men are like that. Are you married, Nell?"

"No, not at the moment." I was still struggling with how to answer that. Well, I wasn't married currently, although I had been once. I was in a committed relationship—that sounded stiff. I had a partner—silly. I lived with my boyfriend? For heaven's sake, he was an FBI agent! Gentleman friend? Paramour? I stuck with the simplest answer: no. "Have you and Tyrone been married long?"

"More than ten years. We met just after college. He was already involved in community organizing activities then, but I decided to get an MBA at Wharton, so I went in a different direction."

"You told me you'd been involved with John Street's initiative—you must have been fairly new here then."

"I was, so I ended up doing a lot of the tedious work. But Tyrone's insights into the community were invaluable to me, and helped me capture the attention of some of the more senior members. And in a sense, that's why I asked you here today. As I told you, that original project has had a fairly decent track record, and now that it's wrapping up, the firm is interested in carrying it forward, at least in spirit, and has asked me to take the lead on it. Have you heard the term *impact investing*?"

"No, I can't say that I have. What is it?"

Vee smiled. "Let me explain it to you, and tell you what it can do for the city of Philadelphia."

CHAPTER 24

"I'm sorry," Vee said, "I'm forgetting my manners—it's been a long day. Would you like something to drink? Tea, coffee, sparkling water?"

I took her offer to mean that this visit would take more than a few minutes. "No, I'm fine."

"All right, then." Vee sat back in her leather swivel chair behind her spotless desk, her back to the spectacular view of city hall through the floor-to-ceiling plate glass windows. "In simplest terms, impact investing is investing that generates both a financial and a social return. It addresses social problems by making capital available from a variety of sources to fund programs that improve people's lives and communities. It's not new—it's been around for perhaps two decades in an organized manner, and now one dollar out of every nine is invested in ways guided by social or environmental concerns. DH has decided to create a

new department within the firm to address ways of bringing new capital to finance community and economic
development."

It took me a moment to translate *DH* to *Dillingham
Harrington*. While I was not versed in the ways of public
finance, I caught the drift of what she was saying. "You're
talking about raising money to support neighborhood
projects? Like Tyrone's?"

"Yes, in essence, although giving to his group would
no doubt be construed as favoritism. But broadly speaking,
we here at DH can bring together a range of investor types,
combining different vehicles, in order to diversify the risk
to the individual investors, who in turn are willing to
accept a somewhat lower return with the knowledge that
they are doing something worthy. Affordable housing has
been the prime example, because there is an anticipated
income stream of rental payments and subsidies. Public
funding, from the City or the state, and pure philanthropy
cannot meet all the demands of projects such as these, but
we can work closely with those entities to assemble successful packages."

It sounded good. It probably looked good on paper.
Did I believe her? I wasn't sure. "Do you need the City's
support, or at least their blessing, for this?"

"The mayor is firmly behind this. But we would also hope
to pull in corporate financing from local companies, and on
the flip side, to create equity investment opportunities to
provide capital for other collaborative enterprises."

"It sounds very persuasive. But isn't there an interme-
diate step? I'm sure you know neighborhoods like the one

I visited with your husband last week. They're dangerous wastelands. How do you persuade anyone to invest in such a disaster zone?"

"That's an intelligent question, Nell, and an important one. No one is promising that this will be easy, but it's something that needs to happen, and we believe in it. We are still in the early phases, but we've spoken to some important construction firms who we think are on board, and as I mentioned, the City is behind us. As well they must be, since they hold a substantial number of properties in the areas we're addressing. This has to be a collaborative effort."

Time to cut to the chase. "I'm impressed. But why am I here? I'm assuming it's not for the money, because the Society has none to give."

"It was Tyrone who first approached you, right? I think he was on the right track. Your Society can provide the human element for what, for want of a better term, will be our sales pitch. You have the resources to show what the city's neighborhoods once were, and what we hope they can be again. We can talk about numbers and wave handsome architectural drawings around, and then watch investors' eyes glaze over; you can make the neighborhoods real to them."

I studied the woman in front of me. About my age, better dressed than I was, clearly intelligent and articulate. Did she believe in this venture? Or did she see it as a stepping-stone to a vice presidency at the firm? Assuming, of course, that the venture wasn't a total bust. It wouldn't be the first time: Philadelphia was littered with failed projects.

"Why do you think this can be successful?" I asked. "Haven't there been other efforts like this, such as Street's initiative?"

"Yes, of course. The neighborhoods problem in the city is not new, and the City, the state, and even the federal government have thrown money at it. Realistically, it's usually too little, and it dries up too quickly. But times have changed. Impact investing has a decent track record. We've been careful about jumping in, waiting to see how other efforts have fared, and what mistakes were made. We think the time is right to move on this now."

"What does Tyrone think?" I said, mainly to satisfy my own curiosity.

Surprisingly, Vee looked away. "If I may be honest, Tyrone thinks I'm selling out. That I'm going to ride this currently fashionable trend to get what I want, which is both money and job security. I won't defend investment banking in general—a lot of established firms managed to tarnish their own reputations and have paid the price—but I believe in DH and their sincerity in advancing this effort. And I want to be part of it."

She looked past me, and I wondered if she was checking to be sure the door to her office was closed. Then she looked back at me. "Nell, I don't often bring this up, but I was raised in the same neighborhood as Tyrone. I know what the problems are. I've worked hard to get where I am today, but in part that's because I feel I can be more effective in bringing about real change from here, rather than on the streets like Tyrone."

That, I would never have guessed. "And how do you

feel about what Tyrone is doing?" *Which may have gotten him shot?*

"I respect my husband, Nell. He is truly committed to saving his neighborhood. My own opinion is that he's pouring a lot of energy into his efforts, but they're too small to really make a difference. It takes too much money and power to make the changes he wants to see happen, and he'll never be able to access that through a small community organization."

I studied her for a moment. "It sounds like your goals are the same, but it's your methods that differ."

"That's true. Philadelphia is our home and always has been. It breaks my heart to see neighborhoods going downhill the way they have, even within my lifetime. I have the chance to make a real difference, and I've fought to make this firm see that. I hope Tyrone will be on my side. We want the same thing."

I gave myself a mental shake. It was getting late, and we needed to get down to details. "What would you like to see from us? And what's your timetable?"

Did Vee look relieved? "We hope to announce a fully fleshed-out project after the first of the year. Any sooner and it would get lost in the holiday muddle. In any event, it will take that long to get all the players lined up. Once we define a specific project, we'd like to see your Society put together a presentation on the 'before' aspects on the area—something we can distribute to investors. Something professional."

"With plenty of pictures? No, I'm not being sarcastic—I know that people like the old pictures, and that sometimes they don't bother to read the words. But bear in mind that I wouldn't want to put out anything that didn't reflect conscientious scholarship, or that misrepresented the past. You know, not just happy children playing in the streets, or colorful festivals. These neighborhoods were diverse and vital—they had schools and shops and churches, and people knew one another, even watched out for one another. I hope that's what you want to convey."

"Exactly. And I wouldn't presume to interfere with your selection."

"I assume there would be some financial consideration?" Awkward phrasing, but not as crude as asking, *How much?*

"Of course." She named a figure that almost made me swallow my tongue. Just for a bit of responsible research? That we might even do anyway, pro bono? If she was trying to buy my support, she was doing an excellent job of it.

I struggled to recover my balance. "If you're successful, perhaps we could consider combining the individual portions as a book, sometime in the future?"

"An excellent idea. So, are you interested?"

"I can't commit for my institution without consulting with my board"—not exactly true, but I was trying to be cautious and allow myself time to consider all sides of the idea—"but I'm sure they'll be interested in your proposal. When do you expect to make a public announcement?"

"Probably in January. Is that a reasonable amount of time for your people to pull together something we could use?"

Maybe the cold and snow will keep the most active criminals behind closed doors and allow for some photo ops, I thought to myself. I glanced at the elegant crystal clock on her side table: nearly five thirty. "I'm sure we could manage that, as soon as you nail down which part of the city you want to target first. I'm sorry—I should be going. I'm meeting someone."

"Of course. I appreciate your taking the time to meet with me. Why don't we walk out together? I'm finished for the day. Just let me gather my things and check with my secretary. Unless you're in a terrible hurry?"

"No, that's fine." Now that she thought she'd won me over, she was certainly being friendly.

"I'll be only a moment." She hurried out to her secretary's desk outside her office and began speaking to her. To give her privacy, I walked to the windows and gazed down at the city laid out below. There was city hall, the heart of the city, at the intersection of Broad Street and Market Street. Just as William Penn had envisioned more than three hundred years earlier. Much had changed, but history was still very much with us. And beyond it lay North Philadelphia, but there was nothing to be seen in that direction, just flat ground or what was left of the old row houses. I had to admit that some of the public commentators had got it right: it looked like images I'd seen of World War I war zones. I wondered if Vee had recognized the irony of her office location: looking back at the place she had come from, to the center of things. She had done well for herself. Maybe she saw this impact investing as her way of giving back, not merely a smart and trendy business idea. If it worked, she would probably accomplish far more in practical terms than Tyrone could hope for. What did he think about what his wife was doing? And why had he come to me before she had? Were they working together, or did they have separate agendas?

Vee came up behind me. "All set. Wonderful view, isn't it?"

"It is. And it looks so different than what you see from ground level." My office, albeit in a corner, had a wonderful view of a defunct night club, a parking lot, and—the only saving grace—one of the city's murals. Maybe this view versus Tyrone's summarized the two differing viewpoints: Tyrone saw individual people on the ground, while Vee saw the big picture, where old and new, rich and poor met.

"Shall we go?" Vee asked.

"Fine." I followed her out to the elevator banks and we took an express to the ground floor. "Do you drive to work or take public transportation?" I asked, mainly to make conversation.

"I walk when the weather permits. You know where we live—it's not far. I call for a car if the weather is bad, or if I have an early or late appointment."

Must be nice. But then, I had a car and driver, at least for the moment—and they should be waiting for me downstairs.

We walked out of the lobby on the Market Street side. Traffic out of the city was peaking. I scanned the curb for James's car, but it wasn't in sight. I wasn't worried, since I was a few minutes early.

"It was great talking with you, Nell," Vee said. "I'll call you when I have more information. I'm heading home now." She turned to walk toward the river, when suddenly her path was blocked by a large black man with a shiny bald head. He looked respectable enough, with a newish leather jacket that fit him well, and a large gold watch on his arm. Vee stopped just in time to avoid walking into him. "What do you want, Raheem?" she asked, her voice icy.

Raheem? It couldn't be a coincidence, could it? Raheem the North Philly drug dealer? Raheem who had arranged for that punk shooter? What was he doing here on Market Street?

"Hey, Ronnie, just wanna talk with you. You don't return my calls or nothin'." His words seemed innocent enough, but his tone was cold. Wait—he knew Vee? Or *Ronnie*?

"We don't have anything to say to each other, Raheem," she said stiffly.

"You be wrong about that, I'm thinkin'. After what I done for you." The man wasn't budging.

I tried to figure out what to do now. I could melt away and pretend I'd never seen him. Or I could jump to Vee's aid, although apparently she knew the guy. Or I could call the police and give them some wild story and they'd send somebody, just to see if it was true. Or I could call James, although if he was driving I wasn't sure he'd answer. I was reaching into my bag to find my cell phone when Raheem's gaze shifted to me. It wasn't friendly.

"You—you the lady been all over the news this week, right? You a friend of Tyrone's?"

Vee turned to me and frowned. Was I supposed to play

dumb? The man had already recognized me from the papers. "We've met," I said neutrally.

He nodded once. "Me and Ronnie here, we got things to talk about. We gonna go somewhere and talk. You can go."

I looked at Vee, and now I thought I saw a flash of fear. "I'm not sure Vee wants to go with you, Raheem."

Raheem had somehow managed to inch closer to Vee, and now he looked down at her. He must have outweighed her by a hundred pounds, easily. If he fell over on her, she'd be flattened. "That right, Ronnie? You don't want to talk with me?"

"I'm not going anywhere with you, Raheem. Leave me alone." She took a step back, but he closed the gap again.

"Jes' wanna talk, Ronnie. About you and that little bitch your man was hangin' around with."

And the pieces came together in my head. Raheem knew Vee. He had seen Tyrone and Cherisse together. Maybe in his mind he thought he was helping her, or that Tyrone was somehow insulting him by running around on his wife in the old neighborhood—Raheem's turf. What conclusion he had drawn might or might not be correct, but he'd landed there with both feet. What had he done?

"Is there a problem here, Nell?" James's voice made me jump. I hadn't heard him come up behind me, but I was overwhelmingly glad that he was there. I took a step back so I was standing beside him. Heck, I wanted to duck behind his broad back and hide, but that would make me look foolish.

The little drama that followed, played out on a broad public sidewalk in the center of a busy city at rush hour, would have been highly entertaining—if I weren't in the middle of it. Vee looked predictably confused; she had no idea who James was and what he was doing there, much less why he had stepped in and come to my assistance. Raheem, on the other hand, realized his control of the scene was being challenged, and somehow managed to make himself look bigger. Like a tomcat trying to scare off an adversary by fluffing out his fur, I thought irreverently. Of course, it didn't work. James didn't react, merely pulled aside his suit jacket so that Raheem could see his badge and gun. He didn't have to say a word. Raheem's expression changed quickly once he knew what he was facing. He took a step back.

His eyes flicked back at Vee. "I can see I ain't welcome here, Ronnie. But we gotta talk. You gonna listen, you hear me? You owe me." He gave James a long look—like a kid on a playground saying, *You don't scare me, nyah nyah*, then turned on his heel and walked away. He turned down the first street he came to and got into a waiting car, which disappeared quickly.

James watched until he was out of sight. "I guess I wasn't late," he said.

I resisted the strong urge to throw my arms around him. "No, I'd say you were right on time."

CHAPTER 25

"Would you mind telling me what was going on here?" James asked. It seemed a very reasonable request—but I couldn't explain much.

I turned to Vee, who was standing stock-still on the sidewalk, looking mortified. I was pretty sure she would rather I hadn't seen that confrontation. But what would have happened if I hadn't been there? "Vee, that was Raheem Hill, wasn't it?"

That made her spin around to face me. "How do you know about him?"

I glanced at James, who appeared to have made the connection, now that he had the name. Then I said, "I think we need to sit down and talk about this. Maybe with the police?"

That startled Vee. "What? Why?"

She actually looked like she didn't understand what I

was talking about. I wavered. *Should we try to sort out what was going on here, or should we go straight to Hrivnak's office before we jump into the story?*

"Raheem Hill is wanted for questioning in connection with Cherisse Chapman's death."

"You mean, when Tyrone . . ." Now Vee seemed completely at a loss. I glanced at James for guidance.

"Call the detective," he said.

I checked to make sure Vee wasn't going to bolt—unlikely in those designer heels—then walked away a few paces to make the call. Luckily Detective Hrivnak answered.

"What do you want?" she barked.

"Don't you ever go home? We've found a link to Raheem Hill, and you need to hear it, now. In fact, he was here just a minute ago, but he's gone now."

"Crap," she muttered. Maybe she had a life outside of work after all. "He didn't happen to tell you where he was going?" Her tone was clearly sarcastic.

"He got into a car and it headed toward the river, but it was a one-way street, so the driver didn't have much choice. No way we could follow him or see where he turned."

Hrivnak sighed. "Where are you?"

"Corner of Market and Eighteenth streets."

"I'll meet you at your place in ten." She hung up.

I walked back over to where Vee and James were standing, as foot traffic flowed around them. "We're meeting her at the Society. Have you two introduced each other yet? I didn't mean to be rude, but I get kind of flustered when cornered by large, menacing men."

"Yes, we took care of the formalities," James told me. "We should get over to the Society. We can't do anything about Raheem right now, so let Hrivnak send her people after him."

"Vee, you okay?" I asked. She still looked stunned.

She straightened her back and looked me in the eye. "Yes, I'll be fine. Let's get this sorted out."

We piled into James's car and circled the block, making our way back to the Society. James scored a parking spot in the lot across the street, mainly by flashing his badge. It could have been a plastic copy of almost anything—the lot attendant didn't examine it too closely, just waved the car in.

We crossed the street and stood huddled in the doorway, watching for the detective. "You've never seen our collections, have you, Vee?" I asked, just making small talk.

"No," she said tersely.

"You should come back sometime, when we don't have other issues to deal with, and I'll give you the grand tour." Unless Vee was somehow implicated in whatever had happened with Tyrone and Cherisse and ended up in jail. So much for that generous consulting fee. Easy come, easy go.

Hrivnak pulled up and parked on the street, oblivious to traffic. She charged up the steps to where we were waiting. "We going in, or we gonna stand here and freeze our butts off?" she asked me while scoping out Vee. Apparently the detective was not in a happy mood. Vee kept her own gaze steady.

"Just waiting for you," I said. "Hang on while I disarm

the alarm." I unlocked the massive front door, then quickly punched in the key code, and the others filed in. I shut the door behind them and said, "Conference room?"

"Yeah, fine," Hrivnak said, and marched off in the right direction. She'd been here before. Too often.

We all trooped into the room and found seats, James taking the farthest one. Once again, he had no active role in the proceedings, yet here he was. Hrivnak was going to think we were joined at the hip.

"Can we get this over with?" the detective demanded. "I'd like to get home sometime today."

"Fine. Detective Hrivnak, do you know Veronica Blakeney? She's Tyrone's wife."

"No, I don't, although I know *of* her." The detective studied Vee, and I wondered if she was trying to picture her and Tyrone together. I had to admit it was an odd pairing.

Vee didn't flinch at the scrutiny. "I go by Vee, detective. As you may already know, I'm a vice president at Dillingham Harrington, and I invited Nell over to my office for a meeting this afternoon."

"And you need me here why?" Detective Hrivnak demanded, glaring at me. Definitely in a bad mood.

Since Vee hadn't volunteered any information, I decided to go ahead and explain what I had seen when we came out of the building, up through the point when James had swooped in and saved us. Well, I didn't put it exactly that way. James did not interrupt. I wrapped up by saying, "I asked Vee if the man was Raheem Hill, and she said yes. After that we decided we needed to talk this over with you."

"Good," she said. Then she turned to Vee. "What's your connection with Raheem Hill?"

"He's my cousin," Vee said curtly, and stopped.

One of Detective Hrivnak's eyebrows twitched; apparently this was news to her. "You are aware that he is a drug dealer, with a criminal record?"

"Yes, I am." Vee stopped again. I was beginning to wonder if it would be legal to shake her with a police officer present.

"Do you know that the police are looking to speak with Raheem Hill in connection with the shooting of your husband and the death of Cherisse Chapman last week?"

That brought the first real reaction from Vee. She cleared her throat, fighting for self-control. Then she said more calmly, "I was not aware of that until Nell told me, a short time ago. I have had little contact with Raheem for years, by my choice, but my . . . relatives have kept me up to date on his activities."

"First cousin, is he?" When Vee nodded, the detective pressed on. "You grow up in North Philly?"

Vee's chin went up half an inch. "Yes, I did. I've never made a secret of that. I did well in school, got a scholarship to college, and never looked back. My parents are dead, and I have had little reason or desire to visit my old neighborhood."

"Huh," Hrivnak said. "But you still know people there. You're married to Tyrone Blakeney."

"Yes."

"He from the same neighborhood?"

"Yes. He was a few years older than I was, so we didn't

meet when we were growing up. We met after college, when we were both working on a community project."

"You know the details of what happened last week, in your old neighborhood?"

"Of course. Tyrone told me about it. In part that's why I wanted to talk to Nell, to see if there was some way to make it up to her for what she stumbled into with Tyrone."

"Did you know Cherisse Chapman?"

"Only by name. Tyrone had mentioned her, said that she worked for the City on abandoned properties. Why is it you think that Raheem had anything to do with that?"

"We caught the guy who did the shooting, and we're holding him for murder. He told the police that Raheem had hired him for the job."

Vee looked sincerely bewildered. "But why?"

"We thought maybe you could tell us that."

"I have no idea," Vee protested. "I mean, I know Tyrone spends time in that neighborhood, but he's never said it was unsafe for him. I don't think he's made any enemies there—certainly no one who would want him dead. He doesn't do drugs, and he doesn't sell them. He's trying to do something good there!"

I broke into their dialogue. "Detective, Raheem said that Vee owed him, after what he did for her. Vee, does that mean anything to you?"

"I have not seen the man in years. I have not called him, texted him, e-mailed him, or passed on a message through friends—nothing. I did not ask him to do anything for me. Nor would I. If he's been trying to get in touch with me, I don't know about it. Maybe he doesn't have the right number. Maybe my secretary has been screening my calls."

"What about at home? He ever call you there?"

"I don't . . . think so. If he didn't leave a message, I wouldn't know. Maybe Tyrone has picked up? He's in and out a lot. Or maybe the calls came to his office. But if he did hear from Raheem, he didn't pass on any messages to me."

"Maybe he and Raheem have something going?" the detective asked.

"Like what?" Vee said.

"Maybe they're cutting a deal to clear the drugs out of part of the neighborhood so your husband's project can go forward?"

Vee shook her head vehemently. "Tyrone doesn't operate that way. He believes in law and order, even though that's not always easy where he comes from, as I'm sure you know. I assume you've checked his record—he's never been in trouble, right? Even a hint of trouble?"

"No, he's pretty squeaky clean," Detective Hrivnak admitted. "Unless he's real good at covering his tracks."

I was having trouble sitting still. Was there a point here? Would it come out before Christmas? "So what was Raheem talking about today, when he said he did something for Vee?"

"I think we'd better have a chat with him and find out," the detective said. "Problem is, we've had some trouble finding him. He moves around a lot. Can you help us with that, Ms. Blakeney?"

"I don't exactly send the man Christmas cards," she said. "I have no address for him."

"Yeah, but you know who his family is. They still there?"

"Some," Vee admitted.

"Write down what you know, and we'll check them out. He's gotta live somewhere, even if he moves around." Hrivnak pushed a pad and pen across the table toward Vee. Vee looked into space for a moment, then began writing.

I glanced at James, who sat in rocklike silence. Okay, fine, this was not his game. I started musing out loud. "So somebody shoots at a car with Tyrone, Cherisse, and me sitting in it, in a lousy neighborhood. The police find the guy with the gun. He says Raheem hired him to do it. Raheem turns out to be related to Vee. Then Raheem shows up on Vee's doorstep today and says she owes him because he did something for her. Vee says she hasn't had contact with him for years. The shooting is really the only connecting link. I'm pretty sure I can say that Raheem wasn't looking to get me. That leaves Tyrone or Cherisse or both. Am I on track here?"

The detective nodded, looking amused. "Yeah, you're doing great."

"Thank you. Vee here says her husband is a saint, although spouses have been known to hide things from each other. Well, let's say as far as any criminal activities Tyrone is in the clear. You checked out Cherisse, you told me, and she's exactly what she appeared to be—a nice middle-class girl from the burbs with a City job. Unless she had a serious drug habit that she hid very well, she would have no reason to cross paths with Raheem."

"ME says no drugs," Hrivnak said.

"So why would Raheem order a hit on the car?" I think by now everyone realized where this discussion was going. "Vee, I don't exactly know you well, and you may find this question offensive, but was your husband having an affair with Cherisse?"

It was almost physically painful to watch Vee's brittle, carefully polished facade crumble. "I don't know," she whispered. Then in a stronger voice she added, "But I have to say I've wondered. They spent a lot of time together."

I thought for a moment that the detective was going to jump on that and run with it, but in the end she didn't. We probably all knew what that kind of suspicion was like. At least in theory. I glanced at James, and he looked steadily back at me. I had a very hard time believing that he could ever cheat on me, but we hadn't been together long. No way could I guess what kind of relationship Vee and Tyrone had.

Detective Hrivnak actually looked kind of pleased. "Okay, then. Let's go with Nell's theory, and say those two were doing the deed. Let's guess that Raheem found out—saw them somewhere they shouldn't have been, or looking too cozy together. What would he do?"

"You're asking me?" Vee protested. "You think I have a clue how a drug-dealing lowlife would think? I have done everything in my power to separate myself from that whole poisonous environment. And things have only gotten worse there since I left that behind."

The detective cocked her head at Vee, with an expression of something like pity. "Maybe I've got a better idea. Say he's a big man in his territory—it's his home turf, he knows people there, he's got family. You may think you cut your ties, but people know about you, where you come from, where you've gotten to. Maybe they're happy for you, or maybe they think you've gotten too big for your designer britches. But to Raheem, you're still family. He sees your man messing around with someone who isn't you—that's an insult to family, and to him. So maybe he decides to do something about it. Kinda like defending the family honor, you know?"

Vee was staring at her with a look of horror. "You're suggesting that because my husband *might* have been involved with a colleague, Raheem *might* have decided to kill him? Or her? Did he mean to? Or was he trying to send a warning?"

"Can't say for sure. The guy he hired wasn't exactly the brightest bulb. Maybe he misunderstood his instructions. Maybe he's a lousy shot. Maybe he saw Ms. Pratt in the car and got rattled. And maybe it's time I sent a car over to your house and your husband's office to see if Raheem shows up looking for him, to finish the job." With that she stood up abruptly and pulled out her phone, walking out into the hallway to make her calls.

Leaving us sitting around the table like dummies. With a start, Vee started rummaging in her bag. "I've got to call Tyrone," she said. She didn't bother to move away, but hit a speed dial button. No answer, apparently. She hit another, and again there was no answer. A third button.

No answer. Vee slumped in her chair, her hands shaking. "Oh God. He's not picking up—not his cell, not at home—and nobody's answering at the office. Where is he?"

I didn't think saying that he could be lying dead at home or in an alley somewhere would help the situation.

CHAPTER 26

Hrivnak returned quickly. "Cars are on their way to your place and his office. You reach him, Mrs. Blakeney?"

"No. Do you think he's in trouble?"

"Could be. Or maybe he stopped for a quart of milk. Or a drink in a bar."

"He doesn't drink," Vee said absently. "You sure about this . . . affair?"

"Of course I'm not. But you seem to think it's possible. He's the only one who's sure, and he may not want to admit it. How's his mood been lately?"

"No different . . . that I noticed. I mean, he didn't complain about how his work was going, not that there have been any major successes or anything lately. He was excited about talking with Nell here. He thought that adding the history piece could make the project more appealing." Vee turned to me. "I know you didn't spend much time together, Nell, but did you notice anything between them?"

I recalled that one poignant touch to Cherisse's cheek, when it was clear she was dead. I decided not to share it; I could have misunderstood it. "No, but as you say, we weren't together for long, and we talked business. Nothing personal." Their conduct with me had been unquestionably professional, so that wasn't a lie.

"Now that you've seen Raheem, Nell," the detective interrupted, "you think he was in the car?"

I shook my head. "I told you before, I was in the backseat and didn't have a clear view. I wasn't paying any attention to a passing car, at least not until Cherisse pointed out that she'd seen it go by before." Obviously she had more street smarts than I did. "Both driver's-side windows were open, but all I really saw was the gun in the hand of the guy in back, and I ducked fast. I could·tell the guys were black, and they didn't have pink hair or colorful clothes on, but that was about it. I wish I could help more. Did you find the car?"

"Still looking. Shooter didn't have it when we picked him up, said he ditched it somewhere. Nothing registered in his name, although that doesn't mean squat around there."

"May we go?" Vee asked.

Detective Hrivnak studied her for a moment. "Go where?"

"Home, I suppose. To wait for Tyrone, or . . . to hear from you. Will there be police waiting outside, if Raheem does decide to come by?"

The detective looked uncertain. "I've got good reason

to ask them to check to see if Tyrone is there, but if he isn't, or if Tyrone is but he chooses not to open the door, there's not much more I can do. I can't commit a police vehicle to keep watch based on a vague suspicion, since the department thinks this case is pretty much closed, at least until this Raheem guy popped up today. Sorry, but you're on your own. Keep your cell phone handy and call if you see anything suspicious."

"And Tyrone?"

"Lady, he's a big boy. Either he comes home on his own, or he calls you, or we find him . . ." She realized what she had been about to say and bit off her words. "Again, we can't go searching for him—we don't have the resources. He's not even missing, officially. If you hear from him, call us."

"Call you, or nine-one-one?" I asked suddenly.

Hrivnak sighed. "Nine-one-one would be faster. Damn, I'd really like to sit down and actually eat dinner once in a while. But don't do anything stupid, you all. This guy Raheem is nothing but trouble." She stood up. "I'm out of here."

We trailed after her to the front door, and I let her out, then stood there, uncertain. Vee spoke first. "I should go home, wait for Tyrone."

James and I exchanged glances, and I gave him a small nod. Telepathy? Not exactly, but I was pretty sure I knew what he was thinking. "We'll go with you, Vee," James said. "You shouldn't be home alone. I'll give you a ride, and if Tyrone is there, we'll be on our way."

"You don't have to do that," Vee protested.

"Vee, a short drive out of our way is vastly preferable to hearing that Raheem found you," I said. "Or Tyrone. Let's go."

Vee did not argue any further.

I locked up after arming the alarm, and we crossed the street to the parking lot, without seeing any large angry black men. James retrieved the car, and we set off for Vee's home, with me providing directions. It might have been faster to walk, but we arrived there in under half an hour, and actually found a parking space on the same block. After James had turned off the engine, we sat in silence for a long moment, scanning the scene. Everything looked normal. There were a few people coming and going, but they looked like they belonged there, and Vee didn't seem alarmed.

"Thank you for the ride. I'll be fine from here," she said, gathering up her coat and bag.

"We'll come in and make sure everything is all right," James said in a level voice that didn't allow for any argument. I wasn't about to protest.

I expected Vee to argue, but she gave in quickly. "Fine."

We straggled out of the car and walked to her front door. She had her keys at the ready and opened it quickly. James lingered behind for a moment, in serious-agent mode, checking the street again. I didn't interfere.

"Tyrone?" Vee called out. No answer. Since it was now full dark and there were no lights on, it seemed unlikely that anyone was home. The house had that peculiar stillness that signaled emptiness. Unless, of course, Raheem had gotten here before us. *No, Nell, don't go there.*

Vee strode ahead of us toward the back, turning on lights as she went, her slender heels clicking on the polished wood floors. James followed more slowly, watching, listening. It would have been a treat to observe him operating in professional mode, but right now I was as nervous as a cat, expecting to see an armed thug or two or three jump out from behind the furniture. Or maybe I wouldn't see it, if it was a bullet that came first.

Vee came back from what must be the kitchen and shook her head, answering the unasked question. "Can I get you something? Coffee? Wine?"

"No, thanks," James answered for us. "You want me to check upstairs?"

"We'll go together," Vee said, and led the way.

I was left alone downstairs. Part of me wanted to tag along with Vee and James, but that would be childish. I pulled my cell phone out of my purse, made sure it was on, and slipped it into my pocket. Just in case. Then I walked into the living room, which ran the depth of the house, with a dining area at the rear, opening onto the kitchen. Having met Vee, I studied the furnishings and artworks on the walls. All very nice: not too showy, but good quality. Somehow Vee had achieved a room that proved how far she had come and how well she was doing now. It was a pleasant home.

There were framed photographs lined up along a mantelpiece, and I moved closer to study them. No childhood photos. A couple of inexpensive studio pictures of older people—parents, no doubt. A wedding picture for Vee and Tyrone, with Vee looking uncomfortable and Tyrone beaming. Ten years ago, had Vee said?

James and Vee were still upstairs when I heard a noise at the front door. At least I didn't shriek out loud, but I backed carefully down the hall so I could conceal myself in the kitchen, out of sight. Was it cowardly of me to leave Vee and James exposed to whatever lay on the other side? No way to warn them quickly without alerting whoever was outside, and James was the one with the gun, not me.

I heard a key in the lock. The door swung inward, and a voice called out, "Vee? You home?"

I slumped against the kitchen wall: Tyrone. I quickly returned to the hall, at the same time that Vee and James came down the stairs. Poor Tyrone looked baffled by the crowd: his wife, me, and a stranger in a suit. "What's going on?" he said.

Vee advanced on him and gave him a solid kiss and a hug. "That's for not being dead. Now you've got to convince me I shouldn't kill you."

"Vee, what the hell is happening here? Nell, nice to see you again, but damned if I know what you're doing in my living room right now. And who's this guy?" He looked at James, still a step or two higher on the stairs.

James came down quickly. "Special Agent James Morrison, with the FBI. I'm with Nell." As if that explained anything.

"Why are you here?" Tyrone demanded.

"Why the hell haven't you been answering your phone, Ty?" Vee demanded.

"Battery ran down. What's it matter?"

James spoke first. "The police have been trying to reach you. Raheem Hill accosted your wife on Market Street after she left her office today, and Nell was with her."

Tyrone looked at Vee. "Raheem?"

"Do you know him?" James asked.

"Mostly by reputation. Not the kind of guy you mess with. What the hell did he want?"

"He didn't bother to explain," Vee said. "You haven't talked to him, have you?"

"Why would I be talking to that lowlife?"

"Because when he approached me this afternoon, he said he'd done me a favor. And then a police detective told me that he was wanted in association with that shooting last week, when Cherisse Chapman was killed."

I wished I had a better view of Tyrone's face, because from where I stood it looked like he had an inkling of an idea about what was going on. He looked around at each of us, ending with his wife. "We really need to talk about this in front of these people?" he asked her.

"These people were nice enough to drive me back and make sure the house was safe. Raheem is still out there, and the police are looking for him. He seems to believe we have unfinished business."

"He wouldn't come here," Tyrone protested, if weakly.

"He came to my building, didn't he?" Vee retorted. "He thinks nobody can touch him. And since Nell ended up in the line of fire, I think she deserves a chance to hear what you have to say."

Tyrone wilted, just a bit. "And him?" he said, nodding at James, who had resumed his stone-faced mode.

"You ready to take on Raheem and his boys, if they show up at the door? Because he is," Vee told him, before James could speak.

I almost felt sorry for Tyrone. Sure, maybe he'd gotten involved with a young, pretty, smart woman who shared his passion for the city and his enthusiasm for his community project. Maybe he and Vee had grown apart, and now she was moving in a different world. But he couldn't have predicted that it would end up with an angry drug dealer trying to kill him, or having to explain his wayward love life to not only his wife but to me and an FBI agent in his own living room. *O, what a tangled web* and all that.

"Maybe we could all sit down?" I suggested.

Vee stalked past us into the living room, and Tyrone followed meekly. They took what appeared to be their usual chairs, leaving James and me the settee. We all sat.

"Let's make this short," Vee said. "Were you having an affair with Cherisse?"

Tyrone looked at her for a long moment, as if trying on different answers. In the end he said simply, "Yes."

"How long?"

"Maybe a year? We've been working together a lot, and . . ."

Vee held up a hand. "I don't want to hear explanations and excuses, and I'm pretty sure these people don't, either. That's between the two of us. Do you think Raheem or any of his boys could have seen the two of you together?"

Tyrone thought for a moment. "Maybe."

"In the neighborhood?"

"Yes."

"You ever talked with Raheem?"

"I told you, no! The guy scares me. I know people who

know him, so he's got to know who I am, but we've never met face-to-face."

"Did Cherisse use drugs? Have you, ever?"

"No, and no. How can you think that? You've lived with me for ten years! I don't do that. We've both seen what kind of damage drugs can do, to people and to a community. Vee, what's this all about?"

She weighed her answer, then spoke carefully. "We're thinking that maybe Raheem saw you two going on behind my back, and he thought it was an insult to him and figured he should make it right. He hired some small-timer to shoot at you, maybe just to scare you, or maybe more. Now he thinks he's done me a favor by getting rid of Cherisse. And he might be wanting to finish the job and take you down."

Tyrone shut his eyes. "I never thought . . ."

"I bet you didn't!" Vee spat at him.

James interrupted, "I'd pull the blinds and keep away from any windows, if I were you," Oh, right, somebody might decide to shoot at us—again.

"Yeah, sure," Tyrone said, and stood up and crossed to the front window. Which shattered just as he reached it. A bullet whizzed by, embedding itself in the back wall. At least it had missed Tyrone, who'd plastered himself against the wall beside the window, then slid down until he was sitting on the floor.

"Looks like Raheem has found you," James said.

CHAPTER 27

Then James shifted quickly into agent mode. "Down, now!" We didn't argue. His next order was, "Nell, call the police." I pulled out my phone, hit 911, and explained quickly. I debated about calling Hrivnak next, but the 911 operator said to stay on the line, so I did. No doubt Hrivnak would hear soon enough.

Oh, goody, *now* I'd get to watch James in action. But at this moment I really did *not* want to watch James in action. I wanted to be home in my nice kitchen with a glass of wine in my hand, eating dinner. People didn't shoot at me there. Why was it I liked Philadelphia?

What was supposed to happen next? I reviewed the situation, while plastering myself as flat as possible against the floor. Someone—Raheem?—was after Tyrone? Or maybe now that same someone had added Vee to the list, since she'd dissed Raheem on the street. Neither one of them was giving him the respect he thought he deserved. The next most important question was, did they know James and I were here? I was no threat to anybody, but James was an FBI agent and was armed and dangerous. With the element of surprise, he was our secret weapon— unless they knew he was in the building and brought in reinforcements with more guns.

James darted a quick look at us. "Stay down," he hissed.

"Are we waiting for the cops?" I hissed back.

"I'd rather not engage in gunfire with one or more unknown assailants. Other people could get hurt."

"Raheem must really be taking this seriously, to come into this part of town and start shooting. You think he's alone, or did he bring friends?"

"I'm guessing he figured he could handle things."

We waited silently. Nothing happened for about two years. Well, more like two minutes, but it seemed a lot longer than that. Tyrone didn't look like he was about to leap to his feet and protect his castle. Vee did not appear to be prepared to take charge and start issuing orders. Terror kind of leveled the playing field. I was content to lie there with my head down, although now and then I peered up to look at James, to see if he sensed anything.

I was not prepared when he did. Maybe he had bat hearing, because I hadn't heard anything. Suddenly he focused his attention on the back of the house, and moments later the kitchen door crashed open and slammed against the wall, and then a very large man with a very large gun came charging through it and thundered down the hall toward where we all lay cowering on the floor. Yup, Raheem, no surprise. How had such a large man managed to sneak around to the back without being noticed?

James had retreated into the corner of the living room nearest the kitchen, out of Raheem's sight line, as he barreled toward us, then stopped. I didn't dare look at James, for fear of giving away his presence and position. Both Tyrone and Vee had their eyes fixed on Raheem. Raheem looked pissed off when he noticed me. "What the hell you doin' here?" he said, waving the gun at me.

"I gave Vee a ride home." I didn't volunteer that it had been after a meeting with a city homicide detective. Where the hell were the cops? How long since I'd called them?

"Too bad for you." Raheem took a step nearer, looking down at Tyrone and Vee. "You gonna talk to me now. You know what this scumbag done?" he asked Vee, pointing his weapon at Tyrone.

"I do now," she told him. "What's it to you?" She got up onto her knees and looked at him squarely.

"I don't let no one mess with my family. You still family, like it or not."

"Your mama still go to church?" Vee demanded, climbing to her feet.

"Every Sunday. Bet you don't. Or this piece of crap you married."

"You hear about forgiveness in church? Tyrone is a good man. He's trying to help the neighborhood," Vee told him. Did she believe that? I wondered.

"Yeah, I seen how he helps. He in bed with the City woman. Bet that helps a lot."

I was beginning to think that Vee was stalling, trying to buy time for the police to arrive. She was certainly putting on a good show. I realized with a start that my phone was still on, and lying under me. Another good reason not to move—I didn't want Raheem to see it. This way the 911 people should be able to hear every word. I hoped.

Raheem took another step closer and kicked Tyrone, who gasped in pain. "You. What you got to say for yourself? Can't keep it in your pants? When you married to this fine woman here?"

"I'm sorry. It was stupid," Tyrone said, sounding unconvincing even to me.

"Raheem, he's my problem, not yours," Vee said. "You in enough trouble without killing him. I'll deal with him." Funny how easily she slipped back into a North Philly accent.

"You can have him. He won't be messing with that girl no more, now she dead."

I felt a moment of panic. Gee, it would be nice to have a confession, with the police recording every word on the 911 line. But if Vee prodded too hard, Raheem might get angry and shoot everybody, to prove a point only he understood. Still no sound from James, and luckily, Raheem hadn't looked in his direction.

"Raheem, you can't fix dead," Vee said.

"Dumb-ass kid don't know how to follow instructions," he grumbled. "Now he in jail. He too stupid to be on the street."

Okay, close enough to a confession for me. The police

were welcome to bust in any old time now. And maybe Raheem didn't know that dumb-ass kid had ratted on him?

"So, you want to keep this piece of shit, after what he done?" Raheem asked Vee, poking Tyrone with a toe, but less harshly than before.

Vee nodded. "I'll make sure he pays. And you need him to keep working in the neighborhood—he's getting things done. He'll keep out of your way, and you keep out of his."

"That's fair. He get to live—for now."

"Thank you, Raheem. Say hi to your mama for me."

"I'll do that." He stuffed the gun in his waistband, then turned and walked to the front door, apparently without a care in the world. But when he opened the door, he found himself looking at a pair of large policemen. It would have been funny if they hadn't all had weapons drawn. I stayed where I was, flat on the floor.

James didn't. He came out of his corner and quietly stepped up behind Raheem before he could make a move, and stuck his weapon in Raheem's back. "Don't even think about it."

Raheem apparently had just enough brains to know when he was beaten. He raised his hands.

The police took his gun away and cuffed Raheem and stuffed him in the back of one of their cars. James followed the group out and spent some time explaining the situation to the cops. I peeled myself off the floor, as did Vee. Tyrone, on the other hand, rolled over onto his back and lay there staring at the ceiling, saying, "Oh, man," over and over. Not much of a fighter, apparently.

When James came back, he said to Vee and Tyrone, "They want to see you at the station in the morning to give your statements."

Tyrone lurched off the floor, wincing from the lingering pain of his healing wounds. At least there weren't any new ones, and I wasn't about to feel sorry for him.

"Everybody, I am so, so sorry. I did a stupid thing, and it got somebody killed. Almost got all of us killed. I never meant for anything like that to happen."

Vee didn't answer him. To me it looked like she was concentrating really hard on pulling herself together, or maybe preparing to launch herself at her husband with claws and teeth bared.

James reached out a hand to me and I grabbed it, pulling myself to my feet. He didn't say anything, but he wrapped his arm around me. I didn't protest; it felt good.

"Vee, Tyrone," James began, "let the police handle it from there. When you give your statements tomorrow, tell them what you know, and what you think you know. Don't try to sugarcoat what was going on. You'll be a lot more effective working in that neighborhood if Raheem's off the street."

"I hear you. Thanks for everything, man," Tyrone said.

"You're lucky I was here. I'm sure you two have plenty to talk about now, so we'll be going. Nell?"

I was so ready to get out of there. "Just let me add that I'm glad we're all safe and sound. Things could have turned out a lot worse."

James walked me out the front door, then paused, checking the street. Everything looked peaceful, ordinary. But then, it had looked like that when we arrived. He shepherded me to the passenger side, then walked around and got in the driver's side. But he didn't start the car immediately.

"What's wrong?" I asked.

He shook his head. "Nothing, or a lot of things. Sometimes I really don't understand what's going on in this world. You were going along, doing your job, and somehow all this happens? Drug lords, shootings, people waving guns around at you? Do you know, for the last few months your job has been more dangerous than mine?"

I stifled a giggle. "True. Not the job description I signed up for, exactly. What would you have me do?"

"You did everything right; that's the problem. You didn't go snooping, you didn't pressure anyone—it all came to you. You're a catalyst, or maybe I mean a magnet. I might argue that you shouldn't have gotten into a car with two people you'd only just met and let them take you someplace unfamiliar, which turned out to be about as bad as could be."

"How was I supposed to know they were in the middle of a hot and heavy affair? And that it would put us in the middle of some of the nastiest street gangs in the city?" I didn't know if I was supposed to be mad, or mad at who. Whom? "I think I did know there was something going on between them," I said in a softer tone.

James turned to look at me. "Oh?"

"After they were both shot, and sitting there in the front seat bleeding, Tyrone reached out and touched Cherisse's cheek. Just once. But there was so damned much tenderness in the way he did it, it broke my heart.

I think he really did care for her—it wasn't just a thing between them. But I couldn't say that to Vee, because under her shiny facade I think she still cares for Tyrone."

"Come here." He pulled me close, and I leaned against him. "When I saw that man with a gun, all I could think about was protecting you. I would happily have shot him if that was what it took to stop him. He could have mowed down Tyrone and Vee, and I wouldn't have cared, as long as you were safe. But I'm not supposed to think like that."

"As far as I'm concerned, you go right ahead. Still, I know what you mean. Love's a bitch, isn't it?"

We sat in the car in silence for a few minutes, with James's arms around me. It was clear that love clouded a person's judgment, even made them do stupid things. It could certainly get in the way of rational thought and action. But what was the alternative? Make a point of staying alone through life? That didn't sound very satisfying. Oh, right, I'd tried that. This was better.

I didn't want to screw up James's career, but I wasn't about to give him up for the sake of the FBI. I didn't expect him to tell me to quit my job at the Society and stay home and knit. There were no guarantees that I'd be any safer sitting in a comfy chair armed only with knitting needles. And the irony was, as he had said, that his job was inherently more dangerous than mine, yet I was the one who kept getting into trouble, and I'd even managed to drag him into it. Were we cursed?

I fell asleep on the way home—all of these confrontations were taking a toll. James nudged me when he'd parked in our driveway. "We're back."

"Are you going to check the environs for drug-dealing gunmen?" I said without opening my eyes.

"Are you actually worried?" he asked.

I struggled to sit up, and unlatched my seat belt. "No, not really. After all, I have an armed FBI agent to protect me. You're doing a great job, by the way, if I haven't said it already."

"I'm trying. Come on, let's go in."

I followed him as he unlocked the door and stepped into our home. "I'm hungry. Or maybe not meal hungry, but comfort-food hungry. What time is it?"

"About ten."

"No wonder! Could we handle cocoa and toast?"

"Probably." He produced both in record time as I sat in the kitchen and watched.

I could have gone upstairs and changed into something comfortable, but it seemed like far too much effort to climb the stairs. "What a truly odd day."

"I won't argue with that," James said, as he slid a plate with buttered toast sprinkled with cinnamon sugar in front of me, then went back to the microwave to retrieve a mug filled with hot cocoa. "There you go." He sat down across from me.

"I have never seen such a tangled mess," I said, blowing on my cocoa to cool it. "Drug wars, illicit affairs, wounded feelings all around, high finance, city government. And poor little us in the crosshairs. I'm beginning to understand why my predecessors stuck with handling places like the Oliver mansion. At least people don't shoot at you, even if you botch a renovation or paint the place pink. They just take you to court. Is this what your life is like, all the time?"

"Sometimes. It's not the norm. As I've said before, there's a lot of paperwork involved, so that means lots of desk time, coupled with court time. You going in to work tomorrow?"

"I have to—there's the board meeting. I hope we're ready for it, because I don't have enough brain cells left to redo anything. We've got a couple of surprises for the board that have come up since we sent out the information packets, but I don't know how much I can say about them yet. But then, I'm not sure how much of the so-called impact banking stuff will survive if Vee gets discredited. Attracting charming people like Raheem is not good for business."

"She strikes me as a very focused woman who knows what she wants and goes for it. I wouldn't count her out just yet."

"Believe me, I won't." I drained my cocoa. "Can we go to bed now?"

"Of course."

CHAPTER 28

The next morning I had trouble getting started. I lay in bed, my eyes closed, trying to sort out what had happened the day before and what it meant. I had to decide whether to take any of the propositions or plans I'd been party to in the past week to the board later in the day. I figured Vee's impact financing department would go forward, because it sounded as though it was trendy in high-finance circles, but she might not play a personal role in it. Or maybe she would. It kind of depended on how much of the whole Raheem-Tyrone mess went public. Vee hadn't done anything wrong, other than remain oblivious to her husband's affair, but public perception could affect matters like finance, whether or not it was logical. If her early background, and her link to drug dealer Raheem, became known, would it hurt her? Maybe it depended on whether her bank had a good PR person who could spin the story. "Vee Blakeney: from the slums to vice president" could play well in the media. But all in all, if Vee was out, I wasn't going to start spending that nice consulting fee she had dangled in front of me. Maybe it would be better to say nothing at the board meeting.

Then there was the issue of the Oliver mansion. At least that was a happier story, but I wasn't sure it was mine to tell, or not yet. It wasn't as though we had to do anything for it, although maybe if we were going to end up with the documents collection, we should factor that into our space planning now, rather than waiting. I should speak to Latoya about it, at least about the collections aspect. I wondered if Eliot had approached her about a role his new institute, or was that also premature? Damn, I couldn't seem to decide anything this morning. Getting shot at and menaced by a drug-dealing thug definitely had messed with my brain.

Before I could decide what else to worry about, James appeared with a mug of steaming coffee. "You look like you need this," he said, handing it to me carefully.

"Do I ever! Everything I'm working on seems to be in some sort of limbo, and I'm not sure what I'm supposed to know, or who I can tell, or when. It's very frustrating. I haven't even had time to fill you in on all of it."

"You can sit back and do nothing," he suggested, perching on the side of the bed.

"I could, but then the board members would be annoyed that I hadn't told them earlier. They regard this kind of insider information as one of the perks of the job. Goodness knows there aren't many."

"Have you talked to Martha lately?" he asked.

"Not since our meeting with Edward Perkins on Tuesday. Which feels like it was a month ago. Why do you ask?"

"Martha has a peculiar way of cutting through the underbrush, so to speak. She might have some insights."

"Maybe," I said dubiously, sipping my coffee. "She'll be around today because of the board meeting. Maybe she has new info from Eliot. Are they serious, do you think?"

"You're asking me? Martha does not share that kind of information, with me or anyone else. But because she has been so closemouthed about this relationship even with you, I'm guessing it may be. She'll tell us when she's ready."

I remembered one other thing to worry about. "I'm concerned that if Eliot is voted onto the board, and if his relationship with Marty becomes known, someone might think there's a conflict of interest."

"You must like to worry. He's very well qualified, right?"

"He is."

"Then the board should welcome him with open arms. What two adults do on their own time is their business."

"All right, then I'll worry about whether Eliot will still *want* to join the board, if he's going to be involved in one of those things I haven't told you about yet. That's going to mean a big-time commitment."

"Have you talked to him about it?" James asked.

"In case you haven't noticed, I've been kind of busy. And Eliot's future role is tied into the whole other thing with Edward Perkins, which you also don't know about, and which is rather convoluted."

"Take it one step at a time, Nell. Drink your coffee. Take a shower. I'll drive you to work."

"Wait—I was going to drive, since I'll be late tonight."

"I'm driving, until I'm sure that Raheem doesn't have any colleagues who think it's their obligation to avenge his honor, or something equally ridiculous. I don't mind coming to the board meeting."

"I wish all the board members felt that way. But I'm sure they won't object to having you there."

"So now you have a plan. I'll deliver you to work, and you will handle whatever comes your way."

"Your faith in my superpowers is touching."

"You can do it, Nell," he said, then leaned over and kissed me. It helped.

———————

There was nothing in the paper about Raheem's arrest, so maybe Vee would escape any fallout from it. As for Tyrone, I wasn't sure how that would play. Would the people he was trying to help be grateful that he had helped to bring down a criminal in their midst? Surely one less drug dealer on the street—especially an upper-level one—would be a plus. Unless the void left by Raheem was filled immediately by someone as bad or worse. Or a turf war resulted to fill that void. My, I was in a wonderful mood this morning. *Stick to your own patch of turf, Nell!*

James let me off in front of the Society. "I'll see you later. Call me if anything changes."

"I'll do that. Thanks for the lift." Outside the car I shut

the door and watched him pull away. He was being so sweet. I didn't really think there was any danger from anyone anymore, but I was beginning to enjoy being taken care of.

When I walked into the lobby, Detective Hrivnak was waiting for me, pacing and fuming. "I had to hear about all this from the street cops?" she said. Bob leaned on the reception desk, listening.

"Good morning to you, too, Meredith. I assume you'd like to talk about this?"

"Damn right." She stalked off toward the room under the stairs, and I had no choice but to follow.

I closed the door behind me. "Would you mind telling me what I was supposed to have done?" I began. "We filled you in right here last night, and then James and I took Vee home. Tyrone wasn't there, but he arrived shortly after we did. We'd barely begun talking when Raheem fired a shot through the front window, then broke down the kitchen door and came raging in waving a gun. I called nine-one-one. Was I supposed to call you, with Raheem pointing a gun at me? I left the line open for nine-one-one."

"I know—I heard the recording this morning."

"Is there anything in there that resembles a confession from Raheem?"

"Maybe. He doesn't play by the same rules you and I do."

"Tell me about it! He actually thought he was doing Vee a favor."

"Yeah, more like building street cred for himself."

"So where do things stand now?"

"We've got him for conspiracy to commit murder, even if he didn't pull the trigger himself. We'll make that stick."

"And neither Tyrone nor Vee is implicated in any of this?"

Detective Hrivnak shook her head. "Ms. Blakeney says she hasn't seen her cousin for years, and I believe her. Mr. Blakeney is guilty of being a cheating jerk, but that's not a crime around here. He's gonna have to live with the fact that he got his sweetheart killed."

"Will he be okay working in that neighborhood?"

"Yeah, sure. Nobody else wants to kill him. Raheem was the only one who cared. You gonna stay out of that part of town now?"

"I . . . don't know. There are a couple of projects that the Society may become involved in that could take me back there, but I can't talk about them yet. So, the answer is maybe. Should I invite you along, if I go?"

The detective produced what passed for a smile. "Nell, I'd really rather stay as far away from you as I can. There are a few other crimes in the city that I need to worry about."

"I understand. How about you try to catch the bad guys before they get as far as me?"

"Deal." The detective stood up. "I'll be in touch if I need anything else. Thanks for your help. And say hi to that guy of yours—he's pretty good at staying on his side of the fence."

"That he is. I'll walk you out."

I led Detective Hrivnak back to the lobby and sent her on her way. We seemed to be sneaking up on something approaching friendship, although I would never think of saying anything like that to her, and I doubted we'd ever go so far to have lunch together, unless there was a crime involved. But it was a good thing to have a friend on the police force.

"Everything okay?" Bob asked, as I turned to go upstairs.

"Just fine. Better than usual, I think, although I shouldn't say that because then something is sure to go wrong. Thanks for asking."

I made it to the elevator and up to the third floor without interruption, but when I emerged from the elevator, Shelby appeared and grabbed my arm. "Come with me—we've got something to show you."

Mystified, I let her drag me to the boardroom, where I discovered most of the staff assembled. The central table was blanketed with documents and photographs, and a few three-dimensional artifacts. I looked around at my staff. "What's this all about?"

Shelby took the lead. "You said you wanted material about all the old neighborhoods in the city. This is what we've put together in the past couple of days. Once we got into it, we got excited—the photos and early maps are wonderful, even some of the advertising flyers. I can see why they'd attract interest from the public. Oh, and you should see this." She handed me a photo in a clear plastic sleeve.

I studied in: it was a brick row house, dating from around 1900, I'd guess. It was flanked by matching row houses. A family sat on the front steps: mother, father, and a couple of kids, dressed up in their Sunday best. Then I looked more closely. "This is the Society's house?"

"It is," Shelby said triumphantly. "I found it in the development files. That's what it looked like not long before it came to us."

Wow. Looking at this small piece of history, I had very mixed feelings. On the one hand, that was where Raheem Hill's hired gun had shot at me and could have killed me. On the other hand, it was a perfect example of what the neighborhood had once been. Taken one way, it could be a condemnation of years of neglect and willful ignorance on the part of the city, letting what had once been a thriving neighborhood rot away. On the other hand, it could serve as a goal—what a conscientious developer could strive for in rebuilding that same neighborhood. Not sterile high-rises where the elevators never worked and the hallways stank of piss; not shoe box housing marching in rows alongside a noisy highway, with no greenery in sight, and only abandoned cars for decoration. A *neighborhood*, where people were happy to live, where they cared about one another and took pride in their homes.

"Thank you all," I said, looking around the table. They'd listened to me, and better yet, they'd heard me. This was a terrific start.

"We thought you might want something to show the board today," Ben said.

"I think you're right." They'd just made my decision for me. Even if neither of these projects ever happened, this was the kind of thing we *should* be talking about at the

Society. Which long-dead poet had said *a man's reach should exceed his grasp*? If we didn't try, if we always played it safe, then we would wither away inside our handsome brick walls, out of step with the world around us. That was not what I wanted the Society to do. "I'm so glad you did this!"

After a number of comments of the "aw, shucks" variety, staff members went back to their usual tasks. Shelby stayed behind. "You know, that was fun," she told me.

"Really?"

"Really. I didn't grow up around here, and I'm still pretty new to the city, but looking at these things"—she waved her hand at the table—"I can see what the place must have been like."

"The question now is, can it be as good again? Or better? The world has changed, and some things aren't coming back."

"But it's worth trying for, isn't it, Nell?" Shelby asked.

"It is. And we will. Starting with the board meeting today."

CHAPTER 29

After Shelby was gone, leaving me alone for a brief moment, I found I was struggling not to cry. For once it was not out of frustration or anger or fear; it was because of what my staff had done for me. They'd heard what I had said, and the results were spread out over the table in front of me. Which, I realized, would have to be cleared in time for the board meeting, but there were a few hours until then. There was no rush.

I walked slowly around the table, taking in the materials that the staff had assembled. I felt so proud—proud of them for helping, and proud of the Society for collecting all these wonderful images and documents for so long. Maybe we hadn't done such a shabby job, for here before me was laid out the history of the city in tangible form. And now we could use this to try to make something positive happen in the city. To give back. That felt right.

On my second pass I started picking up documents, just a few here and there. I needed enough to assemble a small selection that would demonstrate what we could do for Tyrone's agency and Vee's bank and Eliot's institute. Too many would overwhelm our board members, who were not, by and large, academic historians, but a few strong images could get the message across. I wanted to tell a story in pictures and old newspaper clippings and ledger books and school records—but tell it quickly and effectively.

I stuck my head out of the boardroom door. "Eric?" I called out.

"Yes, ma'am?" he replied, bounding up from his desk and approaching.

"I want to pull some pictures to hand out at the board meeting, to prove the point I've been making. Do we have some nice folders or binders, so it all looks good?"

"No problem, Nell."

"Did you have a hand in this, Eric?" I waved at the covered table.

"Just the copying part. I don't know much about local history."

"Well, then you've got a fresh eye. What do you think makes the best case for our neighborhoods project?" I stepped back from the table to give him space to look.

He took his time. Finally he said, "The ones with people. I mean, buildings are nice, but that's not what makes a neighborhood work, right?"

"You're right—thank you. We need the ones with people—all kinds of people. Families. Workers coming home from the factories. Street vendors. Festivals. Elections. Anything that shows that the neighborhoods were alive and thriving back then. I don't know if they can be that again, but we have to start somewhere. Let me put together maybe twenty, twenty-five examples, and then I'll hand them over to you to copy and let you clear the table."

"I'll go find something nice to put them in while you're doing that."

Ten minutes later I dropped a stack on Eric's desk. Back in my office again, I pulled out my meeting agenda and almost tore it up. A lot had changed. But there was a lot I wasn't sure I should mention, since it was far from set in stone. I hated to dangle a lot of hints, but solid facts were hard to come by. I decided I would just wing it. After a couple of weeks during which I'd been shot at, watched a woman die in front of me, and faced down a notorious drug dealer, I thought I could manage a room full of middle-aged guys in suits and ties.

Which did not mean I wasn't nervous when the time came to face them. For once Marty had not arrived early, but came in along with several others and claimed a seat next to me. I leaned over to whisper, "Everything okay?"

"No problems. Eliot will be along later."

"You're assuming he'll be voted in?"

"Of course I am. These guys would be idiots not to." She settled back in her seat.

I waited until we had at least a quorum—there were always a few stragglers—and then nodded to Lewis Howard, the venerable board chair, and he called the meeting to order. It was a larger turnout than usual, and that was before James slid in. Apparently he'd had a word with Eric, who came in with a couple of additional folding chairs. Quite a party we were having.

Lewis began with the agenda, which included a number of minor administrative issues that needed to be addressed. When it came to the vote on Eliot's appointment to the board, there was no discussion and no dissent: he was in. As soon as the vote had been taken, Marty pulled out her cell phone and texted a quick message, but it was still a surprise to see Eliot walk through the door. It was an even bigger surprise to see him accompanied by Edward Perkins, who smiled at me. So we were good to go?

We'd finished the mundane business part of the meeting, and it was time to spring a couple of surprises. I stood up. "Gentlemen? There are several items that have arisen since we mailed you the packet of information last week, but I believe we need to address them sooner rather than later. I'm sorry I don't have all the details for you yet, but it has been a rather challenging week. Let me give you the high points, and we can discuss them at length at another time."

I took a deep breath to calm myself, and then glanced at James, who nodded his encouragement. "Last week I was approached by . . ." And I launched into the story of Tyrone and Cherisse's visit, and the tragic results of that day, and what I had learned and observed since. I left out some of the grittier details, but I tried to convey that what we had discussed in our short time together had led me to reconsider where I thought the Society's responsibility lay. Now and then I glanced around the room and was not encouraged: expressions among the board members ranged from bewildered to bored to annoyed. Not a good start.

I segued into a discussion of the Oliver house that Marty had brought to me, after glancing at her for her approval. She signaled to me to go ahead with it, so I outlined the issues I thought were involved there. And then I glanced at Edward Perkins, who had sat silent with a small smile, listening. "I know this sounds daunting, coming all at once, but I think we may have a solution that should address both problems and also make everyone happy. Mr. Perkins, would you care to share what we talked about?"

"This is a bit unorthodox," grumbled one of the more staid board members, who had been known to fall asleep in meetings.

I turned quickly to respond to him. "Yes, but I think you'll see the relevance, so I ask for some leeway to proceed. I'm sure you have all met Edward Perkins, and he has an extraordinary proposal for us. Mr. Perkins?"

I was relieved when he rose and took my place at the head of the table as I stepped back. "Thank you for indulging me. I have been a member of this institution for many years, and I have known many of you for as long. Recently I have been presented with the opportunity to make an unusual contribution to the local historical community, and I'd like to explain it to you."

I took his seat, next to James, and now I could sit back and watch the reactions of the board members. It took a bit for them to wake up, when Edward began speaking, but I could see them gradually listening more intently, and by the time he had wrapped up his short speech, most looked positively excited. Edward smiled at them, then turned to me. "Ms. Pratt, do you have anything to add?"

"Thank you for your very clear presentation, Mr. Perkins." As he resumed his seat, I surveyed the board. "I'm sure you have questions, and there are quite a few issues to be resolved, but I think you have heard the gist of it. Let me add another thing." I picked up the stack of folders Eric had assembled, and Marty took them from me and began doling them out. "What you have before you is a small example of what we have in our own collections, and what we can provide to any agency or group that wants to take part in reviving the troubled parts of the city. And there's one more piece: the local investment banking firm Dillingham Harrington is committed to creating a new funding unit to address social issues, and the Society has been invited to act as a consultant, providing an historical context for the projects it supports."

"They going to pay?" asked a member I didn't know well.

"Yes, they are."

For a long moment, the board looked confused, leafing through the handouts in front of them. But it didn't take long for Lewis Howard to grasp what had just happened. He stood up, and slowly he began speaking. "My colleagues here may be a bit slow to realize it, but you have done something the likes of which I have never seen during my tenure at the Society. You have discovered opportunities to advance our institution's stature in the community without compromising our core values. *And* to bring in money. Bravo, Nell!" He began clapping, and several other members joined in.

For the second time in one day I wanted to cry, but I didn't think that would be professional. I also rejected saying *just doing my job*, even though it was true. I felt extraordinarily lucky to have found myself in the midst of such an alignment of the stars, and maybe getting shot at was the price I had to pay for that. But all things considered, this was the best possible outcome. "Thank you all. As I'm sure you can guess, there's still a lot of work to be done, but nothing we can't handle. I should have more detailed proposals in your hands after the first of the year."

After that the meeting wound down quickly; everyone was eager to go home, or wherever else they were going. Lewis Howard stayed behind. "Nell, I meant what I said. Under your guidance, the Society is now in a position to take a giant leap forward. Well done."

"Thank you, Lewis. I feel very lucky."

And then he was gone, leaving me with James, Eliot, and Marty; I'd seen Edward Perkins slip out while Lewis was speaking. "We pulled it off," I said, with something like wonder.

"That we did. Although that *we* might be misleading," Marty said. "I think you did most of the work."

And dodged a bullet, literally. "I'll stick to the *we*. We should celebrate."

And so we did, with a long, luxurious dinner that included a lot of champagne. It was close to midnight as we said our good-byes outside the restaurant, and I watched Marty and Eliot head off together toward Marty's house, which was not the same direction as Eliot's. They looked happy even from the rear.

"You are an amazing woman," James said in a low voice.

"I'm just doing my job," I replied. "You know, preserving history, saving the city, solving crimes. All in a day's work. By the way, it's your turn to play hero. Can we go home now?"

"Of course. You and I aren't done celebrating."

Keep reading for an excerpt of
Sheila Connolly's County Cork Mystery . . .

A TURN FOR THE BAD

Available from Berkley Prime Crime!

CHAPTER 1

"John Tully's gone missing."

Maura Donovan looked up from behind the bar at the man who had burst into Sullivan's, sending the door slamming into the wall. She didn't recognize him, but then, she was still sorting out who was who around Leap, even after seven months in the village. The few customers in the pub, local men and regulars, didn't seem to know what the latest arrival was talking about.

"What're yeh sayin'?" one of them asked.

"John Tully," the newcomer said, still out of breath. "Went out this mornin' with his boy to take a walk on the shore, he told his wife. He hasn't come back. No one's seen him since. His brother went out to look fer him, found the boy wanderin' on the beach. His wife's beside herself with worry."

"That's bad," another man said. "After that other thing and all."

Maura was falling more and more behind in this conversation. If she'd got it right, not only had this Tully man disappeared, leaving a young child alone on the beach, but it had happened before? To Tully or to someone else? Nearby or somewhere else? She hadn't heard anything about that, but for all she knew the first disappearance had happened a century earlier. She had learned that memories were long in this part of Ireland. "Is he from around here?" she ventured.

The first man turned to her. "Over toward Dromadoon. Sorry, we've not met. I'm Richard McCarthy, and you'd be Maura Donovan? Used to be I'd stop by now and then when Old Mick ran the place, but not lately."

"I am," Maura said, "and welcome back to Sullivan's. So what's happened?"

"John Tully, a good man, told his wife, Nuala, he wanted some air before the evenin' milkin'. She told him to bring along the youngest child, Eoin, because she was takin' the older ones to something or other. He did so. Nuala came back a few hours later, and there was no sign of the man. It was gettin' cold and she was worried about the little one, so she sent the brother Conor out to collect him. Conor comes back with the child, but not John. It isn't like John to go missin' like that. So she waited fer a bit, then went over to where John liked to walk. He had what he called a 'thinking rock' by the water, and she knew where to look. No sign of him there. She had the other kids with her, and Conor as well, so they all searched and they found nothing. Then she called the gardaí, and they're searching now." The man settled himself on a stool at the bar, and a couple of the other men took adjoining seats. "I could do with a pint, if you please."

"Sure. Rose?" Maura nodded toward Rose Sweeney, who worked in the pub part of the time, as did her father, Jimmy, who'd been listening to the tale.

"Right away," Rose said. "Anyone else?" Rose glanced around the room.

One of the other men at the bar nodded, and Rose started two pints.

Maura turned back to the men at the bar. "You said this has happened before? I mean, someone just disappearing?"

Richard McCarthy nodded, his expression somber. "Terrible thing, that was. Before your time, I'm guessin', a year or two back. Older man, a farmer, married a young American who was visiting here, and they had a child, a little girl it was. Light of his life, he said. But the wife was talking about moving back to the States and takin' the child with her. So the man went out with the girl while the wife was visitin' a friend, and drowned the little one and then himself."

"How awful!" Maura said. "Do you think John Tully . . ." Maura wasn't sure how to finish her question. She didn't know the man, but she couldn't believe he would have taken his young child along if he planned to drown himself.

"God willing, I hope not. Nor is there any reason to suspect it. John's a good man, and he and his wife get on well. He'd have no reason to do himself harm. And he loves the boy—the first son, after three girls."

Rose slid the pints across the bar to the waiting men. "So who's looking fer him now?"

"The neighbors and the gardaí. The wife's waitin' back home with the kids—she had the milkin' to do. The gardaí haven't called the coast guard yet, seein' as there's no reason to think he was out on the water. John has no boat and wasn't much of a man fer the boatin', him raisin' cows and all. But he liked the walk—said it was good for his thinkin'. Ta." He raised his glass to Maura. She realized she probably was expected not to charge him for it since he was the bearer of news, even if the news was bad. Another thing she was getting used to: the odd rules about who paid and when at the pub.

"Will they be needin' help?" one of the other men asked.

"Might do. It'll be gettin' dark soon. No doubt the gardaí will get the word out if it's wanted. And some of you must be volunteers for the coast guard, eh?" McCarthy had finished his pint quickly, draining the last of it. "I'm off to tell the folk at Sheahan's across the street. Pray fer the man, will yeh?"

After McCarthy had left, the remaining men lapsed into glum silence. Maura checked the time: only a couple of hours until dusk, now that it was late October. Would that be enough time to search? She could understand how a man could walk out of his home and just keep going, but to take a small child along and then abandon him? That made no sense.

"Rose, I'm going to talk with Billy for a bit, okay?" Maura said.

"No worries. I think I can handle the crowd here," Rose replied, dimpling. By Maura's count there were five customers in the room, including Old Billy, who lived in a couple of rooms at the far end of the building that Maura now owned and who spent most of his waking time holding court in the pub, seated by the fire. She guessed he was well past eighty, but she wasn't sure even he knew his age. He had known Maura's predecessor Old Mick well, and luckily Billy Sheahan had stayed around to see Maura through the first few rocky months. And since he had lived in the area all of his eighty-plus years, he knew the history of most people and places in West Cork.

Maura walked over to the corner by the fire, where Billy occupied his favorite armchair—which no one else who knew the place dared to sit in—and sat down in the adjoining chair. "Are you ready for another pint, Billy?"

"Not yet, thanks fer askin'. McCarthy's news has put me right off my drink."

"It doesn't sound good. Do you know the Tully family?" Maura asked.

"I knew John's grandfather, years ago. They've a nice little piece of land over west of here, and they keep cows. They make a fair living at it, from what I hear."

Maura thought a moment. "So you're saying John Tully would have no reason to, well, do himself harm?"

"Not likely. And he and his wife are well suited, and they grew up together. And then there's the child. The man was over the moon about havin' a son at last, after the three girls."

"That's what I was thinking—he wouldn't have just

gone off and left the kid. So if John didn't have any problems, where is he?"

"That I cannot say," Billy replied somberly.

"What's the coast guard like around here? I haven't heard much about them. Well, except when a fishing boat goes missing or starts to sink."

Billy smiled. "I'll give yeh the short course, shall I? The Irish Coast Guard is a national organization that rescues people from danger at sea or on land, and that includes the cliffs and the beaches. There are three rescue centers, and the closest is on Valentia Island, over to Kerry. The Volunteer Coastal Units can do search and rescue—the nearest ones are at Glandore, and no doubt you've been past that one, and Toe Head. They'd be the ones would be called in fer this. They're volunteers, local men and women alike, who have to live within ten minutes of the station—which clearly we here in Leap do—and they're always on call."

"I never knew any of that, Billy," Maura said. "How come you know so much about it?"

"One of me nephews has been a volunteer fer years. But he's seldom called in. Still, there are always those daft tourists who think climbing a cliff is a fine idea, until they get into trouble and they have to be rescued."

"Richard McCarthy didn't think they'd been called yet."

"I knew the beach Tully likes, years ago, and I doubt it's changed much. If the man isn't found there, the rescue teams will be called in soon enough."

"Was the coast guard part of that other story?"

"Where the little girl was drowned? They were, as were the gardaí and the local firemen. But neither father nor daughter was found until the next day. The man left a note behind, although it took them a bit to find it."

"And no one saw them go into the water?" Maura asked.

Billy looked at her. "You've not spent much time along the beaches here, have you, now? There's few people near enough to see anything, if they're not lookin' fer it."

"I haven't had the time, I guess, and I don't much like just going for walks. Down along the harbor here now and then, but that's about it."

"Did you not grow up near the sea?"

"Well, yes and no. Boston's got a harbor, and there's plenty of coastline nearby, but I never had the time to go off and look at the water and play in the sand. I was usually working at one job or another, when I wasn't in school." There had always been a job, because she and her gran had never had enough money.

"Do yeh know how to swim?" Billy asked.

"Enough to stay afloat, Billy. My high school got some kind of special grant to give the kids swimming lessons. That's about it. Doesn't mean I like it."

"There's many a fisherman hereabouts who can't swim, so yer ahead of the game there." The front door opened, and Billy nodded toward the newcomers. "You've business to tend to. Maybe there's someone who's had some good news."

"Let's hope so, Billy." Maura went back to her usual place behind the bar and started helping Rose pull pints for the newcomers. It didn't surprise her that the crowd grew throughout the evening, everyone hoping to hear that John Tully had been found. Most of the people who came in knew him, or had bought cows or milk from him, or were related to his mother's cousin over near Clonakilty, and so on. Maura had given up trying to sort out all the invisible connections that existed in this part of Ireland, or maybe throughout the entire country—she hadn't had time to check out more than this small corner.

Mick Nolan, the final member of Maura's staff, had arrived around five and kept busy since. Maura hadn't had time to ask if he had come out of concern for John Tully or because he had heard the news and guessed that it would be a busy night at the pub. As the night wore on, Maura noticed a current of anxiety running through the crowd. No one was drinking much, and Maura hadn't the heart to insist that they keep buying pints. Mostly the people there wanted to be together, either to wait for whatever news came or to share the outcome, good or bad.

It was past ten when garda Sean Murphy walked in. Conversation in the pub came to a halt, and all eyes turned toward Sean. He came straight to the point.

"No sign of the man. They've called off the search until first light."

The mood in the room ratcheted down a notch, and people started draining their glasses and heading for the door: there would be no more news this night. Sean made his way to the bar.

"A pint or coffee?" Maura asked.

Sean rubbed his face. He looked tired, despite the fact that he was younger than Maura's twenty-five years. "I'd love a pint, but it'll be an early day tomorrow. Coffee, if you will."

"Coming up," Maura said.

"I'll do it," Rose volunteered. Maura hadn't even noticed she was still there, they'd been so busy. Rose usually left early in the evening, except weekends, but most likely she had been as anxious as the rest of the people to hear what was going on.

Maura leaned on the counter to ask Sean, "What can you tell me?"

Sean shook his head. "Too little. Everyone's been out hunting half the day, since we heard. The mother's been hovering at the scene, with some of her family around her. The children are staying with the rest of 'em."

"Where'd you find the boy? You must have gone over that beach with a fine-tooth comb. Did you find anything useful?" Maura asked, although she wasn't sure what that might be.

Sean glanced around, but no one was near enough to overhear their quiet conversation. "We found some footprints where Conor told us to look—large and small, together. But they were soon trampled by well-meaning people lookin' fer the man."

"I heard it was John's brother who found the boy and took him home," Maura said. "Is he old enough to tell you anything?"

Sean shrugged. "Hard to say. He's only just turned three, and his mother's barely let him get a word out since he's come home. What he'll remember in the morning is anyone's guess. The best we got was that he kept talkin' about a boat. No surprise, seein' as how he was on the beach."

"Did he seem upset? Did he mention his dad?" If the boy had seen a fight, what would he have made of it?

Sean almost smiled. "Maura, have I not just told you we don't know the details yet? We'll sort it out in the morning. The poor lad was exhausted, as was his mother. We'll all have fresher eyes tomorrow." He drained his cup quickly. "I'd better be on my way so I can get an early start. I only wanted to make sure you knew the story so far, and the others here, so they could spread the word."

"Thank you, Sean. I appreciate it," Maura said softly. Maura wasn't quite sure whether he had been thinking of her concern or only wanted to get the word out as quickly as possible—and what better way than to tell a pub full of worried people? "Safe home."

"And to you," Sean said, then gathered himself up and went out the door.

The crowd cleared quickly after that, and by midnight only Maura and Mick remained, clearing up the last of the glasses scattered around the room.

"Mick, are you planning to stop by your grandmother's tomorrow?" Maura asked, washing the final glasses.

"I might do," he said. "Why?"

"Could you stop by my house? I've got a small problem and I'm not sure what to do." She hated to ask anyone for help, much less someone she worked with, but there were things she was clueless about, and how to manage an old stone cottage in this part of the world was one of them. She needed someone who knew how things worked, and she knew Mick was often down the lane visiting his grandmother Bridget.

"Glad to. I'll look in before I see me gran."

"Thanks, Mick. See you in the morning, then. And we should probably be here early, because people will want to hear the news about John Tully."

"Troubling, that," Mick commented. "Something's not right. John would never have left his son like that."

So what had happened? Maura asked herself. Tomorrow would tell. She hoped.